the
alex
crow

the

alex crow

by
Andrew Smith

Dutton Books
An imprint of Penguin Group (USA) LLC

DUTTON BOOKS
Published by the Penguin Group
Penguin Group (USA) LLC
375 Hudson Street • New York, New York 10014

Ⓟ

USA • Canada • UK • Ireland • Australia
New Zealand • India • South Africa • China

penguin.com

A Penguin Random House Company

Library of Congress Cataloging-in-Publication Data

Smith, Andrew (Andrew Anselmo), date.
The Alex crow : a novel / by Andrew Smith.
pages cm
Summary: The story of Ariel, a Middle Eastern refugee who lives with an
adoptive family in Sunday, West Virginia, is juxtaposed against those of a
schizophrenic bomber, the diaries of a failed arctic expedition from the
late nineteenth century, and a depressed, bionic reincarnated crow.
ISBN 978-0-525-42653-0 (hardcover)
[1. Adoption—Fiction. 2. Death—Fiction. 3. Science fiction.] I. Title.
PZ7.S64257Al 2015
[Fic]—dc23
2014039366

Printed in the United States of America

1 3 5 7 9 10 8 6 4 2

Book design by Christian Fuenfhausen
Edited by Julie Strauss-Gabel

For Chiara Luciana Smith,
my beautiful daughter who went with me to see the great
welcoming mannequin that rises from the water

the
alex
crow

THE ALEX CROW

prologue:
HERE IS A PINWHEEL

"Here, kitty-kitty."

The cat had a name—Alex—but General Parviz always called him in the same generic manner.

General Parviz, all gilded epaulets and clinking medals, a breathing propaganda poster, repeated, cooing, "Here, kitty-kitty."

The Alex cat, a six-toed Manx, an official gift from the Hemingway estate and the people of the United States of America, swept its head from side to side, walking slow like a drowsy lion. The cat paused at the general's slippered feet as though considering whether or not it actually *wanted* to jump up into General Parviz's lap.

The general patted his thigh softly, beckoning.

"Kitty-kitty."

The cat leapt soundlessly.

Then cat, general, palace, bodyguards, and approximately one-third the territory of the capital city blew up.

Here, kitty-kitty.

- - -

Here is a handful of dirt.

As far as its use as a medium for sustaining life—nourishing roots—it is perhaps the least capable dirt that can be found anywhere on the planet. To call it sand would be to give it some unwarranted windswept and oceanic dignity.

It is simply dead dirt, and it fills my hand.

I will tell you everything, Max, and we will carry these stories on our small shoulders.

On my fourteenth birthday, Marden and I played outside the village in one of Mr. Antonio's fields with Sahar, Marden's sister. We would have been in trouble if we had been discovered. There was a funeral that day for Mr. Antonio's cousin who had been killed fighting against the rebels, so it was expected that everyone attend.

At school that morning, we performed a play. I had the role of Pierrot, Sahar my Columbine. One of the boys in our class played a joke on me: At the end of the day when we went to change out of our costumes to prepare for the funeral, somebody had taken all my clothes—everything—so I had to stay dressed as the mute white clown. I didn't mind so much; the costume was loose and soft and made me feel disconnected, like a ghost drifting above the dead fields we played in.

"This is Mr. Barbar's ram," Marden said.

Mr. Barbar's ram had been missing for more than a week.

Sahar and I grabbed small handfuls of dirt. We poured our dirt into the eye sockets on the rotting skull. What else would kids do? Playing with dirt and horned carcasses was a good way to have fun.

The thing looked like a caricature of the devil himself.

When the FDJA came to the village that day—it was just after the mourners arrived back from the funeral—four of them took all the boys and made us go up to the third floor of the school building. I was still dressed as Pierrot; nobody would confess as to who the thief of Ariel's clothing was.

Of course, we all knew what was going to happen next, once the rebels got us into the upstairs classroom. We could already hear gunfire and cries coming from outside the school.

The rebels bribed us with cigarettes and guns.

What boy doesn't want cigarettes and a gun?

One of the men, his face hidden behind a red scarf, said to me, "What are you supposed to be?"

"Pierrot," I answered.

He shook his head, confused.

"You look like a boy-whore."

Ivan, a ten-year-old, puffed on his first cigarette and glared at me. I wanted to slap him. One of the FDJA men patted the boy's head. We were all goners at this point.

Everyone knew. It had been this way all our lives. Here, the deliberate cruelty of violence was a matter of fact, controlling, constraining, and understandable. Not so much in some of my other stories, Max.

The rebels targeted the older boys, many of whom were approaching conscription age for the Republican Army. They taunted the boys with insults about patriotism and loyalty to capitalist puppet masters. One boy, Jean-Pierre, pissed himself when the man whose face was covered with the red snot-stiffened rag prodded his belly with a gun barrel. Naturally, this was very funny to the FDJA men. Who wouldn't laugh at a sixteen-year-old boy who pissed his pants as he was about to be kidnapped by thugs with guns?

I felt bad for Jean-Pierre, who, like the other chosen boys in the schoolroom, recited a robotic pledge of allegiance to the FDJA. He would have done the same thing on his eighteenth birthday to the Republican Army, anyway. So, who cared?

We were all going to go with the FDJA now, or we would never leave this third-floor schoolroom. They promised us that we were old enough to make our way as men, even though some of the youngest boys were barely ten years old.

My friend Marden was sixteen.

When one of the men tried wrapping the red scarf of the FDJA around Marden's neck, my friend swatted his hand away. Marden was always defiant like that—impulsive—and everyone knew it was a mistake. But what could we do?

To make an example of him to the other boys, two of the FDJA men picked up Marden by his feet and threw him headfirst out the window as he kicked and scratched at them. But Marden didn't scream or cry. I heard the impact of his body against the paving stones that lined the street below.

I desperately wished I had my proper school clothes. I felt so isolated and noticeable in my thin white clown suit.

Two of my schoolmates ran for the doorway that led to the stairs. The man with the hidden face fired at them and they tumbled down in a heap across the threshold.

"Let's go!" he said.

I could only see his eyes peering out from a slit on the covering. He waved his gun to goad the remaining boys—there were five of us—over our friends' bodies and out the door.

One of the men videoed the slaughter in the schoolroom with his cell phone, sweeping it around and around until he focused directly on my face. Most of the white makeup I'd worn earlier had been wiped away, but I was still pale and painted. And I was crying.

The video would be uploaded with the usual descriptions blaming all this on the Republican Army. People naturally believe things they see. Nobody argues with the irrefutable postings on YouTube.

I was told that in America, many people believed FDJA stood for *Freedom Democracy Jesus Army*.

They sent money.

I stood by the open window, thinking about Marden and how we'd been playing in Mr. Antonio's field just moments before. What could I do? I was frozen at the edge of the floor, with the fingers of one of my hands resting on the windowsill where my friend had left the room that smelled of sweat and gunpowder.

The man with the red mask, his eyes wild and white, turned toward me. The other boys made their way out into the hallway, tramping through blood. He raised his rifle. The barrel was so slender and short. I was as familiar with these guns as anything in the world—how they smelled, the sound of their report. When he pointed the thing at the center of my chest, I thought it would be a better end than to be thrown after Marden—but when the man pulled the trigger, the thing jammed—dead—and the two remaining FDJA men stared at me as though I were dead, as though the gun had functioned properly and I was done for—I believe they could not accept anything other than this—the wide white staring eyes of them, whiter than the soft clown suit that seemed to flutter around my body.

Then they left and I heard their footsteps clattering downstairs as the others ahead of them yelled at the boys and told them to form a line and get out onto the street.

Happy birthday to me.

Later, I thought, this was the first miracle I had seen. Perhaps my survival was nothing more than an accident. Accident, miracle—I suppose the storyteller retains the right to determine such things.

Picture this, Max: I waited in the classroom for a while, wondering if maybe I really was dead—that this is what being dead is, just a dream that continues on and on—and now I truly was the ghost I'd imagined myself to be when Sahar and Marden and I played that afternoon.

When I was certain the men and their new conscripts had gone, I went downstairs into the school's kitchen and hid inside a walk-in refrigerator.

- - -

Here is nothing but ice.

It is more than ice, more than anyone on the steamer had ever seen. It is the blue-white fist of God, curling calloused fingers to grasp the protesting wooden hull. It is an infinity field of jaws with countless rows of teeth; absolute control and the concurrent absence of control. The hungry ice creaks and moans, stretching forever to become horizon, ceiling, and cemetery; and the ship, frozen and moving, trapped in this relentless vise, is slowly dragged along, endlessly northwest into more and more ice.

TUESDAY, FEBRUARY 10, 1880—*ALEX CROW*

Today is our fifth month in the ice. The ship is held fast. The readings calculated by Mr. Piedmont, ship's navigator, measure the distance the ice has taken us at more than one hundred miles!

It is the cruel reversal of our intent. The men of the *Alex Crow* expedition set off with the expectation that it would be us—the first voyagers here to absolute north—who might inflict our will upon the planet; instead we face the grim truth that nature's will is uncontestable.

I keep such daily accounts as no measure of optimistic entertainment. My overwhelming sense is that the end of our story will not be written by my hand.

I don't think I can endure this imprisonment much longer; I am beginning to wonder if I'll go as insane as Murdoch.

After breakfast, a party of seven men took a team of dogs and one of the sleds out onto the pack to hunt for seal and bear. I stood at the rail and watched in amazement as the men and dogs clambered over the unyielding hummocks of ice that had once been the ocean.

Twenty-five of us remained behind on the *Alex Crow*, including the newspaperman, Mr. Warren, who had crushed his hand three days ago between the ice and forefoot of the hull and is currently under my care. Today, the majority of the men busy themselves with the drudgery of routine maintenance.

Some watch and record wildlife sightings. Wildlife!

In the afternoon we heard rifle fire but could not determine its direction due to the blinding whiteness that smothered everything.

It was then that Murdoch, who has taken to

following me around, said, "Doctor, Doctor, I do believe our men have found something."

- - -

Here we see a two-quart jar of Mason-Dixon-brand sauerkraut.

I believe sauerkraut, along with guns, is some type of national symbol in the Land of Nonsense. Everyone in Sunday, West Virginia, eats sauerkraut and also shoots things. So it isn't a casual act by which I begin a story with the examination of a jar of sauerkraut—the sauerkraut has a purpose; it shapes one of my clearest initial memories since coming to America, as though when the contents of that particular two-quart jar of Mason-Dixon-brand sauerkraut spilled, something began to fill me up after all my emptying and emptying.

I arrived here in Sunday little more than one week after my fifteenth birthday.

A year had passed since the miracle in the schoolhouse.

Happy birthday to me, once again.

Mother—my American mother, Natalie Burgess—has the most confusing habit of making everything seem insignificant and small. My brother Max calls her the Incredible Shrinking Machine.

Here is what happened: When the top jar tumbled from its eye-level placement, it caught the edge of the metal cage basket on the shopping cart and exploded in a fetid shower of cabbage and knife-shards of glass.

Mother was dressed in salmon-colored shorts and pale yellow sandals.

One of the glass shards slashed across her leg, mid-calf.

She said, "Oh."

I had only been here four days, but the way she said it sounded like an apology to me, as though it were her fault for being in that precise spot inside the Sunday Walk-In Grocery Store at the exact moment the jar slipped from the shelf.

We had dropped Max off at school earlier. I was not enrolled yet, because the officials at William E. Shuck High School insisted on testing and testing me to determine whether or not I was an idiot, or could speak English, which I could do perfectly well despite my aversion to talking.

"Oh," Mother said again.

I shifted my weight from foot to foot. I didn't have any idea what I was supposed to do. Maybe I *was* an idiot of some kind. But here I was in this grocery store, which may just as well have been some gleaming palace or gilded mosque, watching in confused silence while Mother bled all over the speckled linoleum floor.

It was a nauseating scene; so much so that I vomited, which made everything just that much more repulsive, and Mother said "Oh" again because we were making such a mess on aisle number seven.

Mother reached into her purse and gave me a handkerchief so I could wipe my face. The handkerchief smelled like perfume and mint chewing gum. Then she pressed some wadded napkins into the cut on her leg.

A clerk wearing a brown apron came running up the aisle toward us. I thought he was mad because of all the mess we'd made, but he was most concerned about the injury to Mother's leg.

"We're calling an ambulance!" he said. "Please sit down!"

And he flailed his arms as though he were swimming toward us.

But Mother said, "No. No. I'll be fine! I'm so sorry for all this."

And while the man pleaded with her, bent forward so she could press her soaked napkins against the wound, she grabbed my clammy hand in hers and led me out to the car.

"I'm sorry. This is so embarrassing, Ariel," she said as we climbed in.

We did not make it home. Mother passed out behind the wheel less than a mile from the Sunday Walk-In Grocery, due to all the blood she'd lost.

She was like that.

- - -

Here is Joseph Stalin telling the melting man what he had to do.

Joseph Stalin's voice came from the air vents on the dashboard of the melting man's recycled U-Haul moving van. Joseph Stalin also spoke to the melting man through the radio.

The melting man tried to do anything he could to make Joseph Stalin shut up.

He removed the radio at a rest stop near Amarillo, Texas, and left its dangling wires atop the hand dryer in the men's toilet, but Joseph Stalin's voice still came through the old speakers.

At the same time Leonard Fountain—the melting man— crossed the border between Oklahoma and Arkansas, Joseph Stalin told him this: "They are coming to get you, Leonard. You know that. You must not let them catch you."

Leonard Fountain drove his recycled U-Haul truck all the way from Mexico City, where he'd assembled the biggest bomb he'd ever seen at a rented flat on the top floor of an apartment house across the street from one of the sixteen Holiday Inns in the city.

Leonard Fountain believed he had to stop the Beaver King.

The Beaver King was hiding somewhere near a shopping mall called Little America. He knew that, because Joseph Stalin told him all about the Beaver King. The Little America Mall had an animated Statue of Liberty in the center of its welcoming gates. The statue could spin its crowned head around in a full circle, and its torch-bearing arm could lower and flash colorful beams of lights at the dazzled shoppers.

No doubt, had the French been more technologically advanced, the original Statue of Liberty would perform the exact same tricks.

Leonard Fountain had a fascination with bombs. He grew up in Idaho, where kids were naturally expected to blow things up.

What else would you do?

When he was thirteen years old, although he spent the majority of his waking hours playing video games or masturbating, Leonard Fountain helped out his neighbors by blowing up beaver dams.

On his fifteenth birthday, Leonard Fountain, who hadn't started melting yet, made a remote-controlled bomb from three sticks of dynamite and lashed it to the neck of a dairy cow.

They never found the cow's head.

Leonard Fountain loved blowing things up.

"They are coming for you, Leonard," Joseph Stalin said. "There is a drone flying directly above our truck. You can see it. When you look at it, it will disappear."

Outside Arkadelphia, the melting man pulled the truck onto the shoulder of the highway. He knew what to do. He pretended to be distracted, and then looked up into the sky behind the rear gate on the U-Haul.

Leonard Fountain saw something in the sky.

What he saw was a perfect rectangular prism that hovered

soundlessly, fifty feet above his head. The thing was metallic and shiny, about four feet long, and as soon as the melting man focused on it, the thing rotated diagonally and vanished—became invisible.

They were watching Leonard Fountain. Leonard Fountain knew it all along.

From time to time, when he'd get out of the van to pee or sometimes vomit alongside the road, the melting man would suddenly jerk his head around and glance up into the sky, and the little floating box—it resembled a package of tinfoil—would always be there, and then it would turn slightly and disappear.

And it was while the melting man drove through Arkansas, in the direction of Tennessee, that Joseph Stalin became particularly nasty.

"Look at you," Joseph Stalin scolded. "You're disgusting. You better get this done before you dissolve into a puddle of pus and goo. Now pay attention."

Leonard Fountain did not want to pay attention. He drove with an old Hohner Special 20 harmonica in his mouth, and he'd blow the loudest noise through it every time Joseph Stalin said anything about what he wanted the melting man to do. But the harmonica didn't work. So Leonard Fountain bought two spring-winding kitchen timers at a drugstore and he taped them over his ears with medical gauze, hoping the metallic *tick-tick-ticking* of them would stop the Communist dictator's voice.

He thought Joseph Stalin's voice must have been beamed into his head from a government satellite. What other explanation could there be?

Actually, there was another explanation, but Leonard Fountain never figured it out.

Leonard Fountain was insane and melting, and he needed to blow something up.

- - -

Here we see the family pet—a crow we call Alex.

The bird is named after a barkentine steamer commissioned by the U.S. Navy in the late nineteenth century. The ship became icebound—trapped—during an expedition to discover a fabled open seaway to the North Pole in 1879.

Alex is a product of my American father's research.

I don't think the research turned out very well for Alex.

What my father does, I believe, is less research, and perhaps more appropriately called "aimless scientific wandering."

And he finds things you'd never know were out there.

Alex is a morbid being, obsessed with his own death, and gruesomely despondent. I know that's an odd set of qualities for a bird, but Alex should not have been saved to begin with. He is a member of a species that has been extinct for more than a century, and I think all Alex really wants to do is go back to where he'd been pulled from.

My father, and the company he works for, are tireless in their obsession with saving things from nonexistence, and by doing so, controlling the course of life itself. Unfortunately, sometimes paths and directions can't be so easily controlled, as the men on the ill-fated steamer *Alex Crow* found out. And sometimes things don't want to be saved or brought back from where they'd been trapped.

WE FIVE BOYS OF JUPITER

It came as no surprise that our interplanetary archery competition was canceled the day Bucky Littlejohn shot himself through the foot with a field point arrow.

What was surprising, Max—my American brother—told me, was this: No kid before Bucky Littlejohn had ever been cunning enough to devise such a foolproof plan for getting out of Camp Merrie-Seymour for Boys.

"Why didn't *I* think of that?" Max said.

Probably because Max was not as self-destructive or desperate as Bucky Littlejohn, I thought.

It was also surprising that Bucky Littlejohn did not cry or scream at all as the arrow drilled through his foot all the way to the plastic yellow feathers of the shaft's fletching. It mounted Bucky Littlejohn like an insect pinned for display to a spreading board, tacking the boy to the soft ground of the lakeside field. And Bucky, transformed into a silent, human version of a draftsman's compass, spun around and around a bloody pinpoint in his sea-foam green plastic clogs, while he stamped out an impeccable circle with his free right foot.

So there was an empty bunk that night in the Jupiter cabin of Camp Merrie-Seymour for Boys, where Max and I slept with a reduced-to-two additional bunk mates and Larry, our counselor.

If only the archery contest depended on our team's willingness to inflict self-injury, we would have beaten the unbloodied boys from the Neptune, Mercury, Mars, Saturn, and Pluto cabins.

There was no populated Earth cabin at Camp Merrie-Seymour for Boys, and the camp's directors had decided to shut down and abandon the Venus and Uranus cabins as well. Those planets came with too much psychological baggage for teenage boys.

The night before—our first night at Camp Merrie-Seymour for Boys—I felt certain that some terrible mistake had been made. Lying in my dingy bed, in a damp room that smelled of urine and sweat, I couldn't sleep at all due to the incessant rustling of bedding, and one of our roommates' depraved sobbing that never slackened in the least.

I believed that Max and I had erroneously been committed to some sort of asylum for insane children.

This was America after all, and there was no shortage of insanity as far as I could see.

It was mid-June here in the George Washington National Forest. I had completed the final months of my ninth-grade year at William E. Shuck High School. That was when our parents sent Max and me off to Camp Merrie-Seymour for Boys.

They told us the experience was intended to get us to bond as loving brothers should. Max and I hadn't made much progress along those lines.

Max, after all, did not like me. He told me as much during my first week with his family.

He'd said this: "Listen, dude, just because they took you in doesn't mean I have to act like you're my brother—because you're not. You're a stranger, just like anyone else I never knew."

Yes, it was a mean thing for Max to say, but I also empathized with his feeling intruded upon.

And as usual, I didn't say anything, so Max went on. "They're nuts, anyway. She doesn't know how to react to setbacks, and Christ knows, every time she turns around she's getting kicked in the teeth. And he—he's a freak."

I shrugged.

And Max had told me, "He's an inventor, you know, and he purposely creates things that destroy people's lives. Like you, Ariel, only you're not going to ruin my life, and neither will Mom or Dad."

So I was convinced Max hated me. He probably had good cause. What fifteen-year-old boy (we were the same age) would welcome the halving of his world with a foreigner who didn't like to talk?

I should explain that Camp Merrie-Seymour for Boys was a sort of disciplinarian's boot camp—a detox center for kids who were unable to disconnect from cell phones and technology. For boys like that, being outside or sleeping in smelly huts crowded with strangers—things I had plenty of experience with—was the same as eternal condemnation to hell. And Camp Merrie-Seymour for Boys was not fun at all, which is exactly why Bucky Littlejohn shot himself in the foot.

You almost couldn't blame him.

Neither Max nor I had a problem disconnecting from such things as technology and video games, and interacting with real human beings. The first time I'd even touched a cell phone happened after turning fifteen and coming to America.

The first time I'd used a cell phone was to call for help when Mother slumped unconscious from blood loss behind the wheel of her Volvo as we drove home from the sauerkraut store in Sunday.

I also found out later that Camp Merrie-Seymour for Boys was free of charge to our parents. It was owned by the lab company our father works for, the Merrie-Seymour Research Group. Every six weeks, the camp alternated its focus between technological addiction and weight loss. Two summers before, during one of Camp Merrie-Seymour for Boys' "fat camp" cycles, Max, who is awkwardly thin, was sent.

The summer he was thirteen, my brother Max lost fifteen pounds.

To this day, Max has nightmares that prominently feature celery.

The campers' beds in Jupiter were arranged along one wall, packed so closely together that they were nearly impossible to make (something we were required to do every morning). We learned that we had to take turns navigating around our sheet-tucking duties. And the only reasonable way to get in or out of one of the beds without risking a fight or awkward bodily contact with another boy was from the foot of each one. Bucky Littlejohn's cot sat empty along the back wall. After he left, which was on our second day—not twenty-four hours into the six-week journey to rediscover "the fun of boyhood" at Camp Merrie-Seymour for Boys—none of the campers in Jupiter wanted to claim the vacated bed by the wall; Bucky peed in it the first and only night he spent in Jupiter. Maybe he only attempted the bedwetting as an initial means for getting kicked out.

Bucky Littlejohn was no quitter.

The arrow-through-the-foot tactic was inarguably brilliant.

The boys of Camp Merrie-Seymour were desperate.

My sleeping spot sandwiched me between a kid Max and I had seen around William E. Shuck High School, Cobie Petersen, a pale-skinned, freckled sixteen-year-old who lived up Dumpling Run, a creek that was only about three miles from our home in Sunday; and a thirteen-year-old boy named Robin Sexton from Hershey, Pennsylvania. Robin twitched his thumbs constantly, as though he were handling an invisible video game controller, and he kept tight wads of toilet paper jammed into his ears because he said he couldn't stand all the noise the world pushed into his head when he wasn't wearing earbuds.

Of course, there were no earbuds—no electric-powered devices of any kind—permitted for the campers at Camp Merrie-Seymour for Boys. In fact, every one of the thirty-three boys assigned to the six planets of the camp was closely inspected upon arrival. Each of us was obligated to bring perfectly matched camper kits: duffel bags, which contained precise numbers of T-shirts, shorts, toothbrushes, and changes of socks and underwear, in which, for reasons I could only speculate, we had to write our names with permanent marker.

They counted everything.

Max's bed was closest to the door.

On our first night at Camp Merrie-Seymour for Boys, Max joked that he would be the lone survivor from Jupiter if our cabin burned down in the next six weeks, to which Larry, our counselor, warned, "Don't get any ideas, fuckheads."

And then Larry proceeded to strip-search all five of us. We even had to turn our socks inside out.

This may have pushed Bucky Littlejohn over the edge.

So we five boys of Jupiter, who would be four the following

night, stood there in our underwear while Larry emptied the contents of our duffel bags and tore the covers and bedding from our cots, just to make certain none of us had smuggled in a cigarette lighter.

During the commotion, boys spilled out from the Saturn, Mercury, Mars, Neptune, and Pluto cabins. They taunted us from outside our screen windows. As long as the lights—kerosene lanterns, which were closely guarded by the counselors—were on in our solar system, everyone could see everything that happened in Camp Merrie-Seymour for Boys.

The other planets chanted and clapped at us.

"Strip search! Strip search! Strip search!"

Larry left the place a complete mess, and we had to clean it up—in our underwear—while the planets outside observed (after all, it wasn't as though they could divert themselves with television or video games) and our counselor watched suspiciously from his bed, which sat uncrowded and isolated on the opposite side of the cabin.

"Hurry up and straighten out your shit," Larry said. "I want lights out in five minutes, and you're all getting up at sunrise tomorrow morning. You're going to *have fun*, fuckheads."

I was fascinated by the word. One more of those American things that made no sense to me whatsoever, I thought. If they'd allowed me to bring my notebook along to Camp Merrie-Seymour for Boys, I would have written a reminder to eventually research the etymology of *fuckhead*.

Still, I had no idea what to expect from Larry's concept of "fun." It had seemed to me that in just a few hours we had been through enough torment already. At dinner, they fed us something called "Beanie Weenie." I had never heard of it before, but it was better than sauerkraut, so I ate it.

It made no sense.

Jupiter, an exact replica of Camp Merrie-Seymour for Boys' other eight cabins (three of which were abandoned), was a strange and primitive design. To me, it most closely resembled an insect cage. The walls, which stood only about three feet high, were built with horizontal redwood slats. The entire upper two-thirds of them were nothing more than mesh screen all the way around, which is why the boys of the other cabins could watch us losers from Jupiter enact our dramatic failure in our underwear for their entertainment. Unless you were a counselor, who got to sleep in actual pajamas and had his own lighted-by-electricity toilet and shower facilities, there was no privacy anywhere in the camp. And we would eventually find out, too, just how miserable and damp it could be during a summer downpour.

Camp Merrie-Seymour for Boys had a motto, which was carved in a sort of rustic hewn-log font on the crossbar over the entry gate. It said this:

Camp Merrie-Seymour for Boys
Where Boys Rediscover The Fun of Boyhood!

It almost made me nauseous—not just the word *rediscover*, which is a ridiculous word—all the *boy, boy, boy* on that sign. You could practically smell balls just by reading it. To be honest, the camp always did smell like balls, anyway.

Someone—no doubt a Merrie-Seymour success story who'd endured the camp before Max and I arrived—had taken the time to vandalize the crossbar by etching in two additional words: OR DIE.

Apparently, the internees at Camp Merrie-Seymour for Boys had been encouraged to carve. This was something that we'd never be allowed to do. After Bucky Littlejohn's archery performance, the counselors removed everything sharp from Camp Merrie-Seymour for Boys.

There were all sorts of things carved into the walls around our cots. Two pieces in particular fascinated me. First, there was a kind of religious depiction of an Xbox controller that was nailed to a cross floating in the clouds, while tangles of skeleton-thin boys looked up at it from the apparent hell of Jupiter cabin. The second thing I admired was a short inscription—a mathematical equation for our cabin—that said LARRY = SATAN.

And there were plenty of names, too, and dates. The name nearest my pillow said ELI 1994. Camp Merrie-Seymour for Boys had been there for decades.

It was almost like sleeping in a graveyard.

So as I lay there that first night, trapped between the twitching kid with toilet-paper earplugs from Hershey, Pennsylvania, and Cobie Petersen—and while I listened to Bucky Littlejohn's pathetic sobbing—I imagined what 1994 Eli was doing right at that moment.

Probably Facebooking, I thought.

Larry extinguished the lantern. There was no electricity in the cabins, naturally.

Our audience disbanded and journeyed back to their respective planets.

The mattresses on our cots were covered with thick plastic. It made sense, I suppose, but whenever any of the boys moved or shifted, our beds made sounds like someone was crumpling a soda can. After about five minutes, Cobie Petersen said to no one in particular, "I can't take this shit."

Larry said, "Shut up and go to sleep."

Larry had a non-plastic mattress. Apparently, Larry could be counted on to not pee his bed, or do the other things some of the campers at Camp Merrie-Seymour for Boys inevitably did.

Max rolled onto his side—*crumple crumple!*—and put his pillow over his head.

Then Cobie shot up in bed and yelled, "What the fuck! The crying kid's pissing!"

And we all heard the dribble of Bucky Littlejohn's urine as it trickled down between the cots and puddled on the floor below us.

Larry said, "Jesus Christ!"

The lantern came back on.

And Larry ordered Bucky Littlejohn, who was steaming and stained in his drooping, piss-soaked underwear, and the rest of us, the four insomniacs with dry underwear, to go to the lavatory—a dark and scary combination toilet, insect sanctuary, and shower facility for the campers—and fetch a mop and pail.

On the way there, Cobie said, "If you weren't covered in piss, kid, I'd kick the shit out of you."

I wondered if Cobie Petersen really meant that, because if he actually did kick the shit out of Bucky Littlejohn, it would really be a mess we'd have to clean up.

It was a very long night.

THE GREAT WELCOMING MANNEQUIN

It was hot and stuffy inside the walk-in refrigerator where I hid the day of the slaughter at the schoolhouse.

It may be difficult for you to believe, Max, but electricity only came to the village once or twice per week, so the refrigerator had never performed its duties as far as I could recall. Maybe it did function as something other than a clown's hideout at some point in time. Maybe there were legends passed down from the elders of the village about an era when the refrigerator was cold, and also contained food.

Despite the fact that there was nothing edible inside the refrigerator, I could not bring myself to pee there when I needed to.

Nobody pees inside refrigerators, even ones with no food in them. I would be in trouble if anyone ever found out I'd peed inside our school's refrigerator.

But, as desperate as my urge to pee was, I was too afraid to go outside.

I thought about things. I wondered who was safe in the village, and if my cousins, my uncle, and aunt had been looking for me—or if they assumed I'd gone off with the other boys to become a rebel with the FDJA.

So I tried to devise a mathematical formula based on the concept of predicting when, exactly, the need to pee would surpass my fear of being shot while dressed in a clown suit. As I thought about this, I curled up on my side and fell asleep on the floor.

It is possible that I was inside the refrigerator for days. Who could ever know? Refrigeration—even when the refrigerator in question does not produce coldness—has a way of slowing down time. But I do know this: The mathematical breaking point at which I overcame my fear of going outside occurred sometime before I opened my eyes.

I needed to go.

So picture this, it is a disturbing image: a fourteen-year-old boy wearing a white clown suit, peeing into the gutter along a street in a village where none of the residents is alive.

Everyone had disappeared or lay dead. Their bodies were scattered randomly as though they simply had the life force sucked away from them while they went about their daily drudgeries.

It was poison gas. We were familiar with such things. It had happened before and certainly would happen again.

A useless refrigerator saved my life.

A second miracle, or possibly just another accident. Who can say about things like this?

It was afternoon—but what day I could not tell—when I came out of the refrigerator to pee among the dead in the street in front of my old school. I say *old* because it certainly was not going to be a school after this. There was nobody left to learn anything.

"Hey there. Where did you come from?"

I spun around to see who'd asked the question. I hadn't finished, so I found myself peeing in the direction of a pair of uniformed Republican Army soldiers carrying rifles. They'd been walking, searching house to house along the street toward the school. The men wore gas masks over their faces, so I could not tell which of them had called to me.

"I came from a refrigerator," I said.

"How long have you been outside here?"

"Not even long enough to pee."

They stood there, watching me as I buttoned up the front of my clown pants.

The soldier on the right turned to his partner and said, "It's a miracle this little boy survived."

"I thought so, too," I said, choosing not to argue about such things as accidents and divinity.

"Why are you dressed like that?"

"We were having a play." I nodded at the school. "In there. Someone stole my clothes and I had to stay like this. And why are *you* dressed like *that*?"

I pointed up and down, at the men's uniforms.

"You're a funny clown."

I shrugged. "I do my best."

I turned as if to leave. "I need to go to my uncle's house."

"Where? In the village? Here?"

I nodded.

The soldier shook his head. "There's nobody left, boy. Just you. You're a damned lucky clown."

"Pierrot."

The man on the right pulled the mask from his face and wiped the back of a shirtsleeve across his eyes. "I suppose if you can breathe, we might take these damn things off now."

"The kid's a little canary," the second soldier said.

"Was there any food inside your refrigerator?"

"No."

"Are you hungry?"

I tried to read his face, but there was nothing there. Only whiskers and sweat. He looked as though he hadn't shaved or slept in days. People commonly had that look in those days—in my first life, Max.

"Yes."

"Maybe you should come with us. There's nothing left here, anyway. You don't want to stay here now, clown-boy."

"My name is Ariel," I said.

- - -

Jacob and Natalie Burgess—my American parents—drove me and Max—my American brother—all the way from Sunday, West Virginia, just so that I could see New York City.

They did it only two days after I arrived in the United States.

It is hard to explain the strangeness of my experience. In a matter of days, I had been taken from the filthy squalor of a refugee camp, and then escorted to America aboard a military aircraft by a man named Major Knott, to the Burgesses' home in a sauerkraut-eating and rifle-admiring hamlet in West Virginia. And then I was whisked away in an automobile with a satellite navigation system for an eight-hour ride so I could gawk in awe at the towers to the sky of New York.

Alex, our crow, came, too. He stayed inside a small plastic crate—the kind you'd keep a dog in—stowed in the cargo area of the Volvo. Alex did little more than stare and stare. The first time I saw him, I thought he was a taxidermist's model.

On occasion, Alex would say awful things.

From his dog crate, he said, "I want to die."

It was one of the strange side effects of Jake Burgess's early work with de-extinction and chipping animals: The resurrected species generally was less than enthusiastic about their sequel-return to the here and now, and the chipped animals—animals that were surgically implanted with mechanical surveillance devices—often manifested extreme psychoses. Alex, our crow, did a bit of both.

Alex stayed in the car while we walked toward the river that looked across to the state of New Jersey. Natalie left a plate of spaghetti inside the crate for Alex to eat.

At the water's edge, Father—his name was Jake Burgess—said, "This is what I wanted you to see, Ariel."

And Father waved his arm out across the water as though he had created everything before my eyes, to direct my attention to an enormous welcoming mannequin that rose from the sea.

It was a strange thing to look at. Of course I had seen photographs of the thing before, but standing here at the edge of the continent, the thing struck me as being threatening—a type of warning. After all, the giant blue woman had sharp horns growing from her head and was holding a burning stick, the way you would hold fire to frighten ravenous predators away from you in the dark.

If I owned a house and wanted to keep myself safe from robbers, I would have someone who looked exactly like the great welcoming mannequin watching my door.

Max said, "I'm hungry."

Mother offered, "There's spaghetti in the car."

"I don't like spaghetti," Max said.

Max was a finicky eater ever since his summer at fat camp.

Father took us to a sandwich place for lunch. Mother's purse was stolen while we ate.

She said, "Oh dear. Our car keys were in there."

Father's car was towed to an impound lot, and we were stranded in New York City for two days.

- - -

THURSDAY, FEBRUARY 12, 1880—*ALEX CROW*

There is something morbidly fascinating in our predicament, wouldn't you agree? To imagine the probability of our present situation was impossible. Think about it—we have created our own island, as it were; our own kingdom, phylum, and class of men who hurled themselves arrogantly against the world and became trapped like flies in pine sap. And yet with each short day and interminable night the men put themselves back out onto the ice, never flagging in their effort to control our fate.

Our last contact with humanity came with our stocking of provisions and fuel at St. Lawrence Bay on 27 August, 1879. The *Alex Crow* became trapped in the ice pack only two weeks later. Captain Hansen maintained a strict and disciplined routine, taking constant measurements while the ice continued to drag our ship farther north toward his desired objective, the North Pole. In November, our expedition discovered a true island, which Captain Hansen claimed for the United States and named Alex Crow Island. It was with much bitterness that we watched that piece of land recede away from us and disappear from view as our other, icebound island of *Alex Crow* pulled us tediously onward.

We forge ahead, if nothing else, simply for the sake of doing.

The condition of Mr. Warren's hand is worsening.

It may be selfish of me (and this is very likely a confession of sorts—for is selfishness not the truest component of survival?), but having a patient to occupy my thoughts during the endless monotony aboard ship proves to be an acceptable diversion, unfortunate as it may be for the newspaperman.

I am afraid that given our circumstances I may soon become overwhelmed by such selfish diversions. Our provisions cannot last. Eventually, we will all succumb to the ice. After the last hunt on the pack ice, the native drivers of the dog teams threatened to abandon us and make an attempt for Saint Michael, their home.

Now Captain Hansen has armed guards watching the native men and their dogs. He has instructed the guards to shoot them if the dog drivers attempt to leave. The situation grows worse with each passing day.

This afternoon, an inspection revealed stresses on two of the hull's reinforcing beams. Before departing San Francisco, the *Alex Crow* had been refitted with new boilers and massive crossbeams below decks in order to withstand the tests anticipated on the journey.

Nobody could rightfully foresee our five-month imprisonment.

Today, while I was rewrapping Mr. Warren's crushed hand, Murdoch said to me that he had been his entire life at sea, but had never endured such a predicament as the one we find ourselves in at this moment.

"The ship will be eaten by the sea," he said. "I know the ship will break apart, and we will all of us be buried in ice."

FRIDAY, FEBRUARY 13, 1880—*ALEX CROW*

The hull of the *Alex Crow* gave in last night.

Murdoch came up from below and woke me by pounding on my cabin's door.

"Doctor! Doctor!" he cried.

At first I believed there was some kind of medical emergency that required my attention, but the commotion of men as they scrambled to remove whatever could be taken from the *Crow* and off-loaded onto the ice that trapped us here confirmed my worst fears.

The *Alex Crow* is sinking.

- - -

It was when he was eighteen—a legal adult in the Land of Nonsense—that Leonard Fountain answered an advertisement to participate in a paid study by a company called Merrie-Seymour Research Group. Leonard Fountain didn't really understand or care about the aim of the study, because a thousand dollars was a lot of money to an eighteen-year-old kid from Idaho.

Unfortunately for Leonard Fountain, the study—which was the first round of such experiments involving the implantation of audio-video feed tissue-based "chips"—was directly linked to schizophrenic hallucinations among the majority of the participants. Merrie-Seymour Research Group decided to go back to the drawing board on newer generations of non-schizophrenia-inducing biochips.

MRS. NUSSBAUM, LARRY, AND THE SNORE WALL

Larry was the only inhabitant of Jupiter who'd slept much on that first night.

But since the incident with Bucky Littlejohn and the field-point arrow through the foot, Larry was more than a little stressed out by the four boys of Jupiter. He looked as though he might toss and turn in his non-plastic bed.

After they packed up Bucky in an ambulance, Larry gathered us together and said, "I'm calling a cabin meeting. And right now."

Max and I learned at "orientation," an absolutely senseless meeting where we filled out the name tags we were required to stick to our chests at all times and counted out our socks and underwear and toured the dreaded lightless, spider-infested communal toilets and showers, that at Camp Merrie-Seymour for Boys, "cabin meeting" times were usually reserved for group sessions with the camp's therapist, a frazzled old woman named Mrs. Nussbaum. During our six weeks, Mrs. Nussbaum ultimately came to the conclusion that at least three of the Jupiter boys were particularly troubled, and trouble for her—I never answered her personal questions, while Cobie Petersen and Max seemed to not fit in with the other planets of campers.

She happened to be waiting inside Jupiter when Larry marched the four of us in for our scolding about suicide attempts and such.

Our first session went something like this:

We sat on our beds while Mrs. Nussbaum eyed each one of us, almost as though she were trying to decide which unattractive and mangy puppy to save from the euthanizing chamber at a dog pound. Ultimately, I got that all wrong. Mrs. Nussbaum had other intentions as far as the fate of her boys was concerned.

Mrs. Nussbaum touched the tip of her index finger to my name tag. It made me flinch, and wonder, as all boys do at times like these, why did I always have to go first?

My name tag said this:

HELLO! MY NAME IS: **Ariel Burgess**
I COME FROM: **Jupiter**

Mrs. Nussbaum said, "*Ariel.* That's a lovely name. Would you care to tell us all something about yourself, Ariel?"

I looked directly at her and shook my head.

And since Mrs. Nussbaum brought it up, let me add something about my unwillingness to talk.

It wasn't that I felt embarrassed speaking English. I was confident in my ability with the language. The truth is this: I did not speak because I was unhappy and I was afraid. I was sorry for where I came from, and for what happened to so many of my friends and family members. I was sad to be an orphan—worse, a sole survivor—even if the Burgesses did graciously make me their awkward second son, Max's non-twinned twin. And it made me feel terrible how much Max hated me, too.

I didn't talk because I wouldn't tell anyone about what happened to me with the orphans in the tent city. But most of all was the feeling that I didn't belong here, as much as everyone had seemed so intent (and self-satisfied) with the notion of "saving" Ariel; and that I would never come to understand all of the nonsense that America presented to me.

That's why the boy from the refrigerator didn't say much.

So when Mrs. Nussbaum asked me if I would care to talk about myself, what would she expect me to say? I would love to *care* about talking about myself, but I did not.

So I said this, as politely as I could:

"No thank you."

Mrs. Nussbaum looked injured.

It was a silly thing. Why would anyone ask a question to someone who has free will and then be surprised—or disappointed—by their answer? This made no sense. She asked, I answered, and then there came an awkward, silent, staring period that lasted for several minutes before Max contributed an opinion.

"Allow me to break the ice," he said. "Ariel just doesn't like to talk."

Besides, Mrs. Nussbaum mispronounced my name—she called me *Air*-iel—which is how most Americans said it. Max corrected her, saying *Ah*-riel.

It almost felt as though he were sticking up for me—something brothers should do, right?—but then Max added, "He's stupid, besides."

So Mrs. Nussbaum asked Max to talk about his anger, and again seemed surprised by Max's response that he A) remembered

Mrs. Nussbaum from when this was a fat camp, and he had never been fat in his life; and B) couldn't give a shit about Camp Merrie-Seymour for Boys.

Apparently, Max still held on to his celery grudge from two years earlier.

"This used to be a *fat camp*?" Cobie said.

Max said, "It still *is* a fat camp. They switch it every six weeks between fat camp and the eighteenth century. When I was thirteen, my parents got me in during a fat camp cycle. It was the shittiest summer of my life. Even worse than now."

Mrs. Nussbaum smiled broadly. "But of course I remember you now, Max!"

And then Cobie Petersen asked Mrs. Nussbaum, "How does it feel having the only vagina here in this entire camp?"

Mrs. Nussbaum reddened.

She stuttered, "I . . . I . . ."

When she regained her composure, Mrs. Nussbaum reminded the boys of Jupiter that this session was *not* about her, but if we felt like we wanted to talk about vaginas, she thought that it could be a healthy thing for boys our age.

I glanced over at Larry when Mrs. Nussbaum mentioned a possible vagina-talk. He looked sick.

Then Mrs. Nussbaum patted Robin Sexton on the knee and said, "Robin? I have a cousin named Robin. His parents named him after the little boy in *Winnie-the-Pooh*. How about you? Perhaps you'd like to begin by telling us how you feel about being here, or maybe you could say something about home, since the other boys seem to want to shut this experience out. You know, build walls around themselves."

When she said *build walls*, Mrs. Nussbaum pressed her flattened palms in the air in front of her face, as though she were acting out a street mime's performance of "Man Trapped in an Invisible Box."

And Robin said, "Huh?"

"He keeps shit in his ears, ma'am," Cobie Petersen pointed out.

"Oh," Mrs. Nussbaum said.

Then Mrs. Nussbaum asked us if we felt guilty or sad about what happened to Bucky Littlejohn that day on the archery field.

We all shook our heads, and Cobie said, "He pissed in his bed last night, and Larry made us all clean it up. He was bound to get shot sooner or later."

Mrs. Nussbaum looked approvingly at Larry and told us, "You boys are off to a great start, I can tell! That's a very nice way to build a team."

I suppose team-building in America depends on getting someone else's pee on your hands.

That day, Mrs. Nussbaum passed out blank index cards and gave us pencils. The pencils were the small kind you'd get inside box games, like Yahtzee. The Burgesses played Yahtzee every Saturday night. Max hated the game. He told me it was the only game he knew of where it was impossible to cheat, plus you had to do math. Both of these features made the whole thing not fun to Max.

The pencils Mrs. Nussbaum gave us had no erasers, which implied to me a prohibition on making mistakes. I noticed how Cobie Petersen rubbed the pad of his thumb on his pencil's point. I was reasonably certain he was estimating things like sharpness and stabbing potential.

My pencil had teeth marks in it.

And Mrs. Nussbaum instructed: "I want each of you to write

on your cards. I want you to write about where you would *most rather be*, if you couldn't be here right now at Camp Merrie-Seymour with your friends."

We all looked around at our cabin mates.

Friends?

"Come on, boys! You can do it!" Mrs. Nussbaum prodded, raising the pitch of her voice about one-half octave above "drunkenly enthusiastic," and just below the sound baby dolphins make.

"Do we put our names on them?" Max asked.

"Oh, heavens no! These are only for you. They are *personal*."

"Do we have to write in complete sentences?" Max said.

Mrs. Nussbaum frowned and shook her head.

When we finished (and I had no idea what any of the other boys wrote), Mrs. Nussbaum told us to fold our cards in half and tuck them under our pillows. Of course, when we did that, it sounded like a beer-can-crushing party. She told us we could revise our answers anytime we wanted to over the next six weeks, and that maybe we would all be able to see changes in ourselves by the time we had to go back home.

I didn't get what Mrs. Nussbaum meant by revising our answers. No matter what I did for the next six weeks, if I unfolded my index card and looked at it again, it was still going to say the same thing. Who didn't know that?

And Bucky Littlejohn saw plenty of change in himself in his less-than-twenty-four hours at Camp Merrie-Seymour for Boys. He saw a hole through his left foot, and at that moment was undergoing surgery somewhere.

This is what I wrote on my index card:

INSIDE A REFRIGERATOR

It was not a very productive first group-therapy session, I think.

After Mrs. Nussbaum left, we all stood and attempted to make our way out of the cabin, but Larry stopped us. While Mrs. Nussbaum was relatively controllable as far as the manipulative and uncooperative puppies of Jupiter were concerned, Larry was another challenge altogether.

I'm pretty sure all of us were afraid of him.

"You're not going anywhere, fuckheads." He said, "Now sit down."

So each of us sat at the foot of his bed, and faced across the cabin at Larry.

"Let's get something straight right now," he said. "I'm in charge of you guys for the next six weeks. You haven't even been here one day, and already one of you dickwads almost died. If I lose my job because of shit like this, they'll send me home and my dad will kick me out of the house, or make me get a *real* job and pay rent and shit."

Cobie Petersen raised his hand, like a kid in a classroom.

Larry was clearly irritated. "What?"

Cobie said, "How old are you, Larry?"

Larry glared at Cobie. I realized then that Cobie Petersen was very good at testing people's resilience.

"Twenty-two. Why?"

Cobie shrugged. "Just wondering. Maybe you *should* get a real job."

Larry clenched his teeth and inhaled deeply.

"Six weeks. Is that too much to ask? Come on, guys; give me a break. Then you can all go back home to your internet porn and video games while I get a new batch of losers who will never touch real girls in their lives."

Cobie raised his hand again. "You must get lonely here, Larry."

"Don't fuck with me, kid."

Then Larry pointed at Max and said, "You. Arsonist. No more shit about burning down the cabin. Okay?"

Max nodded. "I was only joking. Besides, if Jupiter *does* burn down, they'll probably stick us in Uranus."

Everyone except Larry laughed. Even Robin Sexton, who obviously had a selective filter for the things he'd allow to pass beyond his toilet-paper gates.

Larry's finger aimed at Robin. "And you. Jerkoff. There's no wanking allowed in this cabin. You think I didn't hear you last night?"

Robin twitched his fingers and said, "Huh?"

Then Larry pointed at me, "And you. Marcel Marceau."

Well, at least I wasn't first. But I did look down at my bare knees to confirm I was wearing short pants, and not the Pierrot costume, which may have saved my life in another time.

I waited, but Larry didn't have any warning for me. All he said was this: "You just keep shutting up and we'll be totally okay with each other, dude, as long as you don't kill yourself."

Then Larry stood up and looked at his wristwatch.

"Now get outside and look at that big yellow thing in the sky. It's called *the sun*. You have thirty minutes till lunch."

And that was our first cabin meeting.

One of the inventions my American father came up with—this was years before I arrived in America—was a device that helped him sleep better at night.

The problem with Jake Burgess's sleep patterns had nothing to do with him. My mother, Natalie, snores terribly. I sleep downstairs from them, and even with my door closed I can hear her nightly snores. I can imagine a similar sound being produced by a giant tree stump being dragged by a tractor down a rough asphalt roadway.

When Max was only two years old, Jake Burgess went to work on what he called a *snore wall*. The device was rather small—about the size of a deck of playing cards—so it could stay on the mattress between Jake and Natalie. When activated, the snore wall emitted a pulse of electric-charged microwaves that rigidly locked the molecules in the air above it in a perfect line, so they could not be agitated by sound waves.

Natalie could snore like a sumo wrestler on her side of the snore wall, but Jake wouldn't hear a thing.

Jake Burgess was very, very smart.

Unfortunately, the first successful time Jake used his snore wall, two passenger jetliners crashed when they collided with the barrier in the skies over their house in Sunday.

Jake never used the snore wall again, but the Merrie-Seymour Research Group paid Jake an awful lot of money for the device.

That was the kind of research Jake Burgess was good at.

Too bad for all those people in the planes, but progress, you know, marches onward and will eventually trample anyone sleeping in its path.

Jake invented all kinds of crackpot things for the Merrie-Seymour Research Group. Max warned me about them. Sometimes I wasn't sure if Max was actually making the things up in his head just to scare me.

That's where Alex, our crow, came from.

It's another story entirely.

This Is What We Do at Camp

All the planets were tied for last place, depending on how you looked at things.

You could just as well claim we were all racing in yellow jerseys on that night after the cancellation of the archery competition. Every planet in the solar system of Camp Merrie-Seymour for Boys, including the abandoned ones, had a score of zero.

I was uncertain what rewards winning at the end of six weeks at camp would bring; if the object of *winning* in itself provided its own intrinsic riches. But I had been in war, and that was somewhere none of the other kids at Camp Merrie-Seymour for Boys had been. So perhaps I had a polluted perspective on the whole notion of winning—of beating your rivals—and what that meant in the overall scheme of things.

But this is what we do at camp; winners make losers, and losers make winners.

Camp Merrie-Seymour for Boys' mess hall wasn't much of a hall. It was a massive structure that some people might describe as a pavilion, a minimalist construction of more than a dozen or so log stilts that supported a peaked and shingled roof with lots of picnic tables beneath it. And all the tables were notched and carved, too. It seemed that the most popular word in camp-carving language was *fuck*, but I didn't look at every single tabletop, so I can only estimate.

A few weeks after I came to America, I thought it would be nice if I could invent a new language. I didn't tell anyone about it, because the first thing people say to you when you tell them you are making up a new language is this: "Say something in it."

I wasn't ready to start saying things yet.

I was certain about this: In the best new language, there would be no words for *me* or *you*. Those words have caused all the trouble started by the old languages. In any new language, there should only be *we*.

We do everything, and everything *we* do, *we* do to *us*.

That would have to be the first rule.

At dinner we sat beneath the pavilion roof and ate hamburgers and mashed potatoes with gravy. There was red Jell-O, too. I'm not sure what flavor the red Jell-O was supposed to be. It was sweet and rubbery. And red. Robin Sexton spooned some of his red Jell-O into the diamond-shaped opening on the paper carton of low-fat milk that came with every camper's meal. Then he closed it and shook it up. Robin Sexton drank it. What dribbled from the corners of his mouth looked like salmon-colored vomit. He also put his mashed potatoes and gravy *inside* his hamburger.

Max just stared at the kid. Max didn't eat much.

It was a very strange meal. The planets segregated themselves as planets will do, locked in isolated orbits at separate tables. So as much as we probably did not like each other, the four boys of Jupiter sat alone near the outer edge of the pavilion.

Although other counselors sat among their wards, Larry chose not to eat with us.

Some of the counselors brought acoustic guitars to the pavilion. At the end of dinner they were going to sing to us and teach us camp songs, because this was all part of rediscovering the fun of being boys.

"If anyone attacks, we should all run that way," Max said. He pointed to an opening at the edge of the yard that led into the trees of the surrounding black woods. We had walked the trail with Larry that morning before the archery disaster. About a half mile down the path was a spring that filled a cinder-block well house with icy water.

"Are you always thinking about escape routes?" Cobie Petersen asked.

Max nodded. "It's what I do."

Cobie said, "Who would attack, anyway?"

"Some of those fuckers from Mars look like psychopaths."

Max had a point.

"Hey. Kid. Kid."

Cobie made an attempt at getting Robin Sexton's attention. He waved his palm in front of the kid, but Robin had his face down over his Styrofoam plate so that his nose was just an inch above what remained of his hamburger bun.

Cobie Petersen tapped Robin Sexton's head and pointed at his ears.

"Huh?"

"Take that shit out of your ears."

Robin tweezered his fingers into his ears and popped out the two compacted beads of toilet paper. They were impressively large. Also, one of them had a smear of pumpkin-colored earwax on it.

"What?" Robin said.

Cobie Petersen asked him this: "Were you really jerking off in bed last night?"

All the eyes of Jupiter were riveted on Robin Sexton, who, despite the dimness of evening, turned visibly red and bit his lip. This concerned me. I slept about sixteen inches away from Robin Sexton, and so did Max.

"No," Robin said. But if the boys of Jupiter could act as a fair jury, Robin Sexton would have been convicted on the spot.

Robin added, "I. Uh. I sleepwalk. I had to make myself stay awake."

Cobie Petersen shook his head. "Jerking off is not a good way to keep yourself awake, kid. It just makes you tired."

Max nodded. "Punching the clown puts me to sleep, too, but I would never do it in Jupiter, with all you other dudes around. Gross."

I was horrified. This was not the first time since coming to America I had to sit through a conversation about jerking off. Max even talked about jerking off in front of our parents! They never knew what he meant, though, because he'd make up his own words for it, like *punching the clown*. Sometimes he'd talk about *helping his best friend get an oil change*, or *going out for a shake with my best friend*. But one night, he explained it to me in excruciatingly clinical detail. Max told me that all "normal" American boys constantly *cooked soup*, and that I'd have to stop acting like such an uptight immigrant kid and loosen up. And a number of the boys in my classes at William E. Shuck High School talked about jerking off as casually as you'd talk about going to the movies, or what you ate for lunch.

Robin Sexton swallowed hard and then only stared—at Cobie, then Max, then me.

Then he replaced his toilet paper earplugs and put his face back down in his food.

Dinner ended with the agonizing song-singing that was a scheduled nightly event at Camp Merrie-Seymour for Boys. Larry came back from wherever he'd been hiding, and the six counselors, with two guitars, a tambourine, autoharp, and a cowbell, commanded all the planets to join in singing three songs I had never heard before. The first two songs were called "Kum Ba Yah" and "Do Your Ears Hang Low?"

And I was not the only boy unfamiliar with these songs, since they played no part whatsoever in the culture of video gaming and social networking. So the counselors passed out photocopied lyrics sheets and made us sing, sing, sing, until we got the songs stuck in our heads for good.

Also, the counselors encouraged us all to sing the word *balls* instead of *ears* during our multitudinous renditions of "Do Your Ears Hang Low?" Everyone thought this was very daring and funny. I thought it was as demented as having a conversation about *punching the clown* over dinner.

But the worst thing was the third song. Nobody except the counselors and Max knew the third song, because it did not exist anywhere outside the solar system of Camp Merrie-Seymour for Boys. Max knew it because he'd been required to sing this same song during his summer at fat camp. The song was called "Boys of Camp Merrie-Seymour," and it went like this:

> *Merrie-Seymour Boys!*
> *We're Merrie-Seymour Boys!*
> *We're learning healthy habits,*
> *Smart as foxes, quick as rabbits!*
> *When people see us they turn and stare,*

Merrie-Seymour Boys are everywhere!
We're fit and strong, as hard as granite,
We come from every single planet!
So cheer and make a happy noise—
For US, the Merrie-Seymour Boys!
For US, the Merrie-Seymour Boys!

When we shouted "US" in the last lines, we were supposed to clap. We looked like thirty-two (now that Bucky Littlejohn had been hospitalized) barking circus seals. I clapped, but I did not shout. I did not even sing. I moved my mouth like a beached trout and pretended. But the counselors made the boys sing the song at least a dozen times until we were loud enough to please them, all clapped with a reasonable sense of trained-seal rhythm, and had the inane lyrics permanently ingrained into our memories.

Larry was in a good mood while we were singing, but not because of the songs. He was in a good mood because he was drunk. We didn't find out about the bottles of vodka and other stuff Larry kept hidden in the counselors' clubhouse until later, but he was drunk, and I could tell, even if the other boys of Jupiter didn't notice such things.

Before bedtime, all the planets retreated to their individual campfires. I'd heard stories from some of the boys at Camp Merrie-Seymour for Boys that when they stared into their fires they frequently hallucinated they were playing a video game.

The boys of Camp Merrie-Seymour for Boys were seriously damaged.

Larry told us we all needed to go take showers and brush our teeth before he'd light the fire, but we whined and complained about showering in the spider cave, so he backed off and told us we could go ahead and stink if we wanted to.

But he added a warning: "If it reeks like ass and feet in Jupiter tonight, I'm kicking all you fuckheads out and you're hitting the showers—dark, spiders, fucking Sasquatches, whatever."

I was unfamiliar with this new word—*Sasquatch*—but the other boys seemed to understand what Larry meant and take it in stride. Robin Sexton always had the same take-it-in-stride look on his face, anyway, probably on account of the toilet paper in his ears and not being confronted about masturbation, so who could tell whether that kid had any clue what Larry was talking about? Considering the preceding modifier Larry used, I assumed that a *fucking Sasquatch* was American slang for a sexual deviant who preyed on boys at summer camp.

If so, he could have Robin Sexton, I thought.

Larry sat in a folding chair at the edge of our Jupiter fire ring. We had to sit in the dirt.

Larry said, "You guys got any scary stories?"

This was also new to me. I had plenty of scary stories, but I didn't think anyone really wanted to hear them.

Max said, "Why? I thought we already did the Mrs. Nussbaum encounter thing once today."

"No." Larry licked his lips and shook his head a little too quickly. His chair nearly tipped over.

Larry continued, "Don't you guys know *anything*? You're supposed to tell scary stories around the campfire."

Cobie Petersen raised his hand.

Larry sighed. "What?"

"Do *you* know any scary stories, Larry?" Cobie asked.

Larry did.

SCARY STORIES

Let me tell you this, Max: When I came out of the refrigerator, there honestly was no place for me to stay. I had to go along with the soldiers who'd come to the village after the gas attack.

They were nice to me, anyway. I think it may have had something to do with the clown suit—how it made me look like a baby, even if I had just turned fourteen. Although they smoked, they never offered their cigarettes to me.

It seems so long ago, Max. It's why I tell you it was my first life, as though I had been resurrected at some point—at least once—before we ever met.

I asked Thaddeus, the man who'd taken off his mask first, if it was the Republican Army who'd gassed the village, and he told me, no, that it was the FDJA rebels. What else would he say? Depending on how long I'd actually been inside that refrigerator, there were probably dozens of videos that had already been posted on the internet assigning blame to any imaginable party. And everyone knows whichever video scores the largest number of hits would be the one that tells the true story, right?

So I went with Thaddeus.

We rode in the open back of a dusty troop carrier with nine other soldiers. Our truck drove in a convoy of military vehicles, some of which towed weapons that looked like missile launchers. Although there was a metal frame to support a canvas covering for our truck's bed, there was no tent, so we all sat there exposed to the heat, dust, and sun. The men were so tired they slept in the rattling bed, slumped over wherever they fit. The soldiers lay atop coiled serpents of ammunition—bands of oily bullets as long as my forearm. The men were uninterested in me, or how I'd come to be there dressed as I was.

But Thaddeus was nice to me. He'd told me that he had two sons at home, and he promised me that everything would work out for me now that I was safe and away from the village. He shared his water and food with me.

In the afternoon we rode through another small city. I did not know the place; I had never been there. But when the convoy drove down the main avenue, the people lined the street and crowded the balconies above to watch us. It was so quiet, or maybe it was just that any sound the people may have been making was drowned out by the clank and roar of our convoy.

Young men followed along on motorbikes and scooters, or they ran like snakes along the crowded sidewalks, as though it were a sort of festive parade, and this was the best thing that had happened in memory.

From time to time jets flew by, low in the sky overhead. We could hear the explosions from the missiles they fired miles ahead of us, beyond flat farmland and low mountains.

That night we slept outside on a dirt road that ran through a sesame field.

I woke sometime in the darkest part of the night. There was no moon, only stars. I didn't know it, but Thaddeus had been sitting next to me, watching me as I slept. He'd given me a blanket to lie on, and it was so warm that I was damp with sweat.

"Are you all right?" Thaddeus asked.

"Yes. It's hot, and I'm not very tired."

"Can I tell you something?" he said.

"Sure."

"It's not a good thing," Thaddeus said, "but I feel I need to tell somebody. And I think you're the person to say it to."

"Why me?"

Thaddeus shook his head. "I don't know. Maybe it's the white suit."

"It's not as white as it was when I put it on," I said.

"No matter," Thaddeus said.

He scooted toward my blanket and leaned close, so he could whisper. "When I was a boy—I was—how old are you?"

"Fourteen."

"You're fourteen?"

"Yes."

"I thought you were just a baby."

"Maybe it's the white suit," I said.

Thaddeus nodded. "When I was nine years old, my mother became very sick with cancer. She was dying. It was terribly slow and ugly to witness. My father never talked to me about it. Not one time did he ask me how I was feeling, or what I was thinking about. Do you know?"

"I think so."

"I was so angry about everything, but my father never spoke to me about it."

"It must have been sad. I don't have any parents, and now my aunt and my uncle—"

"Yes. Maybe that's why I need to say this." Thaddeus leaned toward my shoulder. His breath was hot as he whispered. "We had a small dog then. His name was Pipo."

"That's a good name."

"I was so mad about everything. Outside our house, there were fields of wheat growing. One morning, I took Pipo into the field and dug a deep hole. Then I put the little dog in the hole and I buried him. Nobody knew what I did. That evening my father asked where the little dog was, and I lied to him and told him I didn't know; that maybe he ran away. It was a terrible thing. I feel so bad about what I did. I think about it every day."

I could see Thaddeus was crying.

"I never told anyone about it until now. I was a monster, but I couldn't control myself."

"Maybe that little dog was the only thing you could control."

"I hate myself still."

What could I say to the man? It was almost as though, in the telling, he were pouring the story of the little dog into me— this receiving vessel dressed in a clown suit—and now it would be my responsibility to carry Thaddeus's story along with me for how many more years.

"Eventually, I suppose you'll have to find a way to make things right," I said.

"That's why I'm telling you. You need to say how I can do this."

"Why me?"

"Because, when I found you, it was as though you'd come out of a hole," Thaddeus explained.

I shrugged.

"It was a refrigerator. I needed to pee."

- - -

Jake Burgess worked in a semiautonomous laboratory owned by the Merrie-Seymour Research Group. It was called Alex Division. This is where nearly everything Jake Burgess invented came from, including our pet, Alex.

Jake always had a fascination with crows. He told me it was due to the birds' uncanny intelligence and their ability to adapt to just about any situation that confronted them. The first Alex crow was a gift from Jake to Natalie just after the birth of Max, my American brother, who did not like me and was exactly sixteen days older than I was.

I say "first" Alex because that bird died when Max was ten months old and I lived in a dirty village halfway around the world from Sunday, West Virginia. Well, to be honest, the crow only sort of died when Max and I were ten months old.

Jake Burgess brought both of the Alex crows back to life. They were like photocopied beings that would never change, and never leave. Alex, our crow, was a member of a species that had been extinct for a century.

At that time, my father, Jake Burgess, was investigating a method for perfecting de-extinction for Alex Division. Of course, both the word and the concept of *de-extinction* are entirely ridiculous.

Extinction can't be undone, or else you were never extinct in the first place. You were just waiting for something better than eternal death.

There was always something a little *off* about the things Jake Burgess brought back to life. At least, that's what Max told me. I couldn't exactly say I *knew* any of the other Alex animals created by Jake Burgess, so I had nothing to compare our pet to. Still, our resurrected pet bird did strike me as being empty of any kind of soul, and overwhelmingly disappointed by his existence.

Sometimes I wondered if Max had been emptied out and brought back to Sunday just like Alex, in some cruel experiment researched by his father, or that perhaps I had been brought back like our crow, too.

It's funny how I remember some events in my life so clearly, and others—often recent ones—seem disjointed and fuzzy. I attribute that to nervousness, I suppose. It's a very frightening thing, when you think about it, being dug up from a hole or extracted from a refrigerator and then finding yourself some kind of display artifact for everyone to marvel over (*See the kid who shouldn't actually be here!*). But I can't clearly remember all the details surrounding my arrival at the Burgess home in Sunday. I remember riding in a van with Jake Burgess and a man named Major Knott from a place called Annapolis, which I had never heard of before. Also, I remember all the trees and water—we crossed so many rivers on the way—things I'd only seen in pictures.

The Burgess house was a single-story brick home built into a hill with a garage and basement underneath the main floor. We walked up a gravel driveway to the front door, where Natalie and Max—who had taken the day off from school to meet his new foreign brother—waited.

Natalie held my face and kissed me on top of my head. It made me feel nice.

And Max said to me, "What's your name, kid?"

"Uh."

Natalie patted Max's shoulder. "Don't be silly, Max. We've told you. His name is Ariel."

Max said, "Oh yeah. Ariel," and walked away.

But they pronounced it correctly.

I went inside with Jake Burgess and Major Knott, who carried a cloth bag containing the new clothes and things they'd given me when I got to Annapolis. The house was dark and smelled like nothing I had ever smelled before. It was the smell of America, I'd supposed, a combination of furniture polish, cleanser, and cooking oil.

In the living room, behind an old tufted chair, stood a type of black rounded perch. And on that perch was the Burgesses' crow, Alex. He was staring at me, holding perfectly still. I honestly thought he was some sort of decoration; I never imagined people kept such creatures in their homes.

But then Alex moved his head slightly and said, "Punch the clown. Punch the clown."

It was nothing more than a frightening coincidence. Eventually I came to realize Alex learned much of his vocabulary from Max.

- - -

Joseph Stalin was not the only voice inside Leonard Fountain's melting head. The melting man also heard someone named 3-60.

3-60 was not as mean or harmful as Joseph Stalin. While Joseph Stalin urged Leonard Fountain to kill people, 3-60 said nice things to the melting man. 3-60 liked to narrate to Leonard Fountain everything that he was doing, as though she were telling the story of the melting man's life while it played out in real time.

"You are turning onto Smale Road."

"Yes. I am," the melting man said to 3-60.

"You are driving past a cemetery. You are looking at the headstones. Your balls are itchy. You are drifting off the road."

The melting man swerved back onto the highway.

"Thank you for saving my life, 3-60."

"You're welcome, Lenny."

That reminded the melting man of his younger brother, who was the only person who'd ever called him Lenny.

"But your balls still itch," 3-60 reminded him.

"Oh yeah."

"Now they hurt."

"Well, I shouldn't have scratched them," the melting man said.

"You're very sick," 3-60 told him. "Maybe you should consider leaving the masterpiece somewhere along the side of the road and just moving on."

"I have to do what Joseph Stalin told me to do. I don't want to make him angry."

"You are driving. You are driving. You are driving," 3-60 said.

"Yes. I am."

- - -

Tuesday, February 17, 1880—*Alex Crow*

While the *Alex Crow* sank, the crew managed to pull two of the ship's longboats, as well as the dog sleds, food, and equipment from the doomed vessel.

Mr. Warren could not assist the off-loading due to his incapacitation. However, in this past week, Mr. Warren's hand has healed significantly, although he has lost a great deal of mobility due to the shattered bones. Imagine the predicament of a newspaperman who lacks the ability to put pen to paper! Mr. Warren has been dictating to Murdoch, but the man is constantly frustrated by Murdoch's deficiencies in skill.

Let me express how disheartening it was to see the last timbers of the *Alex Crow* being shut up behind the mouth of this hellish Arctic ice. It was a mournful event for us all, because despite our predicament there was always some insulating sense of safety provided to our little society by the formidable ship. Now we are stripped of nearly everything and left to make some way, which I fear is only a lengthening of our journey toward doom. I cannot believe any of us will survive now.

After a full day's rest on the ice pack, Captain Hansen and Mr. Piedmont calculated a direction for our attempt at reaching the New Siberian archipelago. The journey has been incredibly arduous—the men work without rest, dragging the burdensome boats over impossible crags of relentless ice. Two days ago, on Sunday, it seemed as though our party had only managed to cover a few hundred feet for the entire day's labor.

The cost on the men has been significant. Yesterday morning, Mr. K. Holme, a naval seaman, succumbed to the cold, and today our expedition's ice pilot, Edgar Baylor, passed away shortly after dawn.

Our crew has lost all hope of rescue. I am afraid that if there was any reasonable alternative to Captain Hansen's strategy to reach New Siberia, there certainly would be mutiny among the survivors.

Sunday, February 22, 1880—*Alex Crow*

A most remarkable occurrence—we reached open water today!

Could it be that those of us who have endured this ordeal will survive? Mr. Murdoch during this past week has taken to uttering a repetitive chant of sorts—"Why bother?" he asks again and again. It does give one pause, at times, to consider the point of it all. Why is the will to survive—in spite of the horrors of one's condition—so profound?

Why bother?

It was entirely unbelievable. When we saw the dark breach ahead of us, Captain Hansen and Mr. Piedmont presumed we were approaching Kotelny Island, and that what we saw must have been the rocky shore. This proved to be incorrect as we neared the edge of the ice pack.

So it was with renewed spirit the men bothered to lower the heavy longboats into the sea. The dog teams, however, were forced to turn back in the direction from which they'd come, since there was not adequate room on our boats for everything. I sensed some great relief among the native handlers when they were finally free to leave our ill-fated expedition.

I am in Captain Hansen's boat. I believe that his leadership has kept the majority of the expedition alive during the difficult journey across the ice, and I have faith that he will bring us safely to the shores of the northern islands where we will find shelter and warmth among the natives there.

This is my hope.

Tuesday, February 24, 1880—*Alex Crow*

We lost sight of our sister boat in a vicious storm last night.

One more of the seamen—Richard Alan Culp—died aboard our vessel this afternoon. Once again, our diminished party feels alone and without hope. It is all I can do to tend to their aching bodies, and attempt to inspire some sense of confidence and optimism. I'm afraid this is entirely useless, though. The least I can do is to ignore the constant questioning of Murdoch.

This afternoon, Mr. Warren and I huddled beneath the gunwale in a small covered space we'd made with one of the expedition's tents. I'd asked him if he was still dictating the narrative of our expedition to Murdoch. He insisted that readers would want to have the full account of the loss of the *Alex Crow*, even if none of us survived.

"Particularly if none of us survive," I said.

To this, Mr. Warren replied, "I cannot think any of us will ever see his home again. Why would anyone think such a thing, given our current state?"

I do not believe we can last one more night in this boat. I have found myself hoping—and that is an odd word to use—that I will not wake to find myself the sole living inhabitant of the boat, that if I am not to make it home again, as Mr. Murdoch predicts, that I die before too many others are dropped into the sea.

I realize that death and survival are both extremes of selfishness.

Just before nightfall, from beneath our covering, Mr. Warren and I heard Murdoch shouting that land had been sighted, but when we came out to look, it was already too dark to see anything more than an arm's reach from the boat's hull.

Imagine our disappointment and dread at Captain Hansen's cautious decision to forgo any attempt at landing until daylight tomorrow.

"Who knows where we will be at daylight tomorrow?" Murdoch wondered.

MARSHMALLOW JEFF AND THE BOYS FROM EARTH

"I'm going to tell you guys something, but you are not allowed to ever repeat it to anyone else as long as you live." Larry pointed his index finger like a spear to emphasize the words *anyone else*.

"That sounds perfectly reasonable, Larry," Cobie Petersen said.

I wondered about Cobie Petersen. Like Max and me, Cobie Petersen just didn't belong here; he didn't fit in with the other kids at Camp Merrie-Seymour for Boys. At that moment, after his smart-ass comment went unnoticed by Larry, I almost wanted to talk to him, to ask him why his parents sent him here, but I couldn't bring myself to do it.

Robin Sexton, on the other hand, was a different story. Of the four boys of Jupiter, he was clearly in the right place.

I watched Robin Sexton. His face was blank, and he stared into the fire with frozen eyes. His thumbs and fingers wriggled over an invisible controller. I was pretty sure he was hallucinating clearing a difficult level in some violent video game.

"I'm going to tell you what happened to Earth," Larry said.

"Before or after the asteroid that killed all the dinosaurs?" Cobie asked.

Robin Sexton rocked back and forth.

"No," Larry said. "I'm going to tell you about the Earth cabin, and why we don't use it anymore at Camp Merrie-Seymour for Boys. And you fuckheads can't say anything to *anyone*, because this is a true story. But you have to tell a scary story, too. It's what *normal* kids do at camp, at night."

Max and Cobie looked warily at Robin Sexton. Then they both promised they would tell a story.

Larry said, "What about you, Marcel Marceau? You in for telling us a story?"

I shook my head.

"You could just act it out," Larry said.

I *was* acting it out. I shook my head again.

"Whatever," Larry said. "Well, two of you is better than none. We already know Earbud's scary story, about the time he got caught jerking off at camp. So here goes: I started working here as a counselor when I was seventeen—just out of high school. My dad wanted to make me join the army, or he said he was going to throw me out of the house when I turned eighteen, which was going to be in a month and a half, so I headed east and ended up answering an ad for a live-in counselor. In those days, there were *three* alternating programs here: a camp for fat kids; this one you guys are in—the camp for fuckheads like you who don't have any *real-life* friends; and a camp for kids with psychological disorders, you know—neurotics, compulsive liars, narcissists, kleptomaniacs, sadists, and arsonists."

It sounded like the future of America to me.

"Lucky thing I missed out on the Camp Merrie-Seymour for Psychopathic Boys cycle that summer," Max said.

"Every day, you'd wake up and it was like Custer's Last Stand," Larry said.

"That's slang for jerking off," Max pointed out.

"It is?" Larry said,

Max nodded his assurance.

Larry went on, "The Earth cabin's counselor was a guy named Marshmallow Jeff. The kids called him that because he was really, really white, and he'd use marshmallows as bribes to get the crazies to behave themselves. And he was super creepy, too. He kept marshmallows in his pockets for the kids, and tucked inside the tops of his socks, too. Nobody liked him, and he never talked to anyone."

For some reason, this last statement caused Max and Cobie to turn and stare at me.

Then Larry said, "But the kids of Earth were like zombies under Marshmallow Jeff's control, on account of all the marshmallows he'd give them. The Earth cabin's still here, too. It's on the other side of the creek from the mess hall, in the woods. After the incident that happened there that summer, they stopped keeping the vines knocked back around Earth, so unless you know it's there, you don't even notice it."

"So, what happened at the Earth cabin?" Max asked.

"I'm telling you, kid. Be patient." Larry moistened his lips and burped a silent blast of vodka gas. "Pretty much as soon as the camp term started that summer, Marshmallow Jeff complained to Mrs. Nussbaum that one of the other planets was playing tricks on the Earth boys—trying to scare them. He said that his kids kept seeing two red eyes in the woods at night, like they were staring in at them through the screen on the cabin. Nobody likes to get stared at by red eyes at night, right? Anyway, it kept happening, night after night, and the eyes kept getting closer and closer and closer to the Earth cabin."

Larry lowered his voice and got a crazy look in his eyes when he said the part about the eyes getting closer. And I'll be honest—I'd never heard stories like this before, so it was making me more than a little scared.

Then something happened that made us all jump.

We heard the fluttering buzz of a vibrating cell phone. Larry jerked his hand down to smother the spot in his cargo shorts where he'd hidden his phone, but it was too late. The thing may just as well have been an air-raid siren as far as the boys of Jupiter were concerned.

"Uh," Larry said.

Robin Sexton's eyes flashed flames.

"You have a phone!" Robin said.

"No—I—uh—"

In other circumstances, with other planets, I could easily imagine a bloody scene ending in Larry's gruesome dismemberment. But clearly, Max, Cobie, and I didn't care about Larry's cell phone. Robin Sexton, on the other hand, began salivating and attempted to get to his feet.

But Larry held out a warning hand and said, "Don't even think about it, kid."

Robin chewed on his lower lip and sat back in the dirt.

It was reasonable that counselors would be permitted to have such luxuries as cell phones and electricity and so on. I could only assume that most of them were more adept than Larry at keeping their secrets concealed.

"Am I going to finish telling this story, or what?"

"If we had our phones, you could group text us," Cobie Petersen offered.

Larry sighed, and put his hands on his knees like he was going to get up and go to bed.

"No. I was just kidding, Larry," Cobie apologized. "Please finish the story."

Larry pointed his spear-finger at Cobie. "You're telling one, too."

"I promised, didn't I?"

So Larry continued, "One night there was a terrible storm. Everyone shut themselves up inside the cabins just trying to keep dry and warm, except for Marshmallow Jeff and the boys from Earth. They'd seen the red eyes in the woods again, right outside their cabin, and Marshmallow Jeff told his campers he'd give them all fistfuls of marshmallows if they would go out in the storm into the woods with him, so they could kick the living shit out of whoever was trying to scare them."

"Were you in Jupiter then, Larry?" Cobie Petersen asked.

"Yeah."

"Six summers in Jupiter." Cobie shook his head. "You must be very, very lonely."

"Shut up. It's not like I spend all year here, kid. I have a life," Larry said.

"Doing what, exactly?" Cobie asked.

"Jesus. Are you guys going to let me tell the story, or what?"

I think we all wondered what Larry did when he wasn't in Jupiter.

"Sorry," Cobie Petersen said. "I just find you endlessly fascinating, Larry."

Larry's jaw kind of hung open slightly, and he stared blankly at Cobie Petersen—probably the way one would look out at a pair of glowing red eyes in the middle of a creepy forest at night. When he regained his composure, Larry said, "We heard screams—the most horrible sound you could ever imagine—coming from deep in the woods that night. The whole camp was terrified, and when we looked, Earth cabin was completely empty. We searched and searched all the following day, but there was no sign at all of Marshmallow Jeff and the boys from Earth. It was like they had completely vanished into thin air."

Max, Cobie, and I glanced at one another, trying to gauge by each other's face whether or not we should believe Larry's story.

Robin Sexton twitched, rocked slightly, and stared into the fire.

Then Larry's voice lowered to a sinister whisper, and he said, "We only ever found one clue that remained of Marshmallow Jeff and the boys from Earth. Out there . . ."

Larry stretched his arm out and pointed off into the woods on the opposite side of the creek from the mess hall. "Their shoes—six pairs, counting Marshmallow Jeff's—were all perfectly lined up by the well house. And there were a few marshmallows scattered on the ground. That was it. Nothing else. It was a mystery, but the boys and Marshmallow Jeff were never seen again. Unless, that is, if you believe the stories some people tell of seeing a big barefoot white man who wanders the woods and hunts for children with baits of marshmallows."

"I call bullshit," Cobie Petersen said.

"Oh yeah?" Larry was irritated. "I dare you kid—right now, I bet you could go out there in the woods past the well house, and you'll see footprints—bare feet—that belong to Marshmallow Jeff and the crazy boys he abducted from Earth."

And Larry added, "I dare you, tough guy. Let's all go take a look inside the old Earth cabin right now, if you have the balls. Marshmallow Jeff and his friends are waiting for you."

DEMIKHOV'S DOGS AND THE ALEX CAT

Max said, "Maybe we should just go to bed now."

Larry shook his head. "No. It's you guys' turn. *You* got to tell a story now. You know—normal kids at camp and all."

"Well, your story was horseshit, Larry, and mine's true," Max said.

"Whatever you say, kid."

Max folded his knees and hugged his shins. He leaned toward the fire with a look of concentration in his eyes, and said, "My father gets paid to think up and make things that should never exist in the first place."

"That's a start," Larry said. "I'm interested, kid. Like what kinds of things?"

Of course, I sat there cringing at the thought of all the stories Max might tell about life in our home, and I was also confident I didn't even know half of the terrible things my American brother could possibly reveal.

"One time, we had a pet cat," Max began. His voice was low and solemn.

This intrigued me. There were no cats in the Burgess home, so I suspected Max's *scary story* was not going to end well for his leading character.

"When I was in third grade, one afternoon my father brought home a cat—one of his projects he'd been developing for the place where he works."

"Awww . . . ," Larry said. "What was the cat's name?"

"What does it matter?" Max shrugged. "It was a cat. Everything our dad brings home is always named Alex."

It touched me that Max said *our dad,* until he pointed at me and added, "Except *him.* For some reason Dad didn't name *him* Alex."

What could I say? I wondered if Max suspected I was one of our father's inventions.

Max went on, "Did you ever hear of a Russian scientist named Vladimir Demikhov?"

"Are you just making that up?" Larry asked.

"No. He was a real person. My father used to tell me stories about him. He was fucking insane. One of the things Demikhov was famous for was something he did to dogs. He used to surgically attach extra heads to dogs. He would make dogs with two living heads, that could eat, and everything."

"That's fucking *sick,*" Cobie Petersen said.

Although what Demikhov did to dogs was sick, Cobie Petersen used the American teenage slang version of the word *sick,* which meant that attaching extra heads to dogs was something Cobie Petersen admired very much.

And Cobie Petersen added, "That means he'd have to actually *cut the heads off* living dogs to do it, right?"

Max nodded.

"How many heads did your cat have?" Cobie asked.

"Just one. It wasn't *that* kind of invention my dad was working on. Demikhov was stupid. Nobody wants a dog with two fucking heads."

Cobie Petersen raised his hand, an earnest look in his eyes. "I would. I would want a two-headed dog."

Max shook his head. "The cat did have extra toes, though. His feet were as big around as billiard balls, but that wasn't something my dad did, either. The cat was born that way. But the cat was really weird, too, because they had done all this tinkering around inside his head and body. Mechanical stuff and things with computers that were made from synthetic animal tissue that you'd never know were in there, but they changed him so much he didn't really *act* like a regular cat. Maybe that's just because he was fucked up on the inside. But I'll be honest; he seemed depressed, like he didn't want to live. And he didn't sleep all the time, or chase bugs and mice and birds like normal cats, either. He just sat around staring and staring and staring at us. The cat—Alex—was one of the first versions of what my dad's company calls a *biodrone*. They were made to spy on people, and to do worse things, too."

"So? What's so scary about that?" Larry said.

"Biodrones are made to kill people," Max said. "And you'd never know it. Some fucker could be sitting at a computer screen at Alex Division, listening to you, maybe watching you *vaporize your excess anxiety*, and then press a button, and—*poof! kablooey!*—you're done."

Everyone got very quiet when Max said that. There was only the crackling of the fire and the metronomic rustling of Robin Sexton's rocking in the dirt.

"It's a creepy thing," Max said. "Because when most people think of spy drones, they think of things that follow you around and you don't know about them. Biodrones are things that *people* follow around—like pets—and you never know what they're actually doing. It's a safe bet that Alex Division has probably made biodrones out of people, too."

Then Max glanced at me, and said, "What do *you* think, Ariel?"

What could I say?

"Why did your dad bring it home if it was made to kill people?" Cobie Petersen asked.

"They were just testing it out, to see how well it performed, and if it fit in with a family," Max explained. "In the lab, they could actually hear and watch on monitors whatever the cat was looking at or listening to."

"Did you *know* it was spying on you?" Cobie said.

Max shook his head. "No. Not until afterward. Neither did my mom. But that's just normal, everyday shit in our house."

"Did it—you know—did the cat ever catch you *punching the clown*?"

Once again, the things American boys felt at ease talking about mortified me.

"Dude. Don't be an idiot. I was eight years old."

"So?" Cobie said.

Max cleared his throat. "Well, no, dumbass. The cat only stayed with us a few months, anyway."

"What happened to him?" Cobie Petersen asked.

"Well, our house is out on the old South Fork Route," Max began.

Naturally, a kid like Cobie Petersen would know the road, since it was the only link between Sunday and Dumpling Run, which is where Cobie Petersen lived.

Max said, "The cat was always trying to kill himself. Seriously. I know that sounds unnatural, but he would wait in the grass on the side of the road, just like a normal cat waits and watches for birds. Only Alex was waiting and watching for cars or trucks to speed by, then he'd try to run out and throw himself into their wheels. At first, my mom just thought it was because the cat was young and inexperienced with cars and stuff. But after enough times grabbing him by the tail at the last second, the coincidence started to kind of wear off.

"So, one day, my mom was taking a load of garbage out to the incinerator and the cat made a try at it again, just as an old Plymouth came barreling down the highway."

Cobie and Larry, caught up in Max's story, leaned closer to my brother.

"My mom had to drop the garbage and make a dive for the cat. But the cat got loose, and my mom broke her wrist on the blacktop."

"Was she okay?" Cobie Petersen asked.

Max shook his head and shrugged. "Who knows? Her arm was broken—anyone could see that—and she got a tooth knocked out, too, but she said she'd be fine, and she refused to let anyone take her in to see the doctor."

That's our mom!

"Wow. Your mom's fucking tough," Cobie said.

Max shrugged again and said, "Yeah. Whatever. Who knows? The thing is, though, when the cat met the Plymouth in the middle of the road, the thing exploded. Blew up. *Kablooey*. Done. It made a five-foot-deep crater in South Fork Route, and the road was shut down for almost two weeks."

"I remember that," Cobie Petersen said.

"Yeah. Well, it was our cat, Alex, the biodrone, that did it." Max said, "The official explanation said that the boys in the Plymouth were carrying barrels of high-octane moonshine, and that's what caused the explosion. But it was actually our cat, which wasn't much of a cat at all."

"That's kind of creepy," Larry said.

"Yeah. So next time you see a basket of free kittens in a Walmart parking lot, or even if you happen to notice a blue jay swooping down from the branches on a nice summer day, you can just stop and think about whether what you assume you're looking at is really something that happens to be looking at you; something that's worse than anything you could ever imagine," Max said.

Then Max did something that surprised and embarrassed me. He tapped my knee with the back of his hand—almost affection-ately, the way that conspiratorial brothers might do when they're pulling one over on someone—and said, "Isn't that right, Ariel?"

What could I say?

I nodded.

And I thought, maybe in some new language, Max and I would become *we*.

TEACHER'S PET AND THE DUMPLING MAN

"Is that for real?" Larry said.

Max frowned disapprovingly. "Dude. Larry. How long have you been working here at Camp Merrie-Seymour for Boys? You must have heard about some of the fucked-up things Merrie-Seymour and Alex Division do to people."

Larry stared off into the dark. I don't think he actually knew anything about the camp's owners. I was also pretty sure Larry drank an awful lot.

"You've been to this camp before?"

"Yes," Max said, "when I was thirteen. For fat camp."

"It looks like it worked out pretty good for you. What are you? Like a buck-ten, if that?" Larry said.

Max exhaled through his nose. "Look, I have *never* been fat. My parents just wanted to get rid of me for a month or so, and I weigh a hundred and five, besides. The only reason I ever came here is 'cause my folks don't have to pay for this shithole."

"Neither do mine," Cobie Petersen said, raising his hand. And

Cobie added, "I weigh one twenty-two, by the way, if we're swapping personal statistics."

It was obvious to me that Cobie Petersen was unlike the other addicted boys at Camp Merrie-Seymour for Boys. Maybe, I thought, his parents worked at Alex Division or the Merrie-Seymour Research Group. I also had a feeling that if I was ever going to make a friend here—or anywhere—or actually start talking to someone, maybe I could talk to Cobie Petersen.

And Larry went on, "Well, I don't remember ever seeing you at fat camp."

I didn't imagine Larry remembered much of anything from one session to the next at Camp Merrie-Seymour for Boys.

Max said, "I was in Venus. The last year that cabin was used."

"You were one of the kids who got beat up all the time?" Larry said.

"Whatever."

Cobie Petersen stretched out his leg and kicked Robin Sexton.

"Hey, kid." Cobie made his familiar take-that-shit-out-of-your-ears gesture to Robin.

Robin Sexton looked worried. The last time Cobie wanted to engage in conversation with him didn't go so well. Robin Sexton pulled out his plugs and said, "What do you want?"

"How much do your parents pay to keep you in this place?"

Robin said, "Five thousand dollars," and put the toilet paper wads back in his ears.

Cobie kicked the kid again.

"I'm not through talking to you. How much do you weigh?"

I was very grateful that Robin Sexton did not answer Cobie Petersen's question, because I didn't remember how much I weighed in American pounds, and I didn't want to talk about it, besides. They weighed me one time at William E. Shuck High School, in my physical education class, which turned out to be something very cruel and barbaric that involved daily nudity and name-calling, kind of like a state-sponsored ongoing performance of *Lord of the Flies*. If pressed, I would just say I weighed whatever Max said—one hundred five. Max and I were identical in size anyway, which was just another reason Max disliked me—sometimes Mom would switch our socks and underwear when they came out of the laundry.

Nobody likes having his socks and underwear swapped out for some other guy's.

Then Larry said, "All right, Teacher's Pet, stop trying to change the subject. It's your turn to tell a scary story."

Cobie raised his hand and asked, "Am I the official *Teacher's Pet* of Jupiter, Larry?"

Larry tossed two logs into the fire. "Sure. If that's what you want to be. Teacher's Pet. Now, do you have anything to tell us?"

"I do," Cobie said. "And this is a true story, too—like Max's was. Not like your steaming mound of shit."

Larry said, "You want to take a walk over to Earth with me right now? Just us four, and maybe we'll drag along Earbuds, too? We'll see how many of us make it back."

"Just tell the story," Max said.

And Cobie Petersen said this: "Okay. Here goes: I have seen the Dumpling Man. He is real."

And in the same way that anyone who lived near Sunday, West Virginia, would know where South Fork Route went, we had also all heard the stories about the Dumpling Man.

Here's what I'd learned since coming to Sunday: Dumpling Run was the name of a creek that spilled down the mountains in a series of falls that created scattered deep pools where the local kids would fish and swim in summertime. Along either side of the creek were homes spaced apart from one another on large acreage covered with old-growth forests.

And every home up Dumpling Run was owned by a family whose last name was either Peterson or Petersen. I might add, too, that the people who live up and down the banks of the creek known as Dumpling Run—families of Petersons and Petersens—pronounce the word *Dumplin*, unwavering in their conviction that the inclusion of the nasal G is a certain indication the speaker is either Canadian or homosexual.

Everyone in Sunday knew the immortal gossip regarding the origin of those family names, too, but they were all unclear as to whether the original had been changed from "son" to "sen," or the other way around, in order to legitimize what would otherwise have been an illegal marriage between half siblings or first cousins.

Uncles, aunts, cousins, brothers, and so on—it all gets a bit muddy when trying to figure out exactly who is related, and by what degree, as you go house to house visiting the Petersons and Petersens of Dumpling Run.

But for as long as Max and I had been alive (the majority of which time we had spent on opposite sides of the planet), people from Dumpling Run and the occasional fisherman or hunter kept rekindling the frightening tale of the pale and monstrous creature who lived in the woods outside the town of Sunday, West Virginia: the Dumpling Man.

So Cobie Petersen explained to Larry, our counselor, what the Dumpling Man was, and he threw in passing references to the killing of Tate Peterson's prize sow and the mysterious disappearance of a four-year-old boy named Cleon Petersen, a cousin of Cobie's whom nobody around Sunday—Cobie included—could actually verify ever having been acquainted with.

"Those are all just crock-of-shit Bigfoot-Sasquatch stories cooked up by moonshiners to keep people out of the woods," Larry said.

I heard the word again.

It was beginning to make sense now.

"Maybe," Cobie Petersen said. "But I know what I know. And I saw the fucker, just as plain as I'm looking at you right now."

Max's jaw hung open slightly. He looked like he was about to drool. But an actual, firsthand sighting of the Dumpling Man was enough to terrify any kid who lived in Sunday.

"When did this supposedly happen?" Larry asked.

"It happened last fall. And it wasn't *supposedly*, Larry. I was hunting coons," Cobie began, "and I was alone except for my dog, Ezra. It was about one in the morning, I guess."

Let me say here, too, that not only was Sunday a kind of spiritual center for people who loved sauerkraut and firearms, nearly all the boys of a certain age hunted and killed things like deer, squirrels, rabbits, porcupines, bears, and raccoons—they called them *coons*—which were something like bloated and angry stripe-tailed rats that would eat just about anything. Usually, boys would start hunting on their own around age thirteen or fourteen. The coons were hunted for their fur, but also for food, something involving a great deal of preparation, including removal of the scent glands from the animal's legs, and then brining the meat overnight to reduce the coon's natural and pungent odors.

And coon hunting only takes place at night, since the raccoon is a nocturnal animal. It was very convenient to the families in that part of West Virginia, too, because a boy could be out all night hunting coons to provide for his family, and still make it home in time to get to school.

As strange as Jake and Natalie Burgess were, it was a great relief for me to know that our parents never encouraged Max and me— alone or as a brotherly team—to hunt coons for our supper, unlike the other boys who lived in the hills around Sunday.

Max tapped Robin Sexton's shoulder. "Hey? You ever hear of the Dumpling Man in Hershey, Pennsylvania?"

Robin, who apparently could hear just fine, shook his head and said, "No. My daddy works in the chocolate offices, and I weigh ninety-four."

Cobie fired a dirty look at Robin Sexton, and continued, "That night, Ezra got on to a strong scent and took off splashing and yelping across Dumpling Run and up through the trees on the other side. I couldn't see where my dog was heading; could only hear his barking and tramping through the brush, but I ran after him and tried to stay up as close as I could, which put me pretty far back considering the number of legs Ezra has to run on, compared to the number of legs I've got.

"Well, maybe a mile on the other side of Dumpling Run, Ezra held up at the bottom of a big chestnut oak, which meant he'd treed the coon we were after. It was terribly quiet and dark that night. There was no moon, so it was hard to see, but when I looked up in the branches of the chestnut oak, I saw something I will never forget as long as I live."

"The Dumpling Man?" Max asked.

Cobie Petersen nodded slowly, the way a doctor would do when he's telling you that you've only got two weeks left to live. "At first, I didn't know what I was looking at. I thought, if this is a coon, then it's the biggest coon in the history of coon hunting. And even in the dark I could see the color was off—not the color of a regular coon hide. This thing looked more like the color of fresh boiled peanuts, all pale and golden.

"So I'm not going to lie, I was terrified, thinking that maybe me and Ezra had treed a mountain lion, and I was about to get my neck broke. I was shaking so bad I could barely hold on to my rifle, and my knees were knocking together. I reached into my back pocket and pulled out a flashlight, so I could see what I was aiming at up in the tree, and all the while Ezra was howling like he was going to lose his mind. So in all the panic—the crazy yelping of my dog, my shaking fear—I was certain we were both about to die. Even though I was right underneath the thing in the tree, I was trembling so bad I knew I wasn't going to be able to shoot him. And then—*flash!*—I turned my light onto the thing. And there I saw it—the Dumpling Man himself."

Like an expert storyteller, Cobie Petersen stopped at this point so we could all imagine how the situation developed.

"What did he look like?" Max said.

Cobie Petersen shook his head again. "Like nothing I'd ever seen. My light caught his eyes. They were as big around as half-dollars, the color of dried pine sap, and sunk deep in his face. The Dumpling Man stared at me, and his teeth were showing like he was trying to make one of those guilty-dog smiles where your dog knows he did something bad, but it looked more like a painful expression to me. And he was crouched down on the branch, the way a bird would perch, so I can't say for certain how tall he was. But I saw he had hands like a person's, except his fingers all had long black claws, like a bear's, and he was all covered with fine golden fur—but it wasn't so much fur as hair, because I could plainly see the pinkness of his skin under it—and on the top of his head, there were two horns that curled back, just like a billy goat's—or, depending on how you see things—just like Satan's himself."

Max, caught up in the story of the Dumpling Man, inhaled deeply and said, "What happened after you put the light on him?"

"Well, I decided I was going to shoot him. I knew I was standing there, face-to-face with this terrible monster, the Dumpling Man, and I thought people would be so grateful if I could bring him down once and for all."

Max, who'd never really demonstrated to me that he had much of a conscience, said, "Wouldn't killing the Dumpling Man be *murder*? I mean, the Dumpling Man is a *man*, right?"

Cobie looked disappointed. "If you mean, *was he a male*, well, his balls were hanging about seven feet above my head. But the Dumpling Man isn't a *man*. He's a monster, straight from the depths of hell, and I didn't give a moment of doubt to killing him after I saw those eyes, his teeth and claws, and demon horns. The problem was, between holding my flashlight and aiming my gun, on top of how shaky I was, I couldn't actually get a clean sight on him for a shot. So when I raised my rifle and got ready to squeeze off a round, the Dumpling Man hissed at me. He said something to me!"

"No!" Max said, "What did he say?"

Then Cobie Petersen made his voice into a sinister rasp and said, "He said this: 'You don't have the guts to kill me, Cobie Petersen.'"

"He knew your name?" Max was horrified.

"I was shaking so bad I didn't realize my finger couldn't even find the trigger. Then the Dumpling Man pooed."

"He *pooed*?" Max said.

Cobie Petersen nodded. "Yep. He pooed. All over me and Ezra."

"Did you shoot him for pooing on you?" Max asked.

"I didn't get a chance. I was so shocked after getting pooed on by the Dumpling Man, I thought I was going to lose my mind. Then the Dumpling Man jumped down from his branch and dug one of his claws into my shoulder. I dropped my gun when he knocked me back over my dog, and then he took off into the woods."

"Dude. The Dumpling Man pooed on you and then he *clawed you*?" Max asked.

"Yes." Cobie said, "I didn't realize I was hurt at first. I just lay there, looking up into the black sky, wondering if I was alive or dead and whether or not I'd ever get all that poo off me and Ezra."

"Bullshit if I can't see a scar," Larry said.

"I still have the scars from the Dumpling Man's claws," Cobie affirmed.

"Prove it," Larry said.

"Care to make a bet on it, Larry?"

"What's the wager, Teacher's Pet?"

Cobie Petersen considered his terms for a moment, and then raised his hand and said, "If I prove there's a claw mark from Dumpling Man in my shoulder, then you and me are going to trade beds for the next six weeks, Larry. If I'm lying, I'll move over to the bed Bucky Littlejohn peed in last night."

Those were daring terms by any standards.

The four boys of Jupiter stared at our counselor, waiting to see if he had the guts to take Cobie Petersen's bet.

Cobie Petersen got to his feet and began to pull his T-shirt up over his head.

"Hold on there," Larry said. "I didn't agree to the bet."

Cobie stood between the fire and Larry, his shirt halfway up over his enamel-white belly.

"You believe me, Larry? Do you believe in the Dumpling Man?"

Larry shook his head. "I just don't want to bet, is all. I'm not giving up my bed for nothing."

"Okay. I guess that's as good as saying you believe my story," Cobie Petersen said.

There was no possible way for Larry to win, and all the boys of Jupiter knew it.

Cobie pulled his shirt down, and Max protested, "Wait! I want to see it! Show us!"

So Cobie Petersen lifted his shirt up over his head and took it off. Then he leaned toward the firelight so we could all see the imperfect pink grooves—four clawed marks in front of his shoulder, and the deeper scar of a powerful thumb claw in the back.

And Max said, "That's probably the scariest story I've ever heard in my life."

FRANCIS MACINNES IN THE CEMETERY

Tick tick tick went the kitchen timers strapped to the melting man's ears.

Tick tick tick.

"You should take those things off your head, Leonard. You look like a fool, and they don't work, besides." Joseph Stalin said, "You can still hear me."

The melting man had tried everything he could think of to stop Joseph Stalin from telling him what to do.

"You're unwrapping the bandages. You're unwrapping the bandages. Oh my! Your hair is falling out!" 3-60 narrated.

"Shut up!" Joseph Stalin said.

"Shut up!" the melting man said.

Leonard Fountain blew a gust through his Hohner harmonica. It didn't work.

"Listen to me. Your van is broken down," Joseph Stalin told him.

"It is?" Leonard Fountain—the melting man—asked.

"No! You have to *pretend* you've broken down," Joseph Stalin explained.

"How can I do that?" the melting man asked.

"Pull over to the side up there. Then get out and raise the hood. People will think you're broken down."

"That's pretty smart." The melting man said, "But why do I want people to think I've broken down?"

"So someone will stop and try to help. I need you to steal a cell phone," Joseph Stalin explained.

"But I have a cell phone."

"You're pulling over. Now you're slowing down," 3-60 said.

"Can't you shut her up?" Joseph Stalin said.

"I can't make 3-60 stop talking," the melting man said.

"You are applying the parking brake. You are turning the ignition to *off*," 3-60 said.

"Why do I need another cell phone?"

Joseph Stalin said, "Because you're going to make a switch with it. For the *masterpiece*."

"Oh! That makes sense," the melting man said.

"You are opening the driver-side door," 3-60 said.

There are a lot of cemeteries in Arkansas.

Leonard Fountain had pulled off the road beside a place called Holland Cemetery. It was spacious and green, with neatly manicured paths and perfectly spaced oaks that shaded the row upon row of gray headstones.

"Get the gun from the back of the van."

The melting man wanted to do exactly what Joseph Stalin had told him to do. After all, he thought it made sense; it was a good idea. Besides, the melting man was insane, so he didn't have much in the way of choices.

He walked along the gravel shoulder of the road to the rear of the van. The melting man was tired and hungry. He couldn't remember the last time he'd eaten.

He opened the rear of the van. Inside was a mess of strewn clothing, plastic grocery sacks, and empty beer cans. There was a white plastic five-gallon bucket with a lid covering it. This was Leonard Fountain's toilet when he spent nights sleeping in the van. Leonard Fountain's plastic-bucket toilet was getting full.

The melting man's masterpiece, the very big bomb, was covered beneath two horse blankets Leonard Fountain stole from a ranch in Oklahoma. The melting man slept in a mass of ragged sheets and bed linens in the part of the cargo area that overhung the cab—the space the U-Haul company referred to as "Mom's Attic."

"Get your gun," Joseph Stalin repeated.

"You are climbing up to *Mom's Attic*," 3-60 narrated.

The melting man coughed, and spit a bloody molar onto his bedding.

"You've lost another tooth!" 3-60 said.

The melting man only had a few teeth left in his mouth.

Inside his sleeping space, the melting man kept a small chrome pistol—a six-shot semiautomatic .380, the type of gun that was easy to carry in trouser pockets due to its size.

Leonard Fountain picked up the gun and slipped it into his back pocket.

"I wonder if I should take a nap," the melting man said.

"No!" Joseph Stalin ordered, "You need to get that extra phone from someone who thinks they're being helpful."

The melting man walked back to the front of the van.

"You are raising the hood of your U-Haul van. You are looking up into the sky," 3-60 told him.

The melting man caught a glimpse of the drone that had been following him. As it always did, the moment the melting man looked at the small metal rectangle floating in the sky, the object immediately pivoted and vanished.

One thing that is true about Arkansas: The people who live there are very polite and also exceedingly helpful. Leonard Fountain only had to wait about four minutes before an old Chevrolet pickup passed him, stopped in the road one hundred yards down, and then backed up until it pulled even with the front of the U-Haul van's raised hood.

The teenage boy at the wheel had to lean across the seat and roll down the passenger window.

"The boy is rolling down the window," 3-60 said.

That afternoon, Joseph Stalin kept telling the melting man he needed to kill Francis MacInnes, the driver of the old dull-orange pickup, but the melting man didn't want to kill him, probably because the redheaded boy was so nice and well mannered in a very simple, corn-scented Ozarkian way. Later, the chubby, freckle-faced eighteen-year-old kid who wore round wire-frame glasses would become momentarily famous when he appeared on every Arkansan news station to talk about the strange man who'd stolen his clothes and coerced him into handing over his keys and phone.

"Good afternoon," Francis MacInnes said through the passenger window on his pickup. "I'd be pleased to offer you some help, if you're in need of it."

"When the boy gets out of the truck, look to see if there are any cars on this road, and if there aren't, shoot him one time in the side of his head," Joseph Stalin said.

"Huh?" Leonard Fountain was confused.

"Hang on, friend. Let me park my truck and then we'll see if we can't get you on the road again." Francis MacInnes smiled warmly and then parked his Chevrolet on the shoulder in front of the melting man's U-Haul.

Francis MacInnes squinted in the bright afternoon sunlight. "Are you moving *to* or *from* Arkansas?"

"Huh?" the melting man said.

Francis MacInnes hitched his thumb at the dented old moving van. "Moving?"

"Murder him," Joseph Stalin said.

"You are standing on the side of the road," 3-60 told him.

"Oh. Yeah. I'm moving," the melting man said.

"Where to?"

"Um. Maryland?"

"Shoot him now. He knows who you are," Joseph Stalin said.

The melting man didn't know what to do. He wanted to obey Joseph Stalin, but before he could do anything, Francis MacInnes was sticking out his hand and introducing himself, telling the melting man that it was just his luck he'd gotten off work at the chicken farm early because he happened to be a "real ace" at getting trucks running the way they're supposed to.

And all the while, Francis MacInnes had this smiling-yet-disgusted Baptist-preacher-confronting-homosexuality kind of look on his face, due to all the blisters and sores on the melting man.

"You are shaking hands with the nice boy," 3-60 told him.

Francis MacInnes wore an embroidered blue one-piece jumpsuit with an elaborate logo on the back, showing a hen sitting on a clutch of eggs. The jumpsuit said TY-BEE EGG RANCH, and on the front was a small oval name patch that said FRANKIE.

"Do something right for once in your life. Shoot him in the head," Joseph Stalin said.

"Why don't you hop up in the cab and try to fire this thing up, and I'll take a look and see what's going on here," Francis MacInnes said.

"Huh? Oh. Hey. Do you happen to have a cell phone?" the melting man asked.

"Boy oh man, I sure do have a cell phone, mister!" Francis MacInnes was almost sexually aroused by the joyous degree to which he was helping out a stranger with horrible skin boils who was moving to Maryland. "It's in my truck! Let me go get it for you!"

"Kill him," Joseph Stalin said.

"Lenny, he's a nice boy. Do not kill him. You are following Francis MacInnes to his truck. You are taking the gun from your back pocket." 3-60 said, "Oh my! You are pointing the gun at Francis MacInnes."

"Do something right for once in your life, Leonard. Shoot him in the head," Joseph Stalin said.

Francis MacInnes was tremendously disappointed in humanity that afternoon. In fact, he would have been less disappointed if the melting man had done what Joseph Stalin ordered him to do, which was to shoot the kid in the head. Francis MacInnes would have never known the tremendous letdown he'd had to endure, which was this: Leonard Fountain stole Francis MacInnes's cell phone and car keys. Then Leonard Fountain marched the redheaded chicken ranch hand out into the middle of the cemetery and forced Francis MacInnes at gunpoint to strip off all his clothing.

Francis MacInnes lost all faith in his fellow man that day. Leonard Fountain stole all the kid's clothes, his eyeglasses, cell phone, and car keys, and then the melting man locked Francis MacInnes's truck, got into his U-Haul van, and drove away.

"You are driving. You are driving," 3-60 said.

"I am driving," the melting man said.

"You never do anything right," Joseph Stalin said.

Francis MacInnes sat down behind a headstone and cried.

Even people in Arkansas are not generally nice enough to stop and help out a weeping naked guy who's stranded in a cemetery.

SO MUCH FOR GOOD LUCK!

"**Shhhh . . . Wake up,** little boy. It's all right now. Wake up, Ariel."

"Huh? What?"

I had fallen asleep in the shade beneath the rear gate of the truck. Thaddeus leaned over me. He was shaking me by the shoulder.

"I didn't know what to do," he said. "I felt so terrible. You were crying in your sleep. I decided to wake you up. I'm sorry. It was awful."

In my grogginess, I remembered that I had been dreaming about my family. I had come into the kitchen, and everyone was seated around bowls of food. But when I came into the room, my uncle, aunt, and cousins all stood and left the kitchen without saying a word to me. And every time I followed them into a different room of the house, they would leave and go into another and another room. Room after room after room, without saying anything to me.

I sat up and rubbed my face. It was wet.

"It was a bad dream," I said.

"You shouldn't be sad," Thaddeus said.

"Why shouldn't I be?"

Thaddeus shook his head. "I don't know. I guess there's nothing we can do about those things."

"I want to go back home," I said.

You know how these things are, Max. It was terribly sad—so sad I could hardly think about what was happening to me. It seems so hard to remember at times.

Over the course of the three weeks I rode with them, I became a sort of mascot—a good luck charm dressed as a little white clown—to the soldiers of the Republican Guard. They believed I'd kept them safe.

"You can't go home. How would you go home?" Thaddeus said.

I pointed down the rocky road behind us. "Walk back that way."

"But there isn't anyone left," he argued. "Besides, what would we do without you? Look at how much good fortune you have brought to us! Three weeks with no losses and no skirmishes. You're our blessing. The men would not allow you to leave now."

"So I'm a prisoner?"

Thaddeus thought for a moment. "No! Of course not."

"But you said they won't let me go."

"I didn't mean to make it sound as though you have no choice. It's just . . . the men have grown accustomed to sharing what we have with you. We saved you, didn't we? You owe us something, after all, and you've been very lucky for us."

And as though to punctuate Thaddeus's conviction that I was some sort of good luck charm for the soldiers, at precisely that moment a rocket, streaming white-hot vapor, corkscrewed out of the sky and slammed into the lead vehicle of our convoy.

Then two more came in, roaring, screaming. The explosions were louder than anything I'd ever heard. I could feel them in the ground, vibrating through my body like electricity. In seconds, everything became chaos—shouting, hurrying for any cover, gunfire from every direction.

What could I do?

I was frozen there, sitting cross-legged beneath the open gate on the transport truck I'd been riding in since I came out of my refrigerator.

"Move!"

Thaddeus grabbed the back of my tunic and pulled me out from beneath the truck. We scrambled into an irrigation canal that ran along the roadway. The trucks were easy targets, sitting there pinned down on the road in the heat of the day. We were being fired upon from multiple directions. The rebels had divided and were attacking from the cover of the tangerine groves on both sides of the convoy.

I was up to my chest in water; could feel my feet slipping and sinking into the warm mud on the steep banks of the canal, and I put my face down into the grass of the bank with my hands pressed over my ears and the back of my head.

I did not look up.

If I could pray—and I'd stopped doing that nonsense long before the miracle of the refrigerator—I imagined praying, but I didn't know who to direct it to.

The gunfire and explosions seemed to expand through time. Although the fighting was over in a matter of minutes, it felt as though I'd been sinking in the mud of the canal for hours. It may have been—how can I tell? My ears rang until the following day. But when Thaddeus and I, soaked and muddy, came up out of the water, I could see the damage that had been done. More than half of the convoy ahead of us had been destroyed, and seven soldiers needed to be buried in the tangerine orchard before we could move on.

So much for good luck!

- - -

Wednesday, February 25, 1880—
Alex Crow

Luck is with us, and it has turned on us as well.

One more crewman succumbed to the elements during the night. The dead man was the naturalist, Mr. Jason Foster, from Napa, in California.

Several hours after daybreak, Captain Hansen and Mr. Piedmont managed to find a safe beach on which to land our boat, but there is nothing visible in the way of shelter or settlements. And the fog is so thick and heavy! The day appears to have a promise of yet more snow. Three more of the men had to remain behind with the boat and provisions, because they are so sick, and unable to join an expedition to search for relief.

With the three sick men sheltered at the boat, the nine of us who can manage work are preparing to split into two groups in order to explore the island in opposite directions. I will go with Piedmont, Mr. Warren, and Murdoch—Captain Hansen will lead the second party eastward.

We are armed with rifles in the hopes we may find a bear or seal. Our food supply is nearly exhausted.

WEDNESDAY, FEBRUARY 25, 1880—
LENA RIVER DELTA

It is remarkable to note how the human spirit can swing so rapidly from despair to ecstasy. One hour into our expedition out of the landing on the beach, Mr. Piedmont spotted a cluster of native huts and fish houses.

The tiny village was evidently occupied, for we could see black smoke rising from the stovepipes on each of the huts, which appeared to be pyramids of ice. We could smell the odor of food on the fire.

Upon realizing our discovery, Mr. Murdoch fell to his knees and wept.

"We will be warm! We will be warm!" Murdoch cried.

Mr. Piedmont and I had to restrain the man from running wildly into the small settlement, for who could guess what manner of society would exist in such a place as this?

After some discussion on the matter, we came to a consensus that the four of us should make ourselves known to the inhabitants of the dwellings before turning back to reunite with Captain Hansen's party and reclaim our sick crewmen.

The village here consists of six native huts and two communal fish houses, in which the residents store meat—primarily fish, but also some whale and seal. It was our great fortune to meet a Mr. Katkov, an exile from western Russia, who could speak several languages, notably the native dialect as well as French, in which Mr. Warren and Mr. Piedmont were both capably versed.

Mr. Katkov and two of the native men from the village have consented to return to the beach where we landed, and help us bring the remains of our expedition into their shelters.

This is truly a gift from God.

WEDNESDAY, FEBRUARY 25, 1880— *LENA RIVER DELTA*

On the way back to the beach we encountered a brutal snowstorm that would have swallowed us all if not for the skilled guidance of Katkov and the native villagers.

There was little we could do, though. Our progress was so hindered by the weather, and by the time we arrived at our boat the three men we had left behind had all succumbed to the conditions and had frozen to death.

Captain Hansen's party was nowhere to be found.

Fate presented no choice for us but to return to the safety of the village's shelters and pray for the others. As for now, I fear there are only four souls who have survived the terrible fate of the *Alex Crow*.

Murdoch has resumed his incessant repetitions: "Why bother?"

THIS IS PROBABLY WHY YOU DON'T WAKE UP SLEEPWALKERS

The morning after our scary stories, Mrs. Nussbaum woke up everyone in Jupiter. She pounded and pounded on the frame of our screen door.

It was five forty-five, nearly one hour *before* we officially were supposed to wake up to the tolling of the breakfast bell, which was a tin coffee can that hung from the eaves of the dining pavilion. Every morning, one of the counselors would beat it with a steel spoon.

"Good morning, boys!"

Nobody answered Mrs. Nussbaum, who knocked and knocked again. "Are you awake? Do you have clothes on? It's me, Mrs. Nussbaum! Can I come in? I have a surprise for you!"

That was an awful lot to process, considering we were all asleep, including Larry. And despite the predawn dimness, Mrs. Nussbaum could clearly see—as anyone standing outside Jupiter's walls of screen would—that not one of the boys of Jupiter was awake, and the only one with what might be considered *clothing* on was our pajama-wearing counselor, Larry, since the boot-camp boys of Camp Merrie-Seymour for Boys were treated like prison convicts and required to sleep in our underwear in order to conform to some mind-altering standard of tech-free brutality. Besides, there was no likelihood that we might mistake Mrs. Nussbaum for anyone other than Mrs. Nussbaum, since, as Cobie Petersen had so bluntly pointed out the day of our group therapy session, she was the camp's one and only female. On top of everything else, there was no possibility any of us could deny Mrs. Nussbaum's entry to Jupiter if that was what she wanted to do, because, with the exception of the counselors' exclusive, private, fully lighted shower and dressing room, there were no locks at all on any of the doors at Camp Merrie-Seymour for Boys.

So, amid the turbulence of wild crumpling atop our plastic-clad mattresses, while we stumbled around in the near dark and struggled to pull on our shorts and T-shirts, in barged Mrs. Nussbaum and her six-foot-tall, duffel bag–carrying *surprise*.

It almost felt as though we were in the military and subjected to a pop inspection, which we boys of Jupiter would certainly have failed. Cobie Petersen's T-shirt ended up inside out and backward, its tag sticking up like the tail of a frightened deer just below Cobie's chin; and Max, who could not find where his short pants ended up, stood there, wobbling, barefoot and yawning, still mostly asleep, in his underwear. Our sheets and pillows lay scattered all over the cabin's floor.

Larry was obviously perturbed by the early intrusion. He sat in his bed and glared at Mrs. Nussbaum.

"Good morning to my dear friends! How are you all feeling today—on your *second morning* at Camp Merrie-Seymour for Boys? I'm so proud of you all for how dedicated you are to breaking the chains of your technology addictions! Did you sleep well? I've brought a *new friend* for the boys of Jupiter!" Mrs. Nussbaum practically squealed with delight and swept her hand like a floor-show model to demonstrate the living thing that could not be missed by any of the blurry eyes of Jupiter.

"Boys," she said, "this is Trent Mendibles, your newest bunk mate in Jupiter. He is fourteen years old, and comes to us all the way from Ohio! Would you like to say something, Trent?"

Trent Mendibles shook his head. "Um. Hello?"

Trent Mendibles looked like a malnourished Christmas tree that had been drained of all color. He stood there, rail thin in his baggy shorts and Camp Merrie-Seymour for Boys log-fonted T-shirt, wearing the telltale name sticker that identified him as a new resident of our planet.

Cobie Petersen, our inside-out-shirt-wearing Teacher's Pet and unofficial general, leaned forward slightly and welcomed the new kid with an observation. "Jesus. You have the hairiest legs I've ever seen in my life."

It was true.

And despite the fact that fourteen-year-old Trent Mendibles from Ohio was giraffe-sized compared to the rest of us, he looked scared to be standing at the epicenter of all Jupiter's attention, which made me feel kind of sorry for him. I think he had the same look on his face that I must have had the day I crawled out of my refrigerator: He was nervous and pale, and had dark circles around his glassy eyes. I imagined he'd probably been awake all night on the drive out here from Ohio, pleading with his parents to turn around and bring him home so he could log back on to the insomniac online gamers' community from which they had kidnapped him.

Mrs. Nussbaum continued, "And Trent, dear, this is Larry, your resident counselor. And these are your cabin mates: Here is Cobie—he's sixteen, from West Virginia—and our two fifteen-year-old brothers, also from West Virginia, Ariel and . . . *oh my!* . . . Uh . . . Max."

Suddenly aware that Max was standing at the foot of his bed wearing nothing but briefs, Mrs. Nussbaum, who'd mispronounced my name again, reddened and turned away.

"And . . . um . . . Where is Robin this morning?" Mrs. Nussbaum looked around the messy cabin and then turned toward Larry, as though she may have been wondering if yet another boy from Jupiter had done something terrible to himself in order to get out of Camp Merrie-Seymour for Boys.

I didn't think Robin Sexton had the guts to do anything remotely comparable to Bucky Littlejohn's archery performance.

But, indeed, Robin Sexton's bed was empty, although everyone could see it had been slept in.

Max offered, "Maybe he had to go *throw out some photocopies*," and then Max made the loose-fist sign language gesture that all boys understand, which he got away with because Mrs. Nussbaum, who was obviously trying to figure out why Jupiter cabin at Camp Merrie-Seymour for Boys would have a photocopier in the first place, was straining to keep her eyes away from my mostly naked fifteen-year-old brother.

I watched Trent Mendibles. He nodded knowingly.

And Max shook his head and said, "I don't know how the heck I'm ever going to make it through six weeks without a few sessions in the copy room myself."

Then Cobie Petersen raised his hand and said, "Um. Mrs. Nussbaum? The kid—Robin—told us he sleepwalks. Also, the hairy giant new guy gets *that* bed."

Cobie pointed at the bed on the end of the row—the one Bucky Littlejohn peed in on our first night.

Mrs. Nussbaum looked concerned and perplexed. "He *sleep-walks*?"

Cobie Petersen nodded. "That's what he said to us."

Larry reached below his quiet, non-plastic bed and pulled up an alarm clock. "It's five forty-five. Really? We get a new camper at *five forty-five in the morning*?"

Mrs. Nussbaum accidentally glanced at Max again—I saw her—then she nervously looked away.

"I apologize, Larry, but he's just gotten here from Ohio!"

She made *Ohio* sound exotic and remote, as opposed to about four hundred miles away from Camp Merrie-Seymour for Boys, which is how far it was. The poor kid—Trent Mendibles—looked sad and unwanted, and he shifted nervously from foot to foot, still hefting his duffel bag.

Larry sighed. "Okay. Let the kids and me get dressed. The new guy—what's his name?—gets that bed on the end. We'll find that Robin dude before breakfast. I'm sure he's just in the showers or something."

"Or maybe he's *working out with the swim team*," Max offered.

Mrs. Nussbaum looked at Max, turned brilliant red, then fixed her eyes on Jupiter's screen door.

"We have a *swim team*?" she asked.

Despite the fact that it was relatively dark in the George Washington National Forest at six in the morning, it only took us about twenty minutes to find Robin Sexton. He was in the woods about thirty feet away from Jupiter, standing up while rocking side to side in a patch of ferns, completely asleep in his underwear.

Cobie Petersen nudged Robin's butt with the toe of his sneaker to try and get the kid to open his eyes. He was out cold.

"People always say you're not supposed to wake up sleepwalkers," Max said.

"Why not?" Cobie asked.

The new guy—Trent Mendibles—had come with us on our hunt-for-the-weird-kid expedition. Larry left us on our own once again so he could take advantage of the counselors' luxurious facilities, or whatever else Larry liked to do away from the responsibilities of his actual job.

Max shrugged. "I don't know why. I just heard you're not supposed to do it. If waking him up accidentally kills him, Mrs. Nussbaum is going to get really mad at all of us, but mostly probably at Larry."

"Eh. Whatever."

Cobie kicked Robin Sexton's butt again. Harder.

"Hey, dork face."

Robin grunted and slowly cracked his eyelids. He had a strangely horrified and drained expression on his face.

Then Cobie Petersen stepped around the ferns, positioned himself directly in front of Robin Sexton, and horned his pointed index fingers up from the top of his forehead.

He snarled, "Wake up, boy, I'm the Dumpling Man."

I think Cobie Petersen most likely picked the wrong thing to say to awaken our ninety-four-pound sleepwalker, Robin Sexton. Maybe Robin Sexton had been having a nightmare about the Dumpling Man, or maybe it was just that Cobie Petersen's story the night before had made some kind of impression that permeated the toilet paper barriers that were still wedged inside the kid's ears. Whatever it was, when Robin Sexton's eyes came into focus, the kid shrieked like a madman and launched himself out of the bushes, swinging and flailing a barrage of fists, and pale, bony knees and elbows at Cobie Petersen.

And Max, my brother, took a step back and said, "This is probably why you don't wake up sleepwalkers."

I glanced at Trent Mendibles, just to see how the new kid was enjoying his first few minutes in Jupiter, and he said to me, "What the fuck is this place? A home for insane kids?"

I really wanted to answer him, but I didn't.

What I wanted to tell him was this: *I've been wondering the same thing for the past two days.*

And we had a full six weeks to go.

Even though he obviously possessed wolverine-like qualities, Robin Sexton was no match for a raccoon-hunting mountain boy like Cobie Petersen. Robin did manage to clip a good punch into Cobie's nose, but in less than three seconds, Cobie Petersen had the smaller boy pinned to his back in the dirt while Cobie leaned over him, clenching Robin's bony wrists, and trying to get the kid to wake up and calm down.

I was surprised at how gentle Cobie Petersen could be with Robin, because after the punch he'd landed, most boys I'd met since coming to America would have beaten the life out of the kid.

"Calm down, kid," Cobie soothed.

It was probably hard for Robin Sexton to calm down, though, because Cobie Petersen's nose gushed blood all over the scrawny boy's face and chest. It looked like some kind of horror movie, there was so much blood on the boys.

"Dude. Come on. Relax. You were sleepwalking," Cobie said, as he dripped and dripped and dripped a steady stream of blood all over the skinny thirteen-year-old twitching kid from Pennsylvania.

And Robin Sexton gurgled and spit.

"Gah! Get off me, you son of a bitch!"

And as soon as Cobie Petersen loosened up on Robin, the kid began swinging punches and spitting all over again.

It was a gory mess.

Trent Mendibles shook his head. "I really wish I could upload this shit on video. I'd get a million hits. This is just like level four in *Battle Quest: Take No Prisoners*, except for the little dude in his underwear, and being in the woods instead of in Stalingrad during World War Five in 2311, and shit."

Larry was very mad at us when he came back to Jupiter and saw what Cobie Petersen and Robin Sexton looked like, which was murder victims or something. I couldn't blame him. We were attempting to make our beds, trying to clean up, but couldn't manage to finish before Larry walked in on us.

Robin Sexton, who looked especially scrawny because he was still in just his underwear, was covered in blood. So was Cobie Petersen, but he never really looked very scrawny at all.

"What did I tell you?" Larry shouted, "What did I fucking tell you fuckheads yesterday? Am I going to have to follow all five of you around twenty-four hours a day so you don't fucking kill yourselves? I am NOT going to do that."

Cobie Petersen raised his hand. "Um. Larry? It's all okay. It was just an accident. The kid got scared when I woke him up, is all. We didn't even fight or nothing. Trust me. He'd actually be dead right now if I hit him."

"That's it." Larry said, "All five of you. I want you out of here and in the showers right now before the rest of the cabins wake up and someone sees you like this. I've fucking had it with this shit.

You're straightening your shit up or I'm going to start kicking your asses. Boot camp begins today for you pieces of shit."

Cobie raised his hand again. "Larry? Big Chief? I'm really sorry. Do you want a hug or something? Would you like me to read you a story?"

It was remarkable to me that Larry didn't completely snap at that exact moment.

But that was that. Larry, gritting his teeth, marched us in a line, like a leg-ironed chain gang carrying toothbrushes, towels, and clean changes of our name-labeled clothes, out to the communal, spider-infested inmate showers just before the sun cracked the top of the trees in the east.

Nobody wanted to get into those showers, but nobody wanted to fight with Larry, either. He was clearly at his breaking point.

Living with the Burgesses, I had seen a lot of very strange things. None of them particularly frightened me, but I have always been acutely afraid of spiders. When the counselors walked us all through the shower room during our orientation two days before, I couldn't help but notice the massive webs up in the black tar-paper corners of the unlit ceiling, and the hanging white tufts of egg masses that looked as big as tennis balls.

None of the boys of Jupiter had taken a shower since we'd arrived at Camp Merrie-Seymour for Boys, which was actually kind of gross.

So I kept my eyes fixed over my head, waiting for something predatory to drop down, while the five of us stood beneath trickles of freezing water, naked and shivering in the hell of the spider cave. And Larry kept ordering Robin and Cobie to be sure and get all the blood off their skin and out of their hair, because he didn't want to lose his job on account of a fight between two shitheads like us.

Cobie Petersen stood under the corroded spigot next to me, and rubbed water into his face.

"Hey. Noisy dude. Did I get all the blood off?" he said.

I nodded.

Cobie Petersen laughed. "That little kid looked pretty much like a walking scab, I guess."

I glanced back up at the ceiling.

"What are you looking at?"

"Spiders."

"Oh. Well, I always heard spiders don't like water."

"And you never heard about how you shouldn't wake up sleep-walkers?"

"Shit. This fucking water is too cold for spiders."

"Maybe they'll go after Larry, then," I said.

"Hey. You can talk," Cobie Petersen said.

I couldn't help but look at the gashing scar on Cobie Petersen's shoulder. It looked like three streaks of melted pink wax.

Three boys from Mars came in to piss and brush their teeth. They laughed at us and made fun of us and called us fags because we were all naked in the showers, but Larry told them to shut up or he'd throw their asses in there with us. Nobody wanted that. It was bad enough showering with the kids from Jupiter. The Mars boys were monsters.

Cobie Petersen turned and faced the boys from Mars squarely and flipped middle fingers with both hands. He stared them down until they looked away.

Outside, someone clanged and clanged on the coffee-can breakfast bell.

And after breakfast, when we all went back to Jupiter to prepare for the day's interplanetary contests, we watched with mild disgust as the new kid with the extremely hairy legs put a set of sheets on the bed that Bucky Littlejohn peed in. It was probably dumb, I thought, because I was certain that every single plastic-coated bed in Camp Merrie-Seymour for Boys had inevitably been peed in—or worse.

SOCK PUPPET JESUS

By the middle of our second week at Camp Merrie-Seymour for Boys, Larry had softened his opinion regarding the five boys of Jupiter, most likely because none of us had tried killing himself and no blood had been spilled since the morning we caught Robin Sexton sleepwalking. The kid still kept paper plugs stuffed in his ears constantly, and usually pretended not to hear anything we said to him. He'd even managed to sculpt his fake earbuds from toilet paper he chewed on—like a wasp—and then he craftily attached kite string to them so it really looked like he had an iPod or something inside his T-shirt. He got the string from the Camp Merrie-Seymour for Boys kite-making competition, which Jupiter won because I made a kite with Jesus on it.

Two of the boys from Mars beat up Robin Sexton one day because they thought he really had an iPod, and they wanted to steal it. Then they beat him up more when they realized his iPod was made from masticated toilet paper and pilfered kite twine.

And Robin Sexton continued to sleepwalk just about every night or so.

Trent Mendibles talked incessantly about his prowess at *Battle Quest: Take No Prisoners*, an online game that was like a massive networked cult to the majority of the boys at Camp Merrie-Seymour for Boys.

Cobie, Max, and I had never seen the game before, although we knew plenty of kids at William E. Shuck High School who were similarly addicted to it.

Trent Mendibles's parents committed him to the camp after finding him unconscious and dehydrated in front of his computer monitor. He was having some type of seizure, he bragged proudly. He said there was even foam coming out of his mouth and nose. Trent Mendibles told us that he had been playing the game nonstop for eighty-three hours, according to his log-in records. He had to be taken to a hospital and hooked up to an IV, and he told us a very scary story: At the hospital, an orderly had to insert a catheter tube inside Trent Mendibles's penis, which, he said, hurt more than anything he'd ever felt in his life. His story made us all cringe, even Robin Sexton, who was clearly paying attention to Trent Mendibles's story about the tube that got shoved inside his penis.

But Trent swore his plan to play BQTNP for more than eighty-three straight hours as soon as he got back home to Ohio, catheter or not.

Trent Mendibles missed *Battle Quest: Take No Prisoners* so desperately he sobbed for three consecutive nights after coming to Jupiter, until Cobie Petersen told him this: "I will choke you to death with my bare hands if you don't shut the hell up."

Three days was enough to cry over any video game, Trent Mendibles must have decided after that. And Max had said, "You should choke him, anyway."

Nobody in the entire solar system of Camp Merrie-Seymour for Boys was daring enough to mess with Cobie Petersen.

Who would ever be dumb enough to screw with a kid who'd survived being pooed on *and* clawed by the Dumpling Man?

Larry had installed a bell on Jupiter's door, which really wasn't a bell—it was a Mountain Dew can with a pebble inside it, tied to the top of the door by a string—and each night at bedtime one of us would be assigned the task of following Robin Sexton if he sleepwalked again, just to make sure he didn't get eaten by wild animals or wind up drowned in the canoe lake. Except for Cobie Petersen, we were all afraid of waking him up. When it was Cobie's turn to babysit the kid, he just took Robin Sexton firmly by the wrist before he got five feet away from Jupiter and pulled him gently back to his crumpling bed.

He said, "I'll be damned if I wouldn't rather get in another fistfight with that son-of-a-bitch jerkoff than lose a couple hours of sleep following his scrawny ass out into the woods."

And Cobie Petersen begged Larry to let us tie the kid down to his bed every night, but Larry, for whatever reasons, thought that was too weird and could probably get him in trouble if someone came into Jupiter and found one of us boys tied up to his bed.

"What if we forgot him like that for a few days?" Larry had said.

And Cobie Petersen said, "Do you really think anyone would care, Larry?"

Robin Sexton pretended not to notice that Jupiter was having a conversation about tying him to his bed.

Another reason Larry found himself with a kinder attitude toward us was that Jupiter had pulled into the lead after a week and a half of interplanetary contests at Camp Merrie-Seymour for

Boys. I think that the biggest factor in securing our lead over the other planets was that three of the five boys of Jupiter were relatively sane. The other cabins, filled with boys like our own Robin Sexton and Trent Mendibles, just couldn't seem to function in the real world much beyond giving us dirty looks, calling us names, and mouthing predictable threats about us being queers, or about our asses, and how they wanted to kick them.

The interplanetary competition that Thursday afternoon was arbitrarily judged and as nonlethal as any contest could be: The planets of Camp Merrie-Seymour for Boys all had to make puppets and then use them to put on shows for the other cabins. We had to make the puppets out of pairs of our own socks.

I didn't like the idea of sacrificing my ink-marker-initialed socks for a contest, much less for the entertainment of the other planets. We had a very limited wardrobe as it was, and it was getting near to laundry day for the five boys of Jupiter. We were all down to our last relatively clean changes of clothing.

Still, I had no choice in the matter of using my socks. What could I do?

So I made a sock puppet Jesus, and Jupiter put on an absurdist, metaphorical one-act play about gluttony and masturbation called *Teen Jesus Goes to Camp Merrie-Seymour for Fat Boys.*

It was a tremendous hit.

In our play, Max and Cobie Petersen performed all the voices while the five of us crouched uncomfortably close to one another in the sweaty plywood box of the puppet theater stage. Max insisted on playing the role of Jesus, which was okay with me, because I would never have been able to talk in front of all those people, even if I was hiding inside a wooden box.

Max also said he was going to jump over the railing and into the audience if we had to make a quick escape. Planning escape routes and stealing things were Max's specialties.

I had cut holes in the sides of my sock puppet Jesus, so I could use my thumb and little finger as Jesus's arms. Nobody at Camp Merrie-Seymour for Boys had ever done something so inventive— the thirty-odd other sock puppets performing that day all pretty much looked the same, which was to say they all resembled saggy white snakes with two black eyeballs and pinching thumb-to-fingers mouths. My sock puppet Jesus had a halo that I'd made from paper clips, and a Spanish moss beard. At first, Cobie Petersen objected to the beard, saying that if Jesus was a teenager at Camp Merrie-Seymour for Boys he wouldn't have been able to grow a beard yet, but Max quickly corrected him by pointing out Kyle Breckenridge, one of the kids who'd called us "fags" in the showers, a fourteen-year-old thug from Mars with a fire-red man-beard.

"Oh yeah." Cobie Petersen nodded in agreement. "Okay, then. You can keep Jesus's beard, but I think we should stab pins or something into his arms so you bleed."

I shook my head. Cobie Petersen was out of his mind.

Cobie Petersen made a sock puppet of Mrs. Nussbaum, who he gave enormous breasts and hair made from dried grass. His sock puppet looked remarkably like Mrs. Nussbaum. Max, Trent Mendibles, and Robin Sexton all made sock puppet campers they named after themselves: Sock-Max, Sock-Trent, and Sock-Robin. We even glued small name tags to their sock chests.

"Make sure you put shit in the ears on yours, kid," Cobie Petersen instructed Robin, who made small spit-wads from dining hall napkins and stuck them to the sides of Sock-Robin's head.

In our play, Sock Puppet Jesus lamented about how boring it was being a teenager and also having to be so perfect and pure all the time. Max, as I fully expected, delivered a passionate soliloquy at the beginning of our play in which Sock-Jesus complained about how desperately he'd like to sneak away into the woods so he could anoint himself and finally have a chance to *sprinkle around his holy water* or *cast out some Israelites* like other normal teenage boys do from time to time.

And Sock-Jesus's Jupiter cabin kept getting in trouble with Sock–Mrs. Nussbaum because Sock-Jesus could turn water into chocolate milk shakes.

"Nothing beats grabbing a nice shake with your best friend!" Sock-Jesus said.

And Sock-Jesus made endless chocolate milk shakes for Sock-Max, Sock-Trent, and Sock-Robin, who kept getting fatter and fatter, and eventually exploded by the end of our play.

And at the end, Cobie and Max sang the Camp Merrie-Seymour for Boys song, but they had written out their own lyrics as a theme for *Teen Jesus Goes to Camp Merrie-Seymour for Fat Boys*.

Their song went like this:

> *Jupiter-Jesus Boys!*
> *We're Jupiter-Jesus Boys!*
> *We're having endless milk shakes,*
> *We could fill the whole canoe lake!*
> *When people see us they cheer and scream,*
> *There's a quarter-billion tadpoles on our swim team!*
> *When we get bored we hitchhike to town,*
> *Don't bother us now, we're punching the clown!*
> *So cheer and make a happy noise—*
> *For US, the Jupiter-Jesus Boys!*
> *For US, the Jupiter-Jesus Boys!*

It was all great fun.

I'll admit, it wasn't high drama, but our sock puppet play was immensely better than any of the other planets' plays, most of which were reenactments starring plain white saggy snakes depicting various levels of *Battle Quest: Take No Prisoners*, which Trent Mendibles and Robin Sexton found mesmerizing.

Trent told us, "I wished they would have put me in one of the *normal kids'* cabins."

But that's how we five boys of Jupiter pulled way out into the lead against the other five *normal* planets at Camp Merrie-Seymour for Boys.

And Larry slept well at night, which presented an opportunity for Max to come up with some clever diversion for us.

RED MERCURY AND BOTTLED WATER

"**Be careful with the** soldering iron." 3-60 cautioned, "You don't want to burn yourself."

Leonard Fountain—the melting man—had rigged a Honda generator in the back of his moving van to provide electricity for his tools and the two-burner hot plate he used to boil things when he was hungry enough to cook. He held the soldering iron in his blistering hand, connecting thin wires onto the board inside Francis MacInnes's stolen cell phone.

The melting man's stomach ached.

Something dripped like warm tree sap from the end of the melting man's little finger. It was a soggy fingernail that had detached from the pudding-like flesh of his hand and fallen onto the overturned watermelon crate Leonard Fountain used as a workbench.

"Oh, Lenny, your little pinkie nail fell off!" 3-60 said.

"Look at you! You're disgusting!" Joseph Stalin said, "You're falling apart."

The melting man tried to ignore Joseph Stalin. He tried to ignore the bloody fingernail that splattered down beside Francis MacInnes's phone. But he couldn't ignore what the tissue-based biochip the Merrie-Seymour Research Group implanted in his brain a decade earlier had been doing to his brain. It was why, in reality, they had been following and watching Leonard Fountain for so long, even if the melting man's brain, which came up with Joseph Stalin and 3-60, also concluded someone called the Beaver King was out to get him.

"Finish wiring the switch," Joseph Stalin scolded him.

"I want to make you happy," Leonard Fountain said.

"If you wanted to make me happy, you would have shot the kid in the cemetery. You can't do anything right, Leonard! How can I count on you to put an end to the Beaver King?"

The melting man groaned and put his fists to his ears. He'd forgotten he was holding the soldering iron, though, and he burned a diagonal gash in his forehead, just above his right eyebrow, which no longer had any hair. His left eyebrow did, however.

"Ow!" Leonard Fountain said.

"You burned your head," 3-60 told him.

"Make me happy," Joseph Stalin told him.

Leonard Fountain was getting crazier and crazier.

"What do I need to do to make you happy?" He said, "What can I do to make you leave me alone and be happy?"

"Put the red mercury into the masterpiece."

Leonard Fountain had a Folgers coffee can filled with mercury. He did not know exactly what *red* mercury was. Joseph Stalin had been asking for red mercury ever since the melting man left Mexico City. In one of his more coherent thoughts, Leonard Fountain considered that if he didn't know what red mercury was, but Joseph Stalin did, then maybe it proved that Joseph Stalin was real; that all of this was actually happening and it wasn't just a dream going on inside the melting man's short-circuited head.

Still, Joseph Stalin never objected when Leonard Fountain stopped at a Safeway supermarket in Texas and purchased some ketchup and a bottle of red food coloring, both of which he emptied into his Folgers can of mercury. As much as he mixed and mixed, nothing happened. He tried stirring the concoction with his bare hands. The melting man enjoyed the feel of mercury on his skin.

Nothing—not even ketchup—mixes with mercury.

"And stop playing with my mercury! Take the mercury out of your pockets," Joseph Stalin said.

The melting man also liked the way mercury felt in the front pockets of his jeans.

"You are taking the mercury out of your pocket," 3-60 said.

Leonard Fountain dropped the mercury.

The back compartment of his moving van was a mess. There was mercury and trash, a festering open toilet, and rotting food everywhere. And Leonard Fountain had to make poo. He scrambled back up into Mom's Attic and uncovered his can of red mercury.

Well, it wasn't actually red mercury.

This was going to be beautiful, the melting man thought.

- - -

FRIDAY, FEBRUARY 27, 1880—
LENA RIVER DELTA

Staying in the company of Mr. Katkov, along with
Mr. Warren, whose condition and spirits improve

steadily now for the past two days. Mr. Piedmont and Murdoch are both housed with one of the native hunters.

It is remarkable how quickly the human soul can be restored with food and shelter! And having acquired those minimal comforts, there is always a drive to venture outward and seize more. The human condition is perplexing, at best.

Katkov's dwelling is efficient but terribly small. From the outside, the home appears to be little more than a hillock of snow with a doorway and a stovepipe. Inside, one can discern the structure had been made entirely from smooth logs, which are peaked in a triangular frame supported by thick pillars. It is very dark, as there are no windows, and the only illumination is provided by a fat-burning lamp. Katkov has a desk for writing and reading, and a stove that provides heat and is used in cooking our meals, and there are but two beds (one of which I share with Mr. Warren, a necessity we both find convenient to our passions). Thankfully, Katkov snores like a demon.

Mr. Katkov's story—told to me through Mr. Warren, who is quite well versed in French—is particularly compelling. Katkov has been here on the Lena River Delta for some two years, having been exiled for his affiliation with anti-Tsarist radicals. He was forced to leave his wife and children behind in western Russia, and here he stubbornly clings to survival, alongside the enigmatic natives in this most desolate post.

"Would you leave this place if given the opportunity to do so?" I asked him.

I had assumed Katkov, being so Western in his manners and sensibilities, would not hesitate to leave the Lena River Delta with our diminished crew of survivors should our rescue eventually materialize.

Katkov, something of a puzzle himself, answered thusly: "Are you a religious man, Dr. Merrie?"

"I attend church as often as possible," I said to him. "What does religious inclination have to do with your staying here or going elsewhere?"

"There is something here," Katkov told me. "It keeps me here for some reason. I am bound to its preservation. It is a miracle."

"I think the man's been isolated too long," Mr. Warren confided, in English.

"What manner of miracle?" I asked.

"You will see, Dr. Merrie. I will show you and Mr. Warren this thing tomorrow, in the daylight. You will see. Both Mr. Warren and you strike me as reasonable men, and you, Doctor, a man with a scientific mind. You will find this particularly enthralling."

"What is it?" Mr. Warren's curiosity was piqued.

"It's a beast," Katkov explained. "A beast, frozen in ice."

Saturday, February 28, 1880—
Lena River Delta

This morning we ate a breakfast of smoked fish, which Mr. Katkov smothered in seal oil before serving. The native inhabitants of this land are accustomed to such meals, but I find the food to be endlessly unappealing. Still, one must do whatever is necessary to survive. If I have learned nothing else from my experience on the *Alex Crow* expedition, it has been this. This is the reason we bother, Mr. Murdoch!

Armed with rifles—for this is a dangerous and daunting land—Mr. Warren, Mr. Katkov, my constant companion aboard ship, Mr. Murdoch, and I set off in the gray cast of daylight, following the course of the frozen Lena River inland for some two or three miles in search of what Katkov had promised would be our glimpse at a miracle.

Saturday, February 28, 1880—
Lena River Delta

I find myself nearly incapable of expressing what Katkov brought us to see.

After hiking inland for several miles, we came to a place where the river had quite obviously changed its course at some point in the distant past.

Here, the former bank along the western edge was made of a continuous and sheer rock face, into which cut dozens of deep fissures. Katkov led me, Mr. Murdoch, and Mr. Warren up to one of these rifts in the rock wall, and told us the thing he wanted to show us was inside the crevasse.

The opening of the rift had been adorned with all manner of strange artifacts: tusks and bones laced into crosses, dyed strings and ribbons, and small painted pebbles. The place looked like an antique and primitive shrine of some sort. Katkov told me it was he who had labored to make the place into a shrine, gathering together what scarce components were offered by nature to construct his crosses and ornaments.

Climbing up the bank to the opening was a matter of some difficulty, for the hill was piled with shards of broken shale, much steeper and higher than it had appeared from a distance.

"You have never seen such a thing as what you are about to see, gentlemen," Katkov promised. "You will question everything you've assumed to be true."

Along the journey, Warren had whispered to me on several occasions his concern as to the sanity of our two companions. By the time we had arrived at the strangely decorated mouth of this cavern, Mr. Warren's worries had claimed some discernible effect on my own outlook. We were both reasonably afraid of following Katkov into the fissure. Murdoch, as was his usual excited manner, acted eager and intrigued.

"This is nonsense," I said to Warren. "We are

reasonable men. Let's see what we've come so far to see, shall we?"

Mr. Warren didn't answer me. He looked pale.

Katkov went in first, followed by Murdoch, then me, and finally the newspaperman. Within moments we found ourselves in complete darkness, led forward as though pulled along by the guideline of Katkov's voice (and Warren's translation) of our path.

"Be careful to step over this rock!" he would tell us at times, or, "Lower your heads here!"

We moved in a single line—in two places the opening became so narrow I was certain Murdoch might have become trapped. But finally, after some time, the walls widened away from us and we stood in what I could only assume was some sort of room-sized chamber.

It was terribly cold here—so much so that I could sense Mr. Warren shivering beside me.

After a moment, Katkov managed to coax light from a lamp that had been left on a ledge in the wall. I looked at the man, puzzled. There was nothing remarkable at all here that I could see.

Mr. Warren released a relieved sigh and exclaimed, "There isn't anything here!"

And Murdoch shouted, "Good God! Good God!"

Katkov positioned his lamp at the height of his waist and pointed at something I hadn't initially noticed. Here there was another opening in the wall, quite small—so that standing erect as I was, it was not something I would immediately have looked for. Inside this groove was the thing that Katkov had promised to show to Mr. Warren and me.

It was a frozen man.

I will call it a man only because that is the most familiar thing I can use to describe Katkov's beast in the ice.

Mr. Warren crouched forward, simultaneously horrified and drawn to the thing, as a newspaper-man would be. He exclaimed, "What in the name of hell is that?"

"Satan himself!" Murdoch said. Then he laughed viciously and shouted, "Great Jupiter Jove! It's Lucifer, and he's trapped in ice!"

"Well?" Katkov asked, "What do you think, gentlemen?"

The creature, bent slightly back as though seated, would stand no more than three feet in height if erect. But I was quite certain the speci-men was an adult, due to the features and wrin-kles on his face. He was quite obviously a male, too, and with the exception of his hands, feet, and face, was covered everywhere in a sparse growth of white hair, through which could be seen his pink manlike skin and nipples, indicating the species was some form of mammal. The eyes of the beast were closed—indeed, he seemed to have the most placid and relaxed attitude. But the most fascinating characteristic of all were the two ivory horns, each perhaps five inches in length, that curved back from the creature's forehead.

If a devil—or anything that might be mistaken for one and thereby misidentified—ever roamed this earth, we stood looking at one here inside Mr. Katkov's frozen shrine.

And at that moment, I was gripped by something I would not be able to resist—the insurmountable and selfish need to remove this thing from the ice and bring him back to America with any survivors of the *Alex Crow*. All the hellish suffering of this expedition had led me here to this revelation, a discovery of my purpose for being here, for having endured the ordeal in the ice. I could save this thing; I was compelled to do it. Katkov may be satisfied in his role as guardian of the creature, but that is not enough. Our place in this world demands the creature be brought back.

I know I have to do this.

- - -

Let me tell you, my brother: There are few things more unnecessary than a good luck charm that has lost its power.

After the battle in the orchard, the soldiers stopped talking to me. Thaddeus chose to ride in a different vehicle, away from me, so I sat alone in a corner of the open truck bed, hugging my knees and pretending to sleep. I was hungry and thirsty, but nobody offered anything to me.

Two days after the attack in the tangerine grove, what remained of our unit rolled into a destroyed border town in the mountains.

Earlier in the morning jets flew past us overhead, so low in the sky the roar they made seemed to trail behind them like starving dogs chasing after a garbage truck. And then came the terrifying din of rockets and bombs as they slammed into the distant city.

Most of the town we came to lay in rubble that piled into the roadway leading away into the mountains. The convoy stopped in the center of the road, adjacent to a square that would have been a marketplace on any normal day that didn't involve aerial bombardment. All the soldiers climbed out of the vehicles, rifles pointed and ready to fire at anyone who might be there, but nobody moved on the street at all.

I waited and watched from the bed of the truck. The soldiers didn't pay attention to me in the silence of the aftermath to the small city's destruction. Eventually, stiff and sweaty from confining myself to the cramped corner of the truck bed, I climbed down into the market square.

There were some bodies. I had learned to not look at them; it was almost a power we had gained that allowed us to make corpses vanish into invisibility.

The men scavenged through the marketplace, looking for anything worth taking.

I saw a gate that was built across the road beyond the last broken buildings in the city. It was an odd thing to me; a simple wooden bar that could be lifted in order to allow one to pass between *here* and *there*, because if you just stepped off the road and into the dirt, you could walk around the gate as though it didn't exist at all.

Gates make eloquent arguments that condition our choices.

Next to the gate was a small office. The roof of the office had been burned away. Smoke rose from its blackened insides.

And there was a man and woman, walking down the road, pulling a wagon toward the crossing. The woman carried an infant. Nobody said anything to me when I walked away from the convoy and followed the people with the wagon. It was as though I had vanished, too.

The man and woman did not look back toward us. They knew that looking at the soldiers was the wrong thing to do, but they must have been fully aware that we had arrived in the square. The trucks were so noisy.

I stepped past a flattened stall. Lying against the edge of a splintered plywood wallboard was an unopened bottle of drinking water. I picked it up. It was a miracle.

It may have been an accident, too, but in any event the water meant I was going to be alive to drink it, and that was something worth holding on to.

And in the act of stooping to grab the bottle of water, I realized there was a dead boy, lying faceup, his curled fingers just inches from my own hand. It was almost as though the boy had passed the bottle of water directly to me, as both his final act on earth and his first act in whatever new place he had gone to.

I made the mistake of looking at the dead boy's face. Maybe it wasn't a mistake; maybe it was an act that somehow I had been directed to do, and so was helpless. Maybe that's the essence of a true miracle. Who can say?

The dead boy wore a red scarf on his head. I recognized him. He was Jean-Pierre, the boy who'd pissed himself in the schoolroom on the afternoon of my fourteenth birthday.

"Thank you for the water, Jean-Pierre."

Here was another story shelved in Ariel's library.

Then I covered my schoolmate with a broken piece of plywood and walked away, following the couple and their wagon, carrying my unopened bottle of water.

"Hey! Little boy! Ariel!"

I turned around and looked back at the soldiers in the market. Thaddeus stood in the rubble of the roadway, his rifle slung diagonally across his thighs.

"Where do you think you're going?" he shouted.

I pointed at the gate. The wagon-pullers had nearly reached it. "Over there," I said.

Thaddeus frowned and shook his head. "Don't go."

"You said I wasn't a prisoner, remember?"

"Well, suit yourself, little boy. Suit yourself."

Thaddeus spit on the ground.

I turned toward the gate and started walking. The man and woman were somehow determined to raise the gate and remain on the road with their wagon. I thought it was a strange thing to want to do, but who am I to say?

They were having trouble managing the gate. The woman held on to her baby, and the man held on to his wagon.

"I can help you through." I waved my bottle of water at them and hurried to help.

"Wait! Little boy! Stop!"

When I turned back, I saw that Thaddeus was aiming his rifle at me.

He said, "I don't want you to leave."

What could I do?

Of course I was scared. My hand began to sweat and I felt the water bottle slipping from my grasp.

Max, I believed Thaddeus intended to kill me on that road leading out of the town.

So I told him this: "I can't make up for what you did when you were a boy. I promise I will not tell anyone about your dog."

Thaddeus lowered his rifle. It was another miracle.

Then I ran and held up the gate so the small family could pass through.

On the other side, the man looked at me suspiciously and said, "What are you supposed to be?"

"A clown," I said.

"I've never seen you before. I would have seen you if you came from here. Where did you come from?"

"A refrigerator," I said.

MALE EXTINCTION

In addition to her duties attending to the psychological afflictions of the boys at Camp Merrie-Seymour for Boys, Martha Nussbaum also worked for Alex Division.

I have heard people in America use the expression "It's a small world" about such correlations. But, actually, I'm fairly certain the world is somewhat larger and heavier than it ever was in the past. In truth, the world is not small, it's just that Merrie-Seymour Research Group and Alex Division permanently encompassed every component of my and Max's lives. The same was true for Cobie Petersen, whose father was chief of security at Alex Division's main facility. Cobie Petersen admitted this to Max when the boys were attempting to figure out why we'd been sent here in the first place.

We eventually came to conclude that we were less our parents' sons than their subjects.

None of us—Max, Cobie, or myself—truly belonged at Camp Merrie-Seymour for Boys. And the research Mrs. Nussbaum had been conducting on boys for all these years turned out to have chilling implications.

Although the specific focus of Mrs. Nussbaum's scientific research was unclear to just about everyone at Alex Division, which was how the company routinely operated, I found out that she had published a controversial nonfiction text the same year that Max and I were remanded to her care at Camp Merrie-Seymour for Boys.

The title of Mrs. Nussbaum's book was *Male Extinction: The Case for an Exclusively Female Species.*

Max, a practiced thief, found a copy of the book in Larry's cabinet the night he stole the key to the counselors' private clubhouse and asked me and Cobie Petersen if we wanted to break in with him. Of course we did. Max theorized there might be a television or a computer in there, and hoped he'd be able to watch cartoons or look at porn and chat with his friends back in Sunday.

There were neither of those conveniences, as it turned out.

But we all saw the book. Mrs. Nussbaum had apparently signed copies for each of the counselors at Camp Merrie-Seymour for Boys. I don't think any of them had so much as cracked theirs open. All the copies appeared to have been buried beneath the personal effects of the six counselors, which turned out to be equally as fascinating as Mrs. Nussbaum's book about eliminating males.

At first, Max told us the book must have been what he called *all-girl porn*, which excited Cobie Petersen. And we would never have figured out that Mrs. Nussbaum had written it, either, if not for the very unflattering author photo on the back of the dust jacket. On the cover, the author had been listed as M. K. Nussbaum, MD, PhD.

Cobie Petersen and Max were disappointed. The book turned

out not to be porn. Max flipped through it and said it sucked if it was porn, because there was nothing but a bunch of words in it.

But what words they were. Mrs. Nussbaum actually endorsed the idea of eliminating all males from the human species.

I can imagine Alex Division and Merrie-Seymour Research Group as being something like a monster with multiple heads—a Demikhov dog where each toothy mouth competes and pulls in opposition against the others. Because on the one hand there were people like Jake Burgess, so convinced of their command over everything that they could resurrect whatever they wanted to from the dark depths of extinction, while on the other, there were people like Mrs. Nussbaum who apparently were bent on hastening the inevitable end of mankind—*malekind*—and *never* allowing for an encore appearance.

It was almost as though Alex Division were divided into warring fiefdoms.

We stole a copy of Mrs. Nussbaum's book, *Male Extinction: The Case for an Exclusively Female Species*, on Thursday night during our second week at Camp Merrie-Seymour for Boys. Our sock puppet performance had been that afternoon, and that was the night Max took Larry's clubhouse key.

It was Trent Mendibles's turn to listen for the sleepwalker's alarm can. Even if he knew what we were going to do—and Trent Mendibles did not—he'd have to stay on duty in case Robin Sexton ended up dead, which would make Larry mad at us again. The three of us snuck out of Jupiter at two o'clock in the morning and left the guy with the hairiest legs any of us had ever seen in charge of the twitching, earplugged, ninety-four-pound sleepwalker from Pennsylvania.

My brother Max stole the key to the counselors' exclusive clubhouse right out of the pocket of Larry's jeans, which Larry always folded and stored beneath his bed every night while he slept in his non-plastic bed wearing a T-shirt and pair of flannel pajama pants with Spider-Man on them.

The other counselors had to have been smarter than Larry when it came to such matters as security, but then again, possibly not, since the other cabins were filled with relatively uninventive boys.

And Larry slept soundly that night.

Larry snored, too—very loudly.

Max had said that he wished he'd stolen one of Dad's snore wall gadgets, but he might feel bad about all the planes he'd bring down by turning it on. Still—and I could fully understand what inspired our father to invent the snore wall in the first place—there is almost nothing worse than sharing the same sleeping space with someone who snored like Larry or our mother did.

So what's a few plane crashes in the name of a good night's sleep?

We'd gone over our plan at dinner, and when we were certain everyone else at Camp Merrie-Seymour for Boys was asleep, the three of us slid out of our beds as quietly as we could manage.

We got dressed.

Max belly-crawled across the floor and slithered beneath Larry's bunk to snatch the key. The three of us went barefoot, too, because Jupiter's floor was made from squeaky pine planks. It was exciting and terrifying at the same time, and, at dinner, when Cobie expressed his concern about getting into trouble, Max argued, "So what if we get caught? What are they going to do to us, anyway? Kick us out?"

Max definitely made a good case for not worrying about consequences.

Cobie Petersen and I, barefoot, at two in the morning, followed Max across the grounds of Camp Merrie-Seymour for Boys and quietly slipped inside the counselors' private locker room.

Compared to the cabins and spider-infested showers and toilets in the rest of the camp, which served as the only yardstick by which we could measure the aesthetics of the counselors' clubhouse, we had just stolen our way into a gilded palace.

Max turned on the light.

"Don't turn that on!" Cobie Petersen whisper-hissed.

"Why not?" Max said.

"What if someone notices the light?"

"Then they'll probably think one of the counselors is in here taking a dump or maybe *doing a little midnight woodworking*."

"You think about jerking off too much," Cobie said.

"Dude. Don't lie. I think about it as much as you do; I just maybe talk about it more."

Cobie Petersen considered Max's point, nodded, and said, "Yeah. You're probably right."

The inside of the clubhouse was as clean as a hospital operating room. The floors were tessellations of gleaming tile, and the walls paneled in cedar. In the center of the floor was a long bench that faced a row of nine tall lockers—each one decorated with the name and picture of the planet the counselor came from. To be fair, they weren't actually lockers, they were more like personalized cabinets since none of them was actually locked.

I jumped slightly when I heard the sound of splashing water. Max had turned on one of the showers.

"What are you doing? You aren't actually going to take a shower, are you?" Cobie asked.

"No," Max said. "Just checking. These fuckers have *hot water*."

And the showers were very nice. There were three of them at one end of the locker room, all separately enclosed in tile with curtains on the doorways—not like the concrete-floored open-room prison setup we were forced to use. And there were urinals with privacy panels between them, and toilet stalls with doors—again, the complete opposite to the barbaric row of open toilets in the boys' bathroom.

Max turned off the water and dried his hand on one of the fresh towels that sat atop a stack of perfectly white folded terry-cloth, each of which had been embroidered in blue script with *Camp Merrie-Seymour for Boys.*

"Look at this shit," Cobie said.

That's when he opened Larry's cabinet of wonders.

One thing was certain: Larry kept his things neatly organized. Inside his cabinet was a drawer containing toiletries—shaving supplies, deodorant sticks, toothpaste, and nail clippers—and a shelf on which were stacks of clean and folded T-shirts, socks, and underwear. Cobie and Max went through it all. They found Larry's cell phone, too, but they couldn't do anything with it because Larry had a security code programmed into it.

"Well, he's not as stupid as I thought," Max determined.

But the screen on his phone showed that he'd received two missed calls from someone named Lenny.

Cobie Petersen reached inside Larry's cabinet and pulled out his entire stack of boxer shorts.

"What are you doing?" Max said.

"Guys always hide stuff behind their underwear, dude. That's where I hide shit in my house. Nobody wants to poke around there," Cobie said. Then he turned to me with the armload of Larry's underwear and said, "Here. Hold these."

I shook my head. There was no way I was going to hold a stack of Larry's underwear just so Cobie Petersen and my brother could snoop around in his stuff.

"Dude. What is wrong with you?" Cobie was irritated. I thought it was because I didn't want to hold Larry's boxers for him, but I was wrong. Because Cobie continued, "Why the hell don't you ever talk?"

"Because he's stupid," Max said. "That's why."

I swallowed and folded my arms across my chest.

"I'm not stupid," I said. "I just don't say anything because why would I want to talk to someone who hates me as much as you do, Max?"

At that, I had to shut up because I felt my voice crack, and I wasn't about to let myself look like I was about to start crying in front of Cobie and Max.

Cobie Petersen looked at Max and said, "The kid's right. Why do you have to be so fucked to him all the time? I wish I had a brother my age to hang around with, instead of two little sisters."

"I never asked him to come here," Max argued.

I said, "Nobody asked me about it, either."

"Well, at least he's talking to us," Cobie Petersen said. "Because I was about to punch him. Now, here. Hold this shit."

And Cobie pressed the pile of Larry's underwear into my chest, pointed a scolding finger at Max, and added, "And you better lighten up on Ariel. You're the only friends I have in this shithole, but I'm not above twisting your arm and making you hug it out with your brother right now."

I was impressed. Cobie Petersen pronounced my name correctly.

"That isn't going to happen," Max said. "Ariel's holding Larry's boxers."

Cobie Petersen was not one to let a challenge go unattended. He grabbed the bundle of Larry's underwear, which was by this time beginning to unfold itself, and said, "You really want to go there? Okay. Now. Hug your brother or I'll kick the shit out of you, Max."

Many thoughts fired through my mind at that moment. First, I wondered at the complexity of Cobie Petersen's orders to Max, which demanded an act of kindness under the threat of violence. I also considered that Cobie Petersen was in effect delivering what our mother and father had said they wanted to happen—that Max and I would somehow bond over our six weeks at Camp Merrie-Seymour for Boys, even if the real purpose of the camp was something sinister and twisted, which to this day I still can't say whether Jake and Natalie Burgess were aware of.

Max's eyes went from Cobie, down to the shiny tiled floor in the counselors' locker room, and then he looked at me.

I can't say for certain what I saw in Max's eyes. Maybe he was sorry. Maybe this was the first time anyone had ever forced Max to think beyond his distanced perspectives. And I thought, maybe what Max had been doing to me these months since I came to Sunday, West Virginia, had been nothing more than a test to determine some measure of my character. Everyone in my life always seemed to be watching, testing, exerting control over things that couldn't be tamed; so what made Max any different?

"Do it," Cobie Petersen urged.

That's when my brother Max, barefoot, stepped around Cobie Petersen and stood in front of me, so close I could feel the heat rising like steam clouds from his nervous chest. Then he put his arms around me and hugged me tightly. I hugged him back, too.

And Max put his mouth to my ear and whispered, "Sorry. I

guess I've pretty much been a dick to you ever since they brought you home."

"Thanks," I said. "It's okay."

And Cobie Petersen, who was not looking at us, said, "Holy shit. Larry's got booze in here."

Max and I let go.

Cobie stuffed the bundle of underwear back into my arms. Some of Larry's boxers spilled onto the floor around our feet. "Fold those back the way they were, Ariel."

"But I don't want to fold Larry's underwear," I said.

"Do it anyway. What if Larry gets mad again?"

Cobie Petersen stood with an attitude of a fisherman holding up the catch of the day. He raised bottles of vodka, held by their necks in each of his hands, showing a toothy smile.

"Come on," Cobie said. "Fold, fucker. You're in this just as much as we are, so you might as well pull your weight."

There was no arguing with Cobie Petersen. So I sat down on the changing bench and began folding Larry's pile of underwear while Cobie and Max rummaged through every one of the other cabinets.

"I'm telling you right now, I am *not* holding anyone else's underwear tonight," I said.

Cobie Petersen proved me wrong on that statement, too.

YOU NEVER KNOW

It turned out that, as a group, the counselors of Camp Merrie-Seymour for Boys—to a man—were not the kind of people most normal parents would give their boys away to for six minutes, much less six weeks.

This is what happened to us while we explored the hidden secrets of the counselors' locker room that had no lockers:

As I sat there folding Larry's underwear into the neat pile from which it had mostly scattered, Cobie Petersen decided he would keep one of the bottles of vodka from Larry's cabinet.

"You guys ever been drunk before?" Cobie asked.

Max shook his head. "I took a couple gulps of my dad's beer one time when he wasn't looking."

"Well, I don't think I'll try Larry's vodka, but I'm gonna steal it anyway," Cobie said. "You never know."

I had heard people use that phrase—*you never know*—many times since I came to America. To this day, it still perplexes me. I never knew what *you never know* was supposed to mean. If you *never* knew, you would probably be incapable of thinking at all.

Max shrugged and said, "Yeah. You *do* never know."

Cobie and Max argued about what to steal. Cobie wanted to take as much as we could carry, but Max insisted on taking what he called "small shit," so our thievery would be less detectable. The boys went deeper into Larry's cabinet. Max pulled out a plastic bag with what looked like wads of velvet moss inside.

"Holy shit. Larry's a pothead," Max said.

Cobie Petersen took the baggie from Max, opened it, stuck his nose in, and inhaled.

"This is good stuff," he said.

I folded, and tried to ignore what Cobie Petersen and my brother were doing. That was another thing I'd noticed since coming to America—particularly since enrolling in the ninth grade at William E. Shuck High School: An awful lot of boys smoke pot. I had never seen pot in my life before starting high school, where it seemed to be just about everywhere. Boys smoked it and sold it in the toilets and locker room as though school were a never-ending orgy of fun, so by the time I entered Camp Merrie-Seymour for Boys with my ninth-grade American brother Max, I was acutely aware of what pot looked and smelled like.

And I could smell Larry's pot from where I sat folding his boxers.

"Don't take it all," Max said.

Cobie pinched two thumb-sized nuggets from the bag and slipped them into the front pocket on his shorts. And they found some rolling papers and a lighter. I knew there would be trouble ahead.

Max flicked the lighter and said, "Now I really *can* burn down Jupiter."

"But don't, okay?" I said.

"Let's see what's in Horace's cabinet," Cobie said.

Horace was the counselor from Mars. Nobody liked Mars. Well, at least, none of the relatively *sane* boys at Camp Merrie-Seymour for Boys liked Mars, which meant Cobie, Max, and me.

"This is like being on a shopping spree with someone else's credit cards," Max added.

And Cobie told me, "Hurry up. Put Larry's underwear back. We're moving on."

At Horace's cabinet, Cobie Petersen announced, "This is like a goddamned pot dispensary."

As it turned out, five of the six cabinets we looked in had pot in them. And every one of them had some type of alcohol. Also, Max found an open box of condoms in Horace's cabinet.

"Check this out." Max held the condoms in front of Cobie Petersen's face.

Cobie said, "Dude. Who would bring a box of condoms to summer camp?"

"Horace would. That's who."

"*Why?*"

"Uh. Why do you *think*, Dumpling Run Boy?"

"But there's only *guys* here," Cobie Petersen pointed out.

"Duh," Max said.

"Oh. That's really gross," Cobie said.

Max pulled one of the condoms out of the box. It was sealed inside a square red foil packet, about two inches wide. "I've never actually touched a real condom before."

"Is there such thing as a fake one?" I asked.

Both Cobie and Max stared at me as though they couldn't believe I had willingly joined their conversation about condoms.

"Well, I'm taking one." Max slid the condom into his pocket.

Cobie Petersen repeated himself. "*Why?*"

"You never know," Max answered. "Might be fun sometime when I need to *squeeze home the runner on third* or something."

"Dude."

"What?"

"Do you play baseball?"

Max shrugged. "Doesn't everyone?"

"You are so gross."

And Max held the box of condoms out to Cobie Petersen.

"Admit it. You want one, too, don't you?"

Cobie Petersen thought about it. He looked at me. I could clearly see his cheeks reddening.

Then Cobie nodded and shrugged. "Yeah. I guess I do."

Max handed one of the red condom packets to Cobie.

"How about you, Ariel?"

I was horrified by the offer. But I was also touched that Max had somehow managed to cross the bridge between us and begin to act as though I existed in his world.

I shook my head. "No, thanks. Horace probably needs them more than I do."

"Yeah. There's only one left, anyway," Max said. "You'd be a real dick if you took Horace's *last condom*."

Before we left, Cobie Petersen summed up his assessment of the six counselors of Camp Merrie-Seymour for Boys.

"These guys are a bunch of drunk, druggie perverts."

And I thought, considering the things we'd stolen from the counselors' cabinets, this was an amusing and hypocritical accusation for Cobie Petersen to make.

"Who apparently don't read books," Max added.

That was because we'd found Mrs. Nussbaum's book on male extinction on the bottom floor of every counselor's cabinet, usually beneath pairs of muddy tennis shoes or piled dirty laundry, which I was enlisted to lift out, because Cobie Petersen said the only place better for hiding things you don't want people to find than beneath your clean underwear is in a pile of a guy's *dirty* underwear.

In the end, we added a small flashlight, three warm cans of beer, and a signed copy of *Male Extinction: The Case for an Exclusively Female Species* to the loot.

I wanted to read Mrs. Nussbaum's book.

Like my American father, Jake Burgess, I was fascinated by the idea of extinction, especially after meeting our anguished family pet, Alex.

We took our stolen trophies and followed Cobie Petersen along the trail in the dark woods that led to the old well house.

It was half past two in the morning.

"We need to find a good spot to hide this shit," Cobie said.

"If anyone comes, we should all take off in different directions," Max offered.

Cobie Petersen nodded. "Probably a good idea."

CRYSTAL LUTZ AND IGOR ZELINSKY

Jake Burgess's first attempt at de-extinction focused on a species of worm with legs.

In those days, just out of graduate studies and newly married to Natalie, Jake had been eager to stumble upon anything at all that might please the directors at Merrie-Seymour Research Group and Alex Division. He had been moved to Alex Division after inventing a type of eyeglass that stimulated the visual centers in the brain and made blind people *think* their vision had been restored.

The higher-ups at Merrie-Seymour Research Group were very impressed by Jake Burgess for his extreme dedication, creativity, and unique talents.

Everyone knew the eyeglasses Jake Burgess invented were absolutely useless, and all the people who tested them injured themselves or walked out into the path of oncoming buses. But Jake and the Merrie-Seymour people weren't as interested in those minor consequences as much as they were interested in finding out what, exactly, the sightless people saw when they put the glasses on.

Since they had no words for the things they saw, none of the subjects of the eyeglass research could precisely say what the eyeglasses showed them.

The ones who survived needed a new language, apparently.

Jake Burgess's resurrection of the worms with legs succeeded, but there were only male specimens from which the Alex worms could be created. Another strange thing Jake noticed about the worms was that in an experiment to test conditioning responses to negative stimuli, the worms consistently moved themselves toward the small metal electrodes they were *supposed* to avoid.

All the worms electrocuted themselves.

Alex, the crow, came from a species of Polynesian crows that had gone extinct in the late 1800s. Jake Burgess was confident sufficient male and female samples of the birds' genetic material had been accumulated in natural history museums around the world to repopulate a self-regenerating species.

The crows had gone extinct because their blue-black neck feathers were highly prized in the British hat-making industry. It took roughly twenty-seven crows to make one hatband.

Jake Burgess's Alex crow project was a resounding success, and he brought home one of the first young crows he created from the cemetery of the past as a gift to his wife, Natalie, just sixteen days after Max, my brother, was born.

That also happened to be the exact day that I was born, and precisely fourteen years from the day when a broken refrigerator would save me from extinction.

- - -

Mr. Warren and I used wood mallets and chisels heated in a fire we'd made at the entrance to the cave to free Katkov's beast from the ice.

While we worked, Murdoch stood guard outside with our bear rifles, even though we knew there was nothing human left to guard against. I am convinced I must be insane, and there is little justification I can present for the selfishness of my actions unless to offer as an excuse the debilitation we have all suffered consequential to what has been nearly a year-long ordeal trapped in this ice.

We are all the same as Katkov's beast, and the time has come for us to be free.

Five months here at the Lena Delta have driven us to once again attempt to seize control of our fate.

This was entirely unplanned—let me assure you. When the argument with Katkov intensified this morning, the drunken Murdoch—in his steadfast loyalty to me—drew a knife and stabbed the man several times, delivering a mortal wound to Katkov's neck.

Most of the inhabitants of the village were away, hunting and fishing in the clear summer weather. Those who remained behind—three men, including Mr. Piedmont—were executed with Murdoch's rifle, and burned inside Katkov's shelter.

I must be insane.

The weather has improved dramatically and it

is our plan to make a crossing to the Russian out-post of Belun, where we hope our tale of survival and the destruction of the *Alex Crow* will earn us transport west, toward civilization.

I have Katkov's map and have studied our course. We will either escape or die in the attempt.

SUNDAY, AUGUST 8, 1880—*BELUN*

Arrived at the Russian outpost of Belun this after-noon, having traveled here with Mr. Murdoch, and the newspaperman, Mr. Ripley Reed Warren.

It is entirely by some miracle that Warren and I managed to bring our small party to the comman-dant here at Belun, where I truly feel that we've been delivered from hell.

Mr. Warren will not speak to me about the in-cident at Lena River Delta.

His distance troubles me greatly.

We are all that remain of the *Alex Crow* expe-dition, and the only survivors—if one could call us that—of the deadly events at the village on the Lena River Delta. Murdoch, poor demented soul, is almost entirely sightless from our months in the ice. He insists he has been stricken blind by Mr. Katkov's beast.

I have bandaged Murdoch's eyes—and we led him here as one would lead a dog on a leash—in the hopes that some days resting the nerves will find his vision restored.

It is the strangest family imaginable—two men
who do not speak, and a third who cannot see.

- - -

So I will say this: As a child, I was adopted by my aunt and uncle,
and after I came out of the refrigerator I was adopted by a soldier
named Thaddeus. Then I suppose I was adopted by the small family at the gate. There were still two more families ahead of Ariel—
three, if you count the time I spent with Major Knott.

I have had many lives before we met, Max. I have been extinct,
and brought back again and again and again.

Once we had all crossed through the gate, the four of us walked
until well after dark. I offered to share my water, but the man—his
name was Garen—told me they had their own water in the wagon,
which was piled quite high with the family's belongings.

"Where are you going?" I asked.

"There is a camp. It will take us two or maybe three days to
walk there," Garen said. "You could go faster if you went on ahead
of us. We are slow."

"I don't mind," I said. And then I thought, what if they didn't
want me to walk with them? So I said, "I don't have anybody. I
don't mean to bother you. Would it be all right if I walked to the
camp with you and your family? I could do things—help out."

The woman—Garen's wife—was named Emel, and the baby—
a girl—was called Thia. I think the woman may have sensed that I
was scared to be alone.

Garen asked, "You're not a thief, are you?"

"No."

"Did you pay for the bottle of water?"

"A friend gave it to me."

"Friend? You told me you weren't from around here."

"I'm not. But it was my friend's. I knew him from school. I found him dead in a market stall. The water belonged to him," I said.

Garen nodded.

"I can pull the wagon for a bit, if you'd like me to," I said.

"Why would you want to do that?" Garen asked.

I shrugged. "To help."

Garen kept his eyes forward, focused on the empty road ahead of us.

He said, "You're too small."

"I'm fourteen years old."

Garen stopped walking and looked at me.

"I thought you were younger. Maybe it's the clown costume."

"Maybe it is," I said.

Then the woman, Emel, spoke. She said, "We have some clothes in the wagon that would suit you better."

"I don't have any money," I said.

"It's all right," Garen said. "Maybe you could pull the wagon for a bit, and I'll find you something better to wear in exchange for helping us. I am tired of pulling this thing."

I looked down at my clown suit. The knees were torn open on both legs, and the seam under my right arm had completely separated.

And I said, "It would be nice to finally get rid of this thing."

- - -

The melting man met Crystal Lutz at a thrift store in Lafayette, Tennessee, where he went clothes shopping two days after wiring Francis MacInnes's cell phone to his red mercury atom bomb.

"Everything is working out perfectly," Joseph Stalin said.

"Well, except for all the boils on your skin, and your bloody diarrhea. And hair loss," 3-60 pointed out.

"Other than that, things couldn't be better," Leonard Fountain said.

Leonard Fountain woke up in the jumble of rags and matting he fashioned into a bed in Mom's Attic in the steaming and gaseous, fetid petri dish of his converted U-Haul moving van.

"Does she ever *shut up*?" Joseph Stalin, as always, was irritated.

"Sometimes she does," the melting man answered.

"You are getting out of bed. You need to pee," 3-60 narrated.

"Yes, I need to pee," the melting man agreed.

Leonard Fountain realized two things while urinating outside his van, which was parked down a dirt road in the woods outside Lafayette. First, the metallic drone that had been sent by the Beaver King was watching him pee, which made him nervous, so it took a long time before he could manage to get a stream going.

Nobody likes being watched by the Beaver King when he pees.

Second, his clothes were pasted to his skin, and he didn't have anything clean to change into.

Leonard Fountain was a nonstop reality show to the people at Merrie-Seymour Research Group, who had actually been watching him for many years.

"The Beaver King is watching you pee," Joseph Stalin told him.

"So are you," the melting man pointed out. "It's hard to pee when Joseph Stalin and the Beaver King are watching me."

"Your clothes are ruined, and I am watching you pee, Lenny," 3-60 told him.

"Everyone needs to stop watching me pee," the melting man said.

It always made Leonard Fountain nostalgic when 3-60 called him *Lenny*. It reminded him of his little brother. He had tried to phone his brother twice the evening before, but there was no answer. The melting man had only a vague idea of where his brother might be; it had been years since the two had actually seen each other.

"You need to find some new clothes, Lenny," 3-60 said.

The melting man's zipper was so clogged with goo and filth, he couldn't close his fly.

"Your zipper's down," 3-60 pointed out.

"I wish I could slap you both," Joseph Stalin said.

Leonard Fountain, his zipper hanging open, shut the cargo compartment of his van, climbed up into the cab, and drove into the town of Lafayette.

Leonard Fountain decided to shop for a fresh change of clothes at the Lafayette First Church of Christ Charity Thrift Store. The thrift store had everything the melting man needed, even underwear. For just a moment, the melting man found himself wondering who would actually donate old underwear to a charitable organization, and what type of person would buy someone else's used underwear? Even the melting man had standards, but despite this reluctance, he selected two pairs of boxers and three pairs of briefs, anyway, along with some socks. And on the top of the rack where the men's underwear dangled from clothespinned hangers was an assortment of hats of all types.

The melting man, who had lost nearly all his hair from the toxic mix of radiation and mercury in his van, thought a hat might be a good idea. He picked up a dark gray homburg and lifted it above his head.

"Hey now! If you try on anything, you're going to have to buy it!"

Leonard Fountain didn't realize a fat man wearing suspenders and long johns behind the counter was watching him.

"Huh?" the melting man said.

"You heard me. No trying on unless you buy it," the man said.

"You should kill him. He's been watching you," Joseph Stalin said.

Leonard Fountain put down the homburg. "I left my gun in the van."

"That plaid stingy-brim would look good on you."

At first, the melting man imagined it was 3-60 who'd directed his attention to the plaid hat, but it was someone else. A woman stood on the opposite side of the rack of men's underwear. She pointed out the hat for Leonard.

Crystal Lutz worked at a sausage factory in Farmington Hills, Tennessee. Her typical eight-hour shift involved preventing traffic jams on the bratwurst line. She monitored quivering chunks of meat and fat as they marched along a metal conveyor belt and into a pulverizing machine.

Leonard Fountain—the melting man—looked like sausage meat to Crystal Lutz.

Of course, Crystal Lutz didn't actually exist. The small, malfunctioning tissue-based machine Leonard Fountain had been paid one thousand dollars to have implanted behind his right eye had been scripting and broadcasting its own show for the past decade.

"Huh?" the melting man said.

"You are turning red and getting aroused because the pretty girl is talking to you, Lenny," 3-60 told him.

"Don't try it on," the man behind the counter said.

"That one there." Crystal Lutz pointed again. "I think it would look good on you. My name is Crystal."

"Um. Hi, Crystal," Leonard Fountain said. He was sweating and melting, and insanely horny. And Crystal Lutz was exactly like Joseph Stalin and 3-60, except for one thing: The melting man could see her.

"What's your name?" Crystal Lutz asked.

"Igor Zelinsky," Joseph Stalin told him.

"Igor Zelinsky," Leonard Fountain said.

Crystal Lutz smiled like she could eat Leonard Fountain on the spot, if she were real, and if she were a cannibal. "Igor's a bitchin' name."

"Say thank you, Lenny," 3-60 instructed.

"Thank you," the melting man said.

With Crystal Lutz accompanying him, Leonard Fountain purchased two pairs of pants, three button-up shirts, two pairs of boxer shorts, three briefs, and a plaid stingy-brim hat.

"You drive around in *this*?" Crystal Lutz said when they got out to Leonard Fountain's repurposed U-Haul van.

"Yes."

"Bitchin'."

"Be polite, Lenny," 3-60 reminded him.

"Thank you," the melting man said.

"Don't let her distract you from what you need to do, Leonard," Joseph Stalin scolded.

"You are climbing in the van with the pretty girl," 3-60 narrated. "You are very aroused."

Leonard Fountain was quite possibly the most insane person on the planet.

THE YOKE OF INAUSPICIOUS STARS

Cobie Petersen raised his hand in his most earnest Teacher's Pet fashion. He looked at his hand; then he looked at Max and me.

"Who wants to get stoned?" he said.

Max raised his hand. "I do."

I shook my head. "Not me."

The three of us sat, cross-legged on a clearing off the trail beside the cinder-block well house, listening to the splash of the spring water as it spilled from the overflow pipe.

I held our stolen flashlight. I shined it onto the pages of section one from *Male Extinction: The Case for an Exclusively Female Species*. Cobie Petersen scooted along the ground and got so close to me his knee came to rest on top of mine.

"I need some of that light," he said. He dug around in his pocket and pulled out the pot and papers he'd taken from Larry's cabinet. He crumbled the weed onto the lap of his beige shorts and began rolling it up in one of the papers.

Staring down at his fingers in concentration, Cobie Petersen, who obviously had skill when it came to rolling marijuana cigarettes, said, "So, how's the book?"

"Oh. It's scary, I guess," I answered.

"Scary? Mrs. Nussbaum? No way, dude."

Cobie bent forward and licked the adhesive edge on his rolling paper, and then started making a second joint. He grabbed his crotch and adjusted himself.

"God! It's been a long-ass time since I've gotten stoned," he said. "It's practically giving me a boner. What's our therapist say in there?"

"Well, I'm only in the first part, but it sounds like she really believes that the only way to save the human species from self-destruction is to get rid of all the males. At the World Conference on Male Declination in 2014, a universal charter was approved, stating that the male human was the principal driving mechanism behind our species' extinction, which the conference's panel of scientists estimated will occur sometime during the coming century. And there were even *men* scientists who participated in the study."

"That's stupid," Max said. "Without males, there wouldn't be a species. Duh. Maybe Mrs. Nussbaum missed that week in junior high school sex class."

"She's a doctor," I offered.

"That never excluded anyone from being fucking insane," Cobie said.

He probably had a point.

"The book says that scientists have discovered a method to make viable, functioning sperm from female stem cells. Mrs. Nussbaum even claims that an American woman has actually given birth to two healthy daughters using *female sperm*."

"That's the dumbest *and* grossest thing I've ever heard in my life," Cobie Petersen said. "Girl sperm? Girls don't have sperm."

"Female *sperm*?" Max asked. "That sounds totally gross."

Cobie Petersen nodded thoughtfully. "Dude. If you ask me, sperm is just like farts. Everyone else's is totally gross except for your own."

"I can see that," Max said. "So I suppose Mrs. Nussbaum has a dick, or what?"

I shook my head. "No. They created the female sperm in a lab."

"So Mrs. Nussbaum likes to *unclog the ketchup bottle* once in a while and thump out some *girl sperm* in her private laboratory? Can't blame anyone for doing that on slow days at work. Unless it gets you fired, I guess," Max said.

"If she doesn't have a dick, where's her female sperm come out of, then?" Cobie Petersen asked.

I sighed. It was so frustrating and embarrassing, talking about sex with Max and Cobie.

"Yeah. That's ridiculous," Max agreed, "impossible. You need to have guys on the planet—guys with dicks—if you think anyone's going to *shake the yokes out of their inauspicious stars*."

And I was impressed by Max's ability to stretch a quote from Shakespeare into a statement on masturbation.

"According to Mrs. Nussbaum, you don't need guys anymore. Females can now make sperm," I said.

Cobie Petersen finished rolling a second pot cigarette.

He reached across me with an open hand extended toward Max. "Dude. Let me have that lighter."

I continued reading, trying to ignore the spark of the flame and the smell of burning pot just inches from my face. Cobie Petersen sucked in a tremendous drag, held it, then exhaled billows of blue-gray smoke. He passed the joint across me to Max.

Cobie Petersen said, "Ahhhh . . ."

I thumbed ahead in Mrs. Nussbaum's *Male Extinction: The Case for an Exclusively Female Species*. Apparently, the first section of the book was entirely devoted to the scientific studies that yielded the female sperm, failed attempts at fertilizing an ovum, and the successful development, just after the turn of our century, that produced two baby girls, born a year apart to the same mother.

Mrs. Nussbaum hailed this era as "the final century of man."

Her dark prophecy was almost biblical in tone.

The second section of the book was a rationale for the argument in support of programmed male extinction. Mrs. Nussbaum made a reasonable point, after all, considering the terrible things males had done in their never-ending effort to push our species toward the precipice of extinction, and control and manipulate everything they ever came in contact with. With viable and genetically diverse female sperm, she postulated, males could rapidly become extinct if females simply decided to refrain from breeding with them. Since female sperm can only create female offspring, male extinction would occur within fifty years. But the most frightening aspect of Mrs. Nussbaum's case for facilitating the extinction of all male humans—she referred to it as "gender die-off"—was that her "Law of Male Uselessness" was primarily based on the results of comprehensive psychological and medical studies she had conducted over the course of the past decade on "a wide variety of males between the ages of twelve and seventeen years."

Wide variety?

Merrie-Seymour Boys!
We're Merrie-Seymour Boys!

We're learning healthy habits,
Smart as foxes, quick as rabbits!

My brother Max erupted into a coughing fit beside me, which caused Cobie Petersen to laugh so hard he farted and fell backward in the dirt.

And Cobie Petersen said, "I am so wasted, gents."

Max held the little yellow cigarette directly in front of my face and said, "Come on, Ariel. Loosen up and have a little fun for once in your fucked-up life."

I shook my head.

"I have had fun before," I said.

"When?"

I thought about it. I honestly didn't have an answer for him. I remembered playing in Mr. Antonio's field with Marden and Sahar on my fourteenth birthday, how I'd been dressed as Pierrot, and had white makeup on my face, and the times I'd played chess in the camp with Major Knott.

"The sock puppet play this afternoon was pretty fun, I guess."

"You just sat there with your fingers sticking out," Cobie Petersen said.

"I moved them once in a while," I argued.

Then Max started laughing and pressed the end of the joint up to my mouth. His fingers felt wet against my lips, and the joint was soggy and smelled so strong.

So I smoked with Cobie Petersen and Max Burgess, my American brother.

What could I do? I realized how sad and lonely I'd been here in America, and I would do anything to keep my brother Max moving toward me.

I inhaled.

The smoke tickled like frayed straw broom whisks inside me, but I managed to hold it in and even to exhale without coughing.

And Max said, "Welcome to America, little brother."

"You're only sixteen days older than I am," I pointed out.

Cobie Petersen softly punched me on my shoulder.

"I bet you've seen some messed-up shit," Cobie Petersen said.

I thought about a time I'd spent with other orphan boys in a camp of tents. I thought about all the stories I'd been carrying with me.

"I've seen worse things than I can ever say."

Max looked at me. There was something in his eyes. I could see it hurt him in some way to think about the reality of where I'd come from, and what was behind me. "Really?"

I didn't want to picture that time, but what could I do? I needed to change the subject, pick a different story from my library. So I nodded. "One time, I spent two days hiding inside a refrigerator."

"That must have been cold," Cobie said.

"It was broken. I only came out because I needed to pee."

We smoked some more.

At first, I didn't feel a thing. But then a few minutes after inhaling the smoke, I had a sensation as though I were sitting in a perfect lukewarm current of water as it flowed and tickled every inch of my skin, tugging on me. It felt so wonderful.

Max grabbed the flashlight and shined it on my face.

"You're smiling," he said.

"No I'm not."

"Cobie. Look. Mister Silent is smiling."

Cobie Petersen leaned into the light and confirmed Max's opinion.

"You're smiling, kid."

I tried to regain my composure by concentrating on something real. I waved the copy of *Male Extinction: The Case for an Exclusively Female Species* in the center of the tight triangle we sat in.

"Look. This book. She's really crazy. Mrs. Nussbaum really *does* want to see all males die off. And she's doing research on *us*."

"Us?" Max said.

"With girl sperm?" Cobie asked.

And then Cobie Petersen raised his hand and said, "Wait. Wait just a second. Have either of you guys ever in your life heard anything dumber than *girl sperm*?"

For the next hour—it may have only been thirty seconds, but then again, it felt as though it were much, much longer—I tried my hardest to explain to Cobie and Max what Mrs. Nussbaum detailed in her book, but I kept getting confused and lost, and saying the same things over and over.

Finally, Cobie Petersen told me: "Dude. Shut up. You're stoned. Max, I have created a monster."

"The Dumpling Boy," Max said.

"I made him start talking, and now he won't shut up."

Which, for whatever reasons, made me suddenly obsess on something I'd been dying to ask Cobie Petersen.

I said, "Were you really telling the truth about the Dumpling Man getting you like that?" I pointed to Cobie's shoulder.

"It's all true. He pooed all over me, then dug his claws in right here."

Cobie Petersen stretched out the neck of his T-shirt to bare the skin of his left shoulder. Max shined the flashlight's beam directly onto the pale moon of his shoulder, and Cobie traced an index finger along the track of the scar.

"Maybe when we get out of here, you and your brother can come up to Dumpling Run and the three of us will go coon hunting and look for the Dumpling Man again. Because he is real. I've heard all the stories, and most of them are pure horseshit, but not what I told you guys last week at scary story time. I really saw him. He really did this to me."

"If you say so," I said.

And Max added, "You never know."

Cobie Petersen straightened his shirt and wobbled to his feet.

"We better get back to Jupiter before we end up in trouble."

We found a place between three moss-covered boulders where we hid the things we'd stolen from the counselors' locker room. I didn't want to think about their reasons, but Max and Cobie decided they didn't want to leave Horace's condoms behind. And we laughed so hard we all nearly peed our pants when Max said he was going to go crazy if he didn't *stir up some of his favorite birthday pudding* pretty soon.

"How do you think up all these things?" I said.

Max shrugged and said, "It's like magic."

Then we turned off the flashlight, stowed it with the rest of our loot, and, barefoot, stumbled back to Jupiter.

Before we came out of the woods, Max added, "And, Jesus, I am *really* hungry."

That was something Max never said.

And Cobie Petersen told him, "We could go look for marshmallows in Earth."

"Let's not," Max answered.

SUCK IT UP, ICEMAN

Jupiter should have won the interplanetary tug-of-war competition that afternoon—we normally would have—but three of Jupiter's boys were too tired after staying up most of the night, committing acts of thievery, reading terrifying nonfiction, and smoking pot in the woods.

It was the most fun I'd ever had in my life.

At least Max ate a big breakfast.

Cobie Petersen propped his elbows on the picnic table and cradled his face in his hands.

"I am so fucking tired. Why don't they let us sleep late like regular boys?"

Robin Sexton twitched his thumbs and rocked back and forth slightly, listening to nothing at all through his toilet-paper-and-kite-string earbuds.

Max spooned a blob of oatmeal he'd topped with milk and grape jelly into his mouth. "Look around you. Let me know if you see any *regular* boys here."

"You should get stoned more often if it makes you eat like that," I said.

Max bit into a bagel. "That fat camp summer almost killed me."

"Mrs. Nussbaum says all us guys only have about fifty years to live anyway," Cobie Petersen said. "We might as well try and die fat."

Trent Mendibles, the boy with the hairiest legs anyone had ever seen, perked his head up and said, "Wait. You guys got stoned last night?"

"No," Max said. "It was just a . . . uh . . . figure of speech."

"Nothing's better than getting zombied out and blasting away assholes on BQTNP," Trent said.

Trent Mendibles didn't think about many things.

"I have no idea what you're talking about, hairy gamer dude from Ohio," Cobie Petersen mumbled into his hands.

"Hook me up with some weed. I want to get high," Trent said.

Cobie and Max answered simultaneously, like they were singing the Jupiter-Jesus Boys song.

They said, "No."

Trent Mendibles leaned across the table and lowered his voice. "Give me some. Or I'll tell Larry what you guys did."

For a moment, it became deathly quiet at our table in the pavilion. I looked at Trent, then Max, and finally to Cobie. Robin Sexton seemed oblivious, as usual.

And Cobie Petersen raised his eyes from his palms and calmly told Trent Mendibles, "I will kill you when you're asleep tonight."

Max added, "He will. Believe me. I'll help him."

Trent Mendibles sat back on the bench. "You guys are fuckers."

Then Cobie put his head down on the table and said, "Ariel. Go get me something to eat."

Horace, Mars cabin's counselor, whose condoms were stolen

the night before by Cobie Petersen and my brother Max, stood up at the Mars boys' table and bellowed, "All right! Clean up and get out to the rec field for competition!"

Cobie Petersen, the strongest boy at Camp Merrie-Seymour for Boys, missed breakfast. It was going to cost our team significantly.

We five boys of Jupiter got dragged through the mud five times that day.

Cobie Petersen was our anchor. But he was useless—dead on his feet. We all were. Well, except for Robin Sexton and Trent Mendibles. But they were useless anyway.

I had played tug-of-war before; who hasn't? But I had no idea that at Camp Merrie-Seymour for Boys the game would involve a wide and deep pit of soupy mud. Every planet at Camp Merrie-Seymour for Boys destroyed our team in the contest. By the time the first four cabins had their way with us, our knees were scuffed and bloodied, our T-shirts were torn and hung from our shoulders like drapes of wet cement, and Robin Sexton was crying because he'd lost his shorts in the mud pit.

At least his earbuds stayed in.

Larry was mad at us—again—but this time it was for losing. If he suspected we'd done something wrong while we were supposed to have been sleeping the night before, he didn't show it. But to make matters worse, the final team to defeat the mud-coated boys of Jupiter was Mars. We were eliminated, humiliated, and out of clean clothes. Robin Sexton had to wallow around in the pit, feeling for his lost shorts.

Larry tossed everyone's sheets and duffel bags of clothes out Jupiter's screen door. He told us not to bother stepping foot in our cabin until everything was clean.

He banished the five of us to the disgusting showers, and afterward, we had to stand in the laundry room, wrapped in towels for two hours while we washed and dried all Jupiter's laundry. Actually, Max, Cobie, and I didn't stand so much as sit down and fall asleep on the damp concrete floor with our backs to the wall and our towels modestly and securely tucked between our legs.

Clean, dry, and a little bit bloodied, we came back home to Jupiter.

It was entirely unrealistic to have held out any hope that we'd be able to rest until dinnertime.

As soon as I came through the cabin door with my bag of everything I owned including the sheets for my plastic bed, Larry pointed an authoritative finger at my forehead.

"You. Marcel Marceau. Mrs. Nussbaum wants to see you in her office. You might as well get it over with, 'cause these four are waiting their turns right behind you. Get going. And she wants you to bring your index card."

It was like having the wind knocked out of me. We all knew there would be some private one-on-one sessions with Mrs. Nussbaum during our stay at Camp Merrie-Seymour for Boys, but it almost seemed brutally unfair that I was chosen to be the first boy from Jupiter to have to go.

Cobie Petersen patted my back. "Have fun, dude. And don't let her get any girl sperm in you. You never know what that shit might do to a guy."

"Yeah," Max agreed. "You never know."

I was terrified and disgusted at the same time. How could I possibly face Mrs. Nussbaum after what I learned about her theories and her years of *scientific studies on a wide variety of males between the ages of twelve and seventeen years*?

I actually considered running off into the woods and attempting some form of escape. And it seemed to me that with every day that passed at Camp Merrie-Seymour for Boys, Bucky Littlejohn's act of desperation became more heroic and godlike.

Larry grabbed the duffel bag of laundry from my hands and tossed it onto my crumpling plastic-coated cot. Then he handed my folded index card to me.

"Suck it up, iceman," he said. "You know where to go."

Mrs. Nussbaum's office was in a small cottage located at the front gate to Camp Merrie-Seymour for Boys. I took my time walking there. My stomach churned as I read the welcoming message on the gate.

> *Camp Merrie-Seymour for Boys*
> *Where Boys Rediscover the Fun of Boyhood!*

I tried to anticipate the questions she might ask me, in order to prepare myself with evasive and shortened answers, but I kept thinking about her book and what kinds of horrible experiments she could possibly be conducting behind closed doors.

What could I do? There was no way out.

We were all doomed to extinction.

I stopped and chewed on my lip when I got to Mrs. Nussbaum's. I flipped my folded index card over and over inside my pocket. In fact, both my hands were tucked deeply into my pockets, which was something I never did.

A brass plate hung on the slatted siding by the front door. It said: MARTHA NUSSBAUM, MD, PHD

And as soon as I stepped one foot onto the porch of her cottage, Mrs. Nussbaum flung the front door open and, in her high-pitched, wildly gleeful tone, squealed, "Ariel! So very nice to see you today! Come in! Come in!"

Mrs. Nussbaum looked like an enormous sock puppet in her white lab smock.

"You said it wrong," I said.

"Huh?"

"My name. It's *Ah*-riel," I pointed out.

"Oh! That sounds lovely when you say it!"

Then she repeated my name three times—a kind of witch's curse, I thought—and told me three more times to *come in! come in! come in!*

ALL IN THE NAME OF RESEARCH, ARIEL

The front room of the cottage was dim and windowless, lit only by a yellowish incandescent lamp that stood behind a tufted chair in the corner.

I half expected to see Alex, our crow, perched on it. The walls, ceiling, and floor were all paneled wood, which made the place seem even darker, and everywhere was the clutter of what looked like medical antiques: a high-backed rolltop desk with a glass case displaying gleaming instruments and leather-bound books; another cabinet as tall as Mrs. Nussbaum with dozens of small square drawers; and a rack of shelves with old cork-stoppered bottles.

It looked like a stage set from a horror movie.

"Oh my! Look at your knees!"

I did what Mrs. Nussbaum said and looked at my knees. They were raw and bloody from being dragged around on a rope all morning.

"It was tug-of-war day," I said.

"Let's fix you up, Ariel! Come, come!"

And Mrs. Nussbaum waved me through a back doorway and into a beige, fluorescent-lighted, and much more modern examination room. It was as sterile as a boiled thermometer. The floor was linoleum with tan and green tiles, and the walls were smooth and spotless with racks of examination instruments attached by coiled black rubber cords to their power sources. Beside these hung a blood pressure device with black rubber balls dangling from thick Velcro cuffs. In the corner of the room, angling out diagonally, sat a green vinyl examination bed that was covered by a long strip of white paper, and there was some kind of tray table on wheels beside it that had a sheet of blue paper partially covering a scary-looking set of stainless steel doctor's implements.

It was even more terrifying than I could have imagined, made worse by the posters on the walls: one showing a front and a back view of the musculature and internal organs of a human, and two others, labeled "The Anatomy of the Eye" and "The Male Reproductive System."

Who would hang an enormous chart of the internal structures of the male reproductive system at a summer camp for deranged boys?

I was nearly frozen in fear.

Then Mrs. Nussbaum said, "Take off your shirt, shoes, and socks, and hop up on the examination table, so I can have a look at you."

What could I do?

"I thought you were a psychologist," I said.

"Well! Aren't you talkative today? It's so nice to see this breakthrough! I happen to be a medical doctor *and* a psychologist! Everything you could ever need all rolled into one!"

And she makes her own sperm, too, I thought.

Then Mrs. Nussbaum put a hand on my shoulder and said, "Now, off with your shirt, young man! I promise I won't hurt you, *Ahh*-riel!"

And that made me feel even worse.

After taking off my shirt and shoes and socks, I climbed up onto the corner of Mrs. Nussbaum's examination table. I nervously kept my hands folded over my fly and tried not to look at the colorful cutaway diagram of the enormous penis and testicles on the wall to my left. Mrs. Nussbaum sat on a small, black rolling stool and slid herself right up to my knees, so close I could feel her breath tickling my leg hairs. She put her cold hand on top of my bare thigh. I flinched when she touched me.

"You seem scared."

I didn't answer her.

"These are nasty scrapes, you poor thing."

Mrs. Nussbaum wheeled away from me and went to a counter with a stainless steel sink. She pulled some blue examination gloves from a paper carton beside the sink and squeaked her hands into them.

My heart sank.

Nothing good ever happens to you when you're all alone in a room with a grown-up who is putting on medical gloves.

She scooted back to my little corner of the paper-topped examination table. Then Mrs. Nussbaum squeezed some slippery goo from a white tube and smeared it with her gloved fingertip onto my scrapes.

It stung so bad tears pooled in my eyes and I held my breath. I also couldn't help thinking about Cobie Petersen's final warning to me—that this was very likely the dreaded girl sperm.

As though she'd read my mind, Mrs. Nussbaum said, "This is antibiotic ointment. So you won't get an infection."

And I thought, why would she care if I got an infection? She wanted all of us to die, anyway.

Mrs. Nussbaum stood up, snapped the gloves off her hands, and dropped them into a small metal waste can beside the door.

"Now I want to have a look at your eyes," she said.

"I can see fine."

"Don't be silly. There's no reason to be frightened."

This wasn't going well. I wondered how many parts of me Mrs. Nussbaum was going to inspect. I glanced at the penis chart and concentrated on a silent prayer to any deity who might be listening that Mrs. Nussbaum would not go there.

She unhooked one of the metal instruments that was connected to the wall with a corkscrewed black rubber cable and pointed it at my face. I had never seen one of these devices before. There was a soft rubber cup on one side that she pressed over my eye. Then a light came on and Mrs. Nussbaum put her face right up to the other side of the instrument and looked through it.

"I want you to keep your eye open and just look directly into the light."

I imagined this was the vision people reported seeing when they died and then somehow got brought back to life.

I swallowed. "Okay."

Mrs. Nussbaum pivoted the thing around as though she were trying to see every tiny spot inside my eyeball. She looked and looked for so long that I thought I would go blind.

"I need to blink," I said.

"Okay. This one looks good."

Mrs. Nussbaum turned the light off and pulled the little machine away.

I rubbed my eye. Half the universe looked like a red blob.

Then she said, "Now, let's take a look inside the other one."

The light came back on; the soft cup pressed down onto my left eye.

"Is something wrong?" I said.

"No. Not at all."

"I'm wondering what you're looking for. I've never had anyone do this to me before."

"Oh! Don't be silly!" Mrs. Nussbaum's voice raised an octave or two. "It's just a normal exam. It's for a study I'm doing on boys' vision."

When Mrs. Nussbaum was finished looking inside my eyes, I sat there, pretty much entirely blind. I nearly jumped off the table when something cold pressed against my chest.

"Ariel! It's only a stethoscope!"

"I can't see."

Mrs. Nussbaum moved the stethoscope around, then pressed it onto my back and told me to inhale.

"Did you bring your little card for me?"

I slid my hand into my pocket and handed her my index card. I listened to the sound of her unfolding it. My vision was taking its time coming back.

"Hmmm . . . ," she said.

Here is another thing I know: It is never good news when a doctor says *hmmm*.

"So. Tell me. Your father is Jake Burgess, from Alex Division, isn't he?"

Why would she even waste her time asking?

I nodded.

"It's a small world!" Mrs. Nussbaum said in her dolphin-pitched voice, "I work for Alex Division, too!"

I had no comment.

Then she asked, "What do you mean, *inside a refrigerator*?"

Although she'd encouraged us to do so, I had not changed my answer from the first time I met Mrs. Nussbaum and she'd asked the question if there was any place I'd rather be than here at Camp Merrie-Seymour for Boys, where it would be.

I began to see shapes. Mrs. Nussbaum looked like an enormous plum with eyes. She leaned closer to me.

"Well, what does this mean, Ariel?"

I shrugged. "I don't know."

"Don't you like it here at Camp Merrie-Seymour for Boys?"

I thought about it. "It's not the worst place I've ever been."

"And where is the worst place you've ever been?" Mrs. Nussbaum asked.

I did not answer her.

"You know what I find striking about you—about all the Alex boys—you, Max, and Cobie?"

"No."

"Well, you're not like the *other* boys, are you?"

That was incredibly observant of her, I thought. But the way she called us *the Alex boys* made me wonder if she meant something else.

Mrs. Nussbaum went on, "I mean to say I find you to be particularly compelling, Ariel."

I frowned.

"Oh! I don't mean that in an inappropriate way, Ariel! I just find you so interesting. I'd really like to hear about your life—you know, what happened to you, and how you ended up here with the Burgesses. That's what I mean."

"Oh."

I wasn't going to tell her anything.

"But the thing that strikes me about you three Alex boys is that I can't seem to grasp why it was your parents sent you here to Camp Merrie-Seymour for Boys in the first place."

"Because it was free," I said.

Mrs. Nussbaum squealed, "Oh! I see! The parents are taking a vacation from their sons!"

I shrugged and gave her a very American teenager "whatever" look.

"Tell me, did you ever meet an English army officer named Major Harrison Knott?"

I had already decided to stop answering her questions, but I sensed she could tell I was lying to her when I said, "No."

"That's fine, Ariel. That's fine."

She handed my card back to me.

"Are we finished?"

"Oh, no! Just a couple more things. I need to look into your ears—I hope you washed them out today!—and your mouth, and then there's just one last thing and I'll let you run back to Jupiter!"

So, as promised, Mrs. Nussbaum—Dr. Martha K. Nussbaum, inventor of *girl sperm*—probed and prodded and shined lights all over inside my ears and mouth, and even up my nostrils. It was like she was looking for something she was certain would be there but couldn't find—like she was searching for a set of lost car keys. I'll admit the examination was upsetting. I wondered if there was any way I could suggest to my American father, Jake Burgess, that he and his friends at Alex Division work on the development of *boy eggs*. But I also concluded that *boy eggs* would have two major setbacks: First, they would be able to produce offspring of either gender, and possibly a third, YY human—whatever that would be—and second, that there would be no place to implant *boy eggs* after you made them. Where would you stick a fertilized *boy egg*? Every scenario I imagined was horrifying.

But even more horrifying was that after the mouth, ear, and nostril exams, Mrs. Nussbaum took me into another small room where she stood me next to a metal screen and took X-rays of every part of my body, from my skull to my bare feet.

"It's all in the name of *research*, *Ahh*-riel!" she squealed.

COFFEE FOR GOD

"You're lost," 3-60 said.

The melting man was, in fact, lost. He had also reattached the kitchen timers to his ears because there were too many voices he didn't want to listen to, and they kept telling him what to do.

The kitchen timers looked nice beneath the low overhang of the melting man's plaid stingy-brim hat.

Crystal Lutz also helped the melting man by playing an accordion whenever Joseph Stalin told him things. The melting man did not know where the accordion came from. Crystal Lutz told him she'd stolen it from the thrift store in Lafayette.

"How could you get away with stealing an accordion?" Leonard Fountain—the melting man, whom Crystal Lutz knew as Igor Zelinsky—asked.

The melting man was completely insane. Also, he was melting, and Crystal Lutz was not real at all.

"Lenny, you're about to crash into a Mennonite in a horse buggy," 3-60 said.

"Keep your eyes on the road, idiot!" Joseph Stalin said.

Crystal Lutz lifted a full-sized piano accordion and began playing an upbeat, polka version of the national anthem of the United States.

Joseph Stalin did not like Crystal Lutz.

"Huh?" the melting man said. He looked up and swerved the U-Haul van back onto the right side of the road.

The Mennonite stuck his middle finger up at Leonard Fountain, and screamed, "Blow me, bitch!"

"You are lost; you nearly killed us all," 3-60 pointed out.

Leonard Fountain had driven the old U-Haul van through a place called Slemp, which was in Kentucky.

"You are pulling onto the shoulder of the road," 3-60 said.

"What's wrong?" Crystal Lutz asked.

"Look at the road!" The melting man's pus-crusted eyes stared wide.

Ahead, the highway became a churning lava flow, crackling and burbling, blazing the most brilliant red and orange. Red-eared turtles the size of Volkswagens paddled through the lava, and albino kangaroos stood on opposite banks, playing volleyball across the river of molten rock using live kittens as balls.

"Look!" Crystal Lutz said, "Kangaroos!"

"White ones," the melting man said.

The melting man's brain was turning into pudding.

"You are looking at the kittens and kangaroos," 3-60 narrated.

"Keep driving!" Joseph Stalin said.

The melting man didn't know what to do.

And the kitchen timers ticked and ticked.

- - -

I took off the clown suit I'd been wearing for weeks.

I asked Emel to turn away from me when I changed because I didn't have anything at all underneath it. I don't like undressing in front of women. When I dropped the tattered suit onto the ground at my feet, it was almost as though it had become part of the road, that it disappeared.

Garen handed me a pair of worn jeans. They were old and faded on the knees, but clean, and with the belt he gave me, they fit properly. Then he passed me an undershirt. It was pink. I didn't mind. In my first life, I had no concept of *boy colors* or *girl colors*; this was something I was unaware of until I came to America, where there are specific rules about such things. My favorite thing Garen gave me was an old sweater—it was soft and loose, narrowly striped black, white, and blue, with a wide neck that laced shut with three sets of metal eyeholes.

I felt different, like I'd been emptied out at some point in my past, and now that I'd come through the gate and changed my clothes—for the first time since my fourteenth birthday—I was filled up with something strange and new.

When I was dressed, Emel turned around and gave me an approving and sad look.

"You look like a new person," she said.

It was a miracle, I thought; the opening line of another story.

I slipped my feet back into my shoes. Something didn't make sense.

"Thank you for the clothes. They are very nice," I said. "Who did they belong to?"

Garen said, "You told me you would pull the wagon. We have a long way to walk. Let's go now."

I could tell you the story of where the clothes Garen gave me came from, Max. It was the second terrible story—after the one about Thaddeus and his little dog—that someone had given to me to carry along in my library of all the terrible stories that happened to me.

"He was fourteen," Garen said.

I was pulling the wagon and it was night. We were all very tired, although the baby did not fuss at all. Garen was looking for a suitable place for us to stop and sleep. On either side of the road were a few starving cherry trees.

"Who was?"

"My brother."

"Oh."

Of course I knew he was talking about where the clothes he'd given me came from. I didn't want him to tell me about the boy, even though I knew he would.

"I am fourteen," I said.

Garen nodded. "You look like him."

"Oh."

"He was named Ocean. Did you ever know anyone named Ocean?"

"Never."

"Our parents were reckless like that, you know? Names like that are not allowed for legal matters and such."

"I think it's a good name," I said.

"It was destined to make him difficult."

"Do you think?"

"Yes." Garen said, "Two days before the bombing. Ocean used to serve coffee at a stall in the market. He did it for tips, a few coins a day maybe. He was a very stubborn and outspoken boy."

"You don't need to tell me about him."

"You asked."

"That was a few hours ago."

"I've been thinking about him all this time."

"It stands to reason," I said, "he was your brother, after all."

"After everything, yes. We are still brothers, I suppose."

Garen continued, "Two days before the bombing, a man who'd come for coffee overheard Ocean saying how could anyone who lived in war believe there was a god; that if God himself sat down there, Ocean would not get coffee for him. The man—he was FDJA, do you know?—was outraged at my brother's words. He grabbed Ocean by the neck and struck him and called him a blasphemer and a polytheist. At least, this is what I was told afterward."

"He doesn't sound like a polytheist to me," I said.

Garen shook his head. "It's hard to understand where some people get their ideas. Then the man said *this is what God does to blasphemers*, and he shot Ocean two times in his face. Then he finished his coffee. Everyone in the square saw what happened. They told me. He just sat there with his legs crossed and quietly finished his coffee. There were flecks of my brother's blood on his face, and he smoked a cigarette. Then the man got up and walked away, and left my brother lying there in the street."

"I'm sorry."

"What can you do about such things?"

"Feel sick, I suppose."

"Yes. And then the planes came. And I found myself looking at Thia, our daughter. It's difficult to think about the future when somebody is shooting at you."

"I never thought about that, but, yes, I think you're right," I said.

"When someone is shooting at you, you don't think about the

future, and you don't care about God," Garen said.

I couldn't answer him. What could I say? He was right. Ocean was right.

"Do you care about God?" Garen asked. "No. I don't think you do. You're too much like Ocean. I can see that. Who else would have helped open the gate for us?"

"Well, we were all heading the same way."

That night we slept in a collapsing mechanic's shop on the side of the road. All the windows were broken, and there were no doors on the building, not even the big one for vehicles to drive through, but being inside a *place* made us all feel safer, I think.

- - -

Thursday, August 12, 1880—*Belun*

Mr. Murdoch's vision has not improved. I am afraid his blindness is permanent, poor demented thing that he is.

This morning Mr. Warren and I finally spoke to each other about what happened at the village on Lena River Delta. If this is any manner of a confession, then so be it. He and I both knew that when the opportunity to leave the delta manifested that we were driven to take Katkov's beast with us to the West—to save it—it was something we had to do.

We did not stop Murdoch in his mad rampage, and we are both troubled beyond measure by our unwillingness to intervene.

"He would have killed us, too," I offered.

To which, Mr. Warren replied, "You know fully well he would not have harmed you, Dr. Merrie."

And I am afraid Mr. Warren is correct.

MONDAY, FEBRUARY 7, 1881—*LONDON*

Having settled last week into my old lodgings in Whitechapel with the newspaperman, Mr. Warren, who tells me he is unwilling to ever attempt an ocean crossing again. I can't fault him for the opinion, and we have become such close companions in any event.

Our relationship would be deemed corrupt, but I have an enduring attraction for the American. It is also the case that Warren and I are bound to each other by something that goes beyond mutual fondness.

And to think that my journey from here, to San Francisco, and the subsequent ordeal on the expedition of the ill-fated *Alex Crow* have brought me entirely around the world and home again!

Poor blind Murdoch has been confined to an asylum. He will be better off for it, I should think. Tonight, Mr. Warren and I will display our oddity at Hastings's Penny Gaff.

Iain Hastings's Penny Gaff occupies a former fishmonger's stall on Broad Street. On Monday nights, Hastings offers as many as six performances, each of them packed noisily with nearly two hundred unclean factory or errand boys, and far fewer factory girls who infrequently are daring enough to attend such events. These are shows for working boys of the lowest demeanor.

The factory boys—orphans for the most part—live in rookeries, which are rooms where the boys pay a penny per night to sleep on the floor. Landlords crowd them into such an extent that oftentimes latecomers are forced to squat against a wall or in a doorway. There is one such deplorable building two doors down from us here. The working boys come to the Penny Gaff in throngs on Monday nights.

Iain Hastings's establishment promises the bawdiest and most shocking of entertainments, and it is never an uncommon thing to witness surprised spectators turning their reddened faces away from the performers or covering their modest ears—boys and girls alike. For it is here at Hastings's Penny Gaff where audiences stand slack-jawed, amid the ancient smells of cod, salmon, and plaice that fog above the damp musk of sweat, ale, and shag tobacco, at once spellbound and repulsed by Hastings's predilection for human oddities: the "Mirror Man," a small Portuguese fisherman with a complete miniature twin sprouting limp and lifeless from his breastbone; or the unaccountably formed half man–half woman, "Little Christopher," a dwarf who unashamedly poses and displays the neighboring sets of male and female genitalia, completely naked before the fascinated and appalled spectators.

Naturally, as a man of medicine, I find these human rarities somewhat remarkable. Mr. Warren is consistently fascinated by the spectacle as well.

But Hastings's Gaff is also the place where Mr. Warren and I make a show of our oddity—the creature in ice, Mr. Katkov's Siberian Devil.

THE VERNACULAR OF MAX

When I came back to Jupiter from my private session with Mrs. Nussbaum the day after Cobie Petersen and Max talked me into smoking pot with them, Mrs. Nussbaum put my brother, and then Cobie, through pretty much the same routine of head-hole inspections, knee repair, and X-ray exams that I'd gone through.

I never asked Trent Mendibles or Robin Sexton what Mrs. Nussbaum did to them. As far as I could tell, Mrs. Nussbaum considered boys like Trent and Robin to be the normal ones—the boys she was depending on to steer the extinction of males (and if anyone could do it, the *normal* boys of Camp Merrie-Seymour for Boys would)—but she was highly suspicious of the other three boys of Jupiter.

So I told Max and Cobie the details of everything that had happened to me in Mrs. Nussbaum's examination room, even how I was scared that the ointment she put on my scraped knees might have contained some of Mrs. Nussbaum's *girl sperm*. They laughed at me. But every one of us was a little bit bothered by the colorful poster of the male reproductive system that hung on Mrs. Nussbaum's examination room wall.

How could you *not* look at something like that? It was like standing on the edge of an empty field and witnessing a bloody car crash on the road you're about to cross.

Then I told them about the questions she'd asked me—about what I meant when I wrote "inside a refrigerator" on my index card.

"Yeah," Max said, "why *did* you write that?"

I shrugged. "It was the first place I could think of that was better than here."

We were alone in Jupiter—well, except for Robin Sexton who just lay on his cot and stared up at the ceiling, pretending to be listening to music. Larry, as usual, was gone, and Trent Mendibles at that moment was probably sitting shirtless on the examination bed and having his hairy knees salved by Mrs. Nussbaum.

Max told us that Mrs. Nussbaum asked him a lot of questions after she read what he'd written on his index card. Unlike me, my brother kept adding to the card nearly every day, so Max had run out of room on one side and asked Mrs. Nussbaum if she would give him a new one.

Max said that she was thrilled he had kept writing on his card about where he'd rather be than at Camp Merrie-Seymour for Boys, because it meant my brother was focused on better things and more positive experiences, and thinking like that motivates boys to take action. After seeing what Max had written on his card, I had to agree that Max was definitely motivated to take action on his positive experiences. He proudly showed Cobie Petersen and me what he'd been writing. And Max did not have the most legible penmanship, but these are some of the things I could decipher from Max's scrawl:

Where I would rather be than at Camp
Merrie-Seymour for Boys:
  Agitating my youth group
  Encountering heaven through dance
  Whipping up some jelly
  Icing the jewelry store
  Painting some sea monsters

My brother was an artist with words.

Max said Mrs. Nussbaum spent several minutes staring at his card. Then she looked at him, looked at his card again, looked at Max. This went on for some time, according to Max.

Finally, she said, "Max, tell me, what does all this *mean*?"

Max told her they were titles of poems he was planning on writing, when he had bigger pieces of paper.

Max said she came right out and told him this: "These all sound like they might be references to masturbation. Are they? Have you been *masturbating* since you came to Camp Merrie-Seymour for Boys, Max?"

And Max said, "How could you even *think* that? What kind of sick kid would waste his time writing poetry about *masturbation*?"

He said Mrs. Nussbaum turned red (Max was awfully good at embarrassing her), gave him a new index card, and then sent him on his way, back to Jupiter.

Since we were in a sharing mood, after Mrs. Nussbaum was finished with his examination, Cobie Petersen also showed us his index card. Like me, Cobie never amended his choice since the first day. His card read: *Fishing or coon hunting up Dumpling Run with Ezra and nobody else.*

We already knew Ezra was Cobie Petersen's dog—the one

who'd gotten pooed on by the Dumpling Man in Cobie's scary story.

"Well," Cobie told Max, "I could change my card now to say I wouldn't mind if you and Ariel came along. I would kind of like that, I suppose."

"Awww. I'm touched," Max said.

"I'd go fishing or coon hunting with you, Cobie," I said.

"*Coon hunting* sounds like slang for jerking off," Max said.

"Everything sounds like slang for jerking off when you say it," Cobie Petersen replied.

He was right.

He told us Mrs. Nussbaum asked about Cobie's real name, which was Colton Benjamin Petersen, and about Dumpling Run.

"It's a beautiful part of the state of West Virginia," Mrs. Nussbaum had said.

Cobie Petersen said he liked to lay on the West Virginia–boy accent extra thick when he talked to Mrs. Nussbaum.

"'Deed it is," Cobie told her.

"And interesting how many people up along the run are all named Peterson or Petersen," she said.

"It ain't very interesting to me, ma'am," Cobie said. "But I am wondering something."

"Oh! You can feel free to ask me anything, Cobie!" Mrs. Nussbaum said.

"I'm wondering why you have that big poster of a penis on the wall of your examination room."

"Oh! Ha-ha!" Mrs. Nussbaum said, "You know, boys around your age are always so curious about those parts of their bodies, Cobie!"

"Well, if we were *that* curious, I reckon we wouldn't have to look as far away as the wall of your examination room to find out pretty much everything we wanted to know," Cobie Petersen pointed out.

Cobie told us this observation flustered her, too.

"Did she take all those X-ray pictures of everything in your body?" Max asked.

Cobie Petersen nodded.

I said, "I think she is suspicious of us because we're not like the other kids here—the *normal* kids at Camp Merrie-Seymour for Boys. And she asked about our dad working at Alex Division."

"She asked about my dad, too," Cobie added.

"I bet she thinks we're biodrones or something, and that the other scientists at Alex Division are using us to keep an eye on her," Max said. "None of those Alex Division guys trust each other."

The thought of that terrified me. What if one of us actually *was* an Alex Division biodrone? How would any of us even know?

I looked at Max's face for a long time, trying to see if maybe there was something hidden behind his eyes. Then I did the same thing to Cobie Petersen.

"Dude," Cobie said, "quit staring at me. It's freaking me out."

Our little Jupiter cabin powwow fell silent. Trent Mendibles came back from his visit with Mrs. Nussbaum. Robin Sexton was lying on his back on his rumply cot, staring up at the black ceiling and rocking his head to nonexistent music.

"It's your turn," Trent Mendibles said.

Robin Sexton didn't respond.

Cobie Petersen punched Robin Sexton's shoulder. "Hey. Fucker. It's your turn to see Mrs. Nussbaum."

Robin Sexton got up, and as he headed toward the door, Cobie added, "And when she tells you to take off your shirt, you might as well just strip naked, 'cause she's going to want to have a look at everything you've got, and you're going to have to give a sperm sample, too."

Robin looked horrified and sick.

When he left, Trent Mendibles said, "She didn't do that to me."

"I know, hairy dude. I just wanted to fuck with the kid," Cobie Petersen said. "He looks scared enough to piss himself right about now."

Cobie and Max were sitting next to each other on Cobie Petersen's bed, directly across from me. I leaned toward them and whispered, "*Do you think they would actually do that to one of us?*"

"What? Strip us naked and ask for a sperm sample? Mrs. Nussbaum makes her own sperm. She doesn't want guy sperm," Max said.

"No. I mean the biodrone thing. What if one of us..." I couldn't bring myself to say it.

"Nah," Max said.

The way he said it made me feel better—like the thought of it was so completely ridiculous as far as my brother was concerned.

But I wondered how I was ever going to sleep peacefully again, now that Max had planted that little thought about one of us— maybe me—blowing up someday. My library of terrible stories was getting fuller and fuller.

And then Cobie Petersen asked, "Did she make you guys pee?"

"That's really disgusting," Max said. "Why'd you pee for her?"

"No." Cobie said, "It's not like I whipped it out and started peeing right in front of Mrs. Nussbaum. She gave me a plastic cup and told me to go in her bathroom and *urinate* in it, and then leave the cup of my *urine* sitting on the edge of the sink, so I wouldn't have to be embarrassed about handing over a plastic cup of my *urine* to her. And she told me not to put my fingers inside the cup because it would contaminate my *urine*, and I was, all, like, *why would I want to put my fingers in a cup of my own urine?"*

"Did you pee for her?" Max asked.

Cobie Petersen shook his head. "Dude, there was no way I was going to pee for her after smoking pot last night. But I did need to poo, so I went inside and shut the door. That bathroom was the nicest one I've been in in a couple weeks, and no one standing around watching me poo, too, so I took advantage of the luxury. Then I decided I better leave something else in her cup besides pee, and I came out, thanked her for letting me poo, and left."

"What did you put in the cup?" Max asked.

Cobie Petersen grinned and shrugged.

And Max said, "Wait. Are you saying you actually *released your combat troops* in Mrs. Nussbaum's cup?"

Cobie nodded. "She's just going to figure I'm a dumb hick from Dumpling Run who doesn't know what *urine* means."

Max fell back on the bed, covered his face with his hands, and said, "I am going to die!"

"You guys smoked pot. I fucking hate you," Trent Mendibles said. "You ever go online, I'll shred all your asses at BQTNP."

Cobie Petersen answered the kid with a pair of stiffened middle fingers.

THE STRANGE CASE OF DR. ALEXANDER MERRIE'S SIBERIAN ICE MAN

On Monday of week four, we were more than halfway to our freedom.

And on that Monday of week four, Camp Merrie-Seymour for Boys was struck by a torrential thunderstorm that started just before lunch.

The competition that afternoon was supposed to send us down to the waters of the cold, deep, and green canoe lake for interplanetary swim relays from the muddy shores of the rec field to the floating wooden dock that was anchored in the center of the lake. The counselors decided to cancel the contest on account of the incessant lightning strikes.

Most people don't want to watch teenage campers getting electrocuted.

More than half the boys at Camp Merrie-Seymour for Boys couldn't swim anyway, but that was to be expected. There was no way to avoid participating in the relays, though; non-swimming swimmers were forced to wear bulky life vests. Even the most determined Bucky Littlejohns among us was not going to be able to drown himself.

We had practiced swimming every Tuesday, Thursday, and Saturday during our internment at Camp Merrie-Seymour for Boys. Cobie Petersen was a powerful swimmer, and Max and I were reasonably good; so even with the floundering Robin Sexton and unmotivated Trent Mendibles, who complained that there was no water level in *Battle Quest: Take No Prisoners* (so how could he be expected to swim?), Jupiter would have most certainly beaten all the other planets.

With just under three weeks to go at Camp Merrie-Seymour for Boys, Jupiter was well in the lead of the camp competition, even with our terrible showing at tug-of-war. Despite all our differences, the boys of the six planets were unified in feeling like prison inmates who were notching off the days remaining until our collective parole.

It was a miserable day.

And we learned something new about the hairy kid from Ohio: Trent Mendibles was morbidly terrified of thunder. In defense of Trent Mendibles, the spring and summertime thunder in the mountains of the George Washington National Forest sounded like bomb blasts—so frighteningly loud that I was certain there must be trees snapping like matchsticks beneath the concussion of the booms. When the first thunderclaps exploded, Trent Mendibles blanched pale—well, paler than his usual never-go-outside Ohio complexion—and then whimpered and squeezed himself into the dark space beneath his bed.

Larry tried to get him to come out when the lunch bell rang, but the kid refused to budge.

And Larry said, "Hey. Furball. Don't make me drag you out by your ankles."

Cobie Petersen shook his head. "So. Hairy."

From under the bed came the quavering voice of Trent Mendibles.

"I'll smear my own shit on your hands if any of you fuckers touch me."

It was surprising how easily Larry gave up trying to coax Trent Mendibles out from under the bed. Nobody else in Jupiter cared whether or not the kid with the hairiest legs any of us had ever seen joined us for lunch, anyway.

Max tapped the oblivious Robin Sexton on the shoulder and said, "Hey. Kid. Why don't you squeeze under there and keep your bro company?"

And the thunder boomed and boomed all around Jupiter. With each explosion, Trent Mendibles would chirp like a little bird or say "Fuck!"

Beneath his plastic cot, the kid shook from fear so hard we could actually see the bed vibrate, which naturally caused Max to speculate that perhaps Trent Mendibles was *seeing off some of his departed loved ones.*

Just walking to and from lunch was like jumping in the lake fully clothed. So it was no surprise to us that Larry stayed behind and waited in Jupiter, claiming that someone sensible had to keep an eye on the kid hiding under the bed. And when we got back to Jupiter, the rain had been coming down so hard that with the wind pushing it through the screen walls, all of our beds were soaked. Well, all of them were soaked except for Larry's. Larry was experienced with the shortcomings of the cabin design at Camp Merrie-Seymour for Boys, so he had rotated his bed sideways and slid it into the center of the floor, which was a narrow band of dry planks floating in the ocean of Jupiter.

"This fucking sucks," Cobie Petersen observed.

Larry sat, smug and smirking at us from his dry and warm, non-plastic bed.

That was the other thing: Despite it being summertime in the George Washington National Forest, what with being soaked to the skin and inside a windy and wet cabin, the four non-hiding boys of Jupiter were shivering with the cold.

Trent Mendibles was shivering with something else.

Max sloshed down onto the foot of his bed. He said, "I fucking hate this place."

Larry just grinned, enjoying the opportunity to have nature get back at us for all the grief we'd given him through our first twenty-four days at Camp Merrie-Seymour for Boys.

"Yeah. Live it up, Larry," Max said. "You're going to be extinct before we are, anyway."

Then Max slid his duffel bag out from beneath his bed and dug through it, looking for dry clothes.

"Dude. Don't change into your dry stuff. It would be stupid." Cobie Petersen told him, "You'll only end up getting everything you own soaked. And where would that leave you?"

Another explosion of thunder, another startled squeak from beneath Trent Mendibles's bed, a gust of wind, and more rain coming sideways through the screen wall above our pillows.

It went without saying that Cobie Petersen—Larry's Teacher's Pet—was our commanding general of Jupiter. Without him, we other boys would be constantly going in different directions, and wet, too. Colton Benjamin Petersen made sense, and was easy to follow, even if he sometimes suggested doing stupid things like smoking pot with him in the middle of the night.

Cobie Petersen had a rain plan.

Dripping wet, freezing, Max, Cobie, and I removed all the wet sheets and pillows from our cots and then upended the crumpling plastic mattresses to block the back window screen where the rain was coming into Jupiter heaviest and getting onto our stuff. It was the one and only day when I had any kind of appreciation for the fluid-resistant beds we slept on.

We moved all our duffel bags into the dry swath beside Larry's cot in the center of Jupiter. Larry sat cross-legged on his non-rained-on sheets, while Robin Sexton just stood by the door, dripping and watching us work.

Max glared at the kid from Pennsylvania with the toilet-paper-and-kite-string earplugs. He said, "One of these days, before we get out of here, I'm going to kick you in the balls for all the shit we have to put up with from you."

This also made me realize that tonight was my night to be on sleepwalk duty, which caused me to want to kick Robin Sexton in the balls, too.

The last mattress to go up came from Trent Mendibles's bed.

He whimpered, "Put it back, fuckers. Leave me alone."

Trent Mendibles, who was dry in comparison to the other boys of Jupiter, had been curled up on his side on the damp floor with his hands covering his ears and his forearms hiding his eyes.

Cobie Petersen told him flatly, "No. You're taking one for the team."

Trent Mendibles was so scared he was crying. I felt sorry for him, but only a little, because I knew what it was like to be that scared. But thunder was just thunder. The kid had no grasp on reality.

Maybe they didn't have bad weather in *Battle Quest: Take No Prisoners.*

Max sat on the edge of his wooden cot frame and slipped off his sneakers and socks, which splatted onto the cold floor like slabs of raw liver. "Can I get dressed now?"

"No," Cobie said, "we still have some things to do. But it probably is better if we ditch our shoes and socks."

Barefoot, Max and I slogged through the mud of the deserted grounds of Camp Merrie-Seymour for Boys, following Cobie Petersen out to the dining pavilion. We splattered our way into the kitchen and stole a big carton of plastic garbage bags, a pair of kitchen shears, and two rolls of duct tape.

It was brilliant.

Back inside the reasonably drier Jupiter, we changed into our unemployed swim trunks, and then stuffed all our wet bedding and clothes inside garbage bags. Robin Sexton just watched us, sitting on the foot of his cot frame.

Cobie Petersen glared at the kid as he slipped on his trunks. "Dude. You're a creep. Stop looking at me."

Robin Sexton just stared and stared. Trent Mendibles whimpered in the corner. Larry snored, napping on his dry cot in the middle of Jupiter.

We cut holes in three of the garbage bags so we could make rain ponchos with them. The duct tape made them heavier and secure around our necks and wrists so they wouldn't leak so much.

Then Cobie Petersen tapped Robin Sexton on the forehead.

"Kid. Take that shit out of your ears."

Robin Sexton complied.

"You've got only one chance if you want your shit put in the dryer. Bag up your clothes and sheets right now or we'll leave you here to freeze to death. I don't really care either way."

Robin Sexton said, "I fucking hate you."

Larry snored.

But Robin reinserted his earbuds, quickly stripped and changed into his swim trunks, wadded up his wet laundry, and stuffed it into a plastic bag. I picked up Trent Mendibles's sheets.

"What are you doing?" Cobie Petersen—our general—asked.

"Helping Trent. I feel sorry for him."

Cobie gave me a disappointed look and shrugged *whatever*.

Then Robin Sexton pulled out another garbage sack and started to measure it for a rain poncho. Cobie Petersen snatched the bag from the twitching kid's hands.

"No. You are *not* coming with us. We'll be back when we're done."

We did not go directly to the laundry room. Cobie Petersen had other plans.

Carrying our laundry sacks like muddy, barefoot thieves, the three of us padded out into the woods to find the spot where we'd hidden the things we stole from the counselors. Wrapped in our duct tape and garbage-bag rain suits, we must have looked like alien spacemen, if anyone possibly had been looking at us.

The trees in the forest stopped most of the rain, but it was so loud hitting the leaves, it sounded like we were walking inside a popcorn cooker. And the thunder boomed and rattled above the treetops.

"What are you thinking?" Max said when we got far enough into the cover of woods that nobody could possibly know we were there.

"No one's coming outside in this rain," Cobie Petersen said. "We might as well have a little fun."

"We can't smoke pot in the middle of the day," I argued. "People will know. We'll act too stupid."

"Don't be dumb," Cobie Petersen said. "We can't smoke pot because the joint is going to be too fucking wet."

"Yeah, Ariel," Max added, "don't be dumb."

It didn't matter that they were joking. I was still scared that Cobie Petersen was going to lead us into trouble.

We spent a good ten minutes trying to find the hiding spot. Things change after ten days in a forest. And as Cobie Petersen predicted, our stash was fairly well soaked. I felt bad for Mrs. Nussbaum's book, *Male Extinction: The Case for an Exclusively Female Species*. I didn't like seeing books damaged. I'd seen enough burned-out schoolhouses and libraries in my first life.

Cobie Petersen dropped his laundry sack onto the leafy ground, reached inside the mossy hole and lifted up a can of beer, which he handed to my brother Max.

"What if they make us go swimming or something?" I protested, "You'll drown."

I sat on one of the small mossy boulders that hid our contraband.

Cobie Petersen shook his head. "You worry too much."

"Yeah, you *do* worry too much. Lighten up, Ariel," Max said, and he popped open the can of beer.

Cobie picked up the two remaining cans of beer and passed one to me.

"Nobody will ever know," he promised.

So we drank warm beer in the rain, dressed in swim trunks and garbage bags.

I couldn't tell, exactly, if one can of beer had any effect on me. My knees felt rubbery and disconnected from my body, though, and I fell down twice on the way back to the camp, so, probably. Max and Cobie laughed at me. Even with our makeshift rain gear, we were wet and muddy up to our thighs. And we all had to stop and pee in the woods before we came out into the clearing of the campgrounds.

I noticed I didn't feel cold anymore. I also didn't care about the spiders in the disgusting shower room, or that it was disgusting at all. The three of us rinsed the mud and leaves off our skin after we loaded all our wet things into the dryers.

I'd hidden Mrs. Nussbaum's book inside my sack of laundry. I figured it would give me something to do while we waited for our stuff to dry. Cobie Petersen and Max occupied themselves by talking too loud and laughing about things I tried not to pay attention to.

Max told Cobie Petersen that the beer he drank made him feel like sneaking away to somewhere private so he could *deport some troublesome settlers*.

Cobie laughed and called Max a pervert, which he was.

In the last section of Mrs. Nussbaum's book, she explained about the difficulties scientists at Merrie-Seymour Research Group had encountered when attempting the de-extinction of species from which there were only male genetic samples. This furthered her argument for the uselessness of males in general. Among these species were an invertebrate worm with legs, a rat, and one experiment in which both males and females were created from a species of extinct Polynesian crow—this was our pet, Alex. She also wrote about one of the first trials of hominid de-extinction in a chapter called "The Strange Case of Dr. Alexander Merrie's Siberian Ice Man."

I was sitting on the dryer, reading, while our clothes tumbled around below me. It was a warm place to sit. The dryer stopped. A buzzer rang.

Cobie Petersen slapped my knee and said, "How's the *girl sperm* book ending up?"

"It's really weird," I said. "I think the people at Alex Division have an obsession with control. Controlling *everything.*"

"Let me see," Cobie said.

Max grabbed the book from my hands, but let it slip and fall to the floor with a damp *thud.*

"Sorry," he said.

"You're drunk," I said.

Cobie Petersen laughed. "Duh! And he's a pervert, too."

Max bent down and picked the book up, opening to its title page.

"Holy crap, Ariel. Did you see this?"

And Max held the book right in front of my legs, so we all could see the smearing wet inscription on the title page. It said this:

> *I hope you're enjoying my book, Ariel!*
> —M.K. Nussbaum

"I bet the book's chipped," Max said.

Chipping was what our father called it when the Alex Division people turned animals into biodrones. It's why Mrs. Nussbaum examined the three of us so closely when we had our private therapy sessions with her. She was looking to see if there was any sign one or all of us were actually being used by Merrie-Seymour Research Group to keep watch on her, or on anyone else for that matter. It stood to reason that if they could chip a cat or a crow, they could chip a book, too. Or a boy.

I nearly choked. What could I say? I looked from Max, to Cobie, and back to my brother. They looked scared. I was scared. Mrs. Nussbaum was watching me.

And outside, thunder exploded, and the rain poured down so hard the roar on the roof was nearly deafening.

Then Cobie Petersen said what I was thinking—but what I did not want to hear.

"Or one of *us* is chipped."

At exactly that moment the door to the laundry room opened. I nearly jumped out of the towel I was wrapped in, convinced that I'd see Mrs. Nussbaum coming for us. But in walked a dripping Kyle Breckenridge, the red-bearded lad from Mars who'd called us fags when he saw us in the showers. He was wrapped in a soaked bedsheet and wearing only his boxers, carrying an armload of wet laundry.

The Mars boys' rain strategy was not very intelligent.

Cobie Petersen looked at him. I could tell our general was already formulating a plan. We pulled our warm trunks out of the dryer and put them on.

"Did you lose the go-do-the-Mars-boys'-laundry bet, fucker?" Cobie asked.

Kyle Breckenridge had obviously made the same assumption we had when we left Jupiter to go drink beer in the woods: that nobody else at Camp Merrie-Seymour for Boys would go outside in the torrent of the storm.

He was scared and alone.

And he remained scared and alone until the storm broke and the dinner bell rang and people found him, because Cobie Petersen put Kyle Breckenridge in an arm lock and wrestled the struggling kid outside into the dining pavilion, where Max and Cobie duct-taped Kyle Breckenridge in his underwear to one of the roof's outer support posts in the perfect spot where a steady stream of rainwater hosed down on the kid from Mars.

They also threw all the Mars boys' laundry and sheets into the mud.

While Cobie Petersen and Max put the finishing touches on their living gargoyle, I decided I really wanted to read about Dr. Merrie's Siberian Ice Man, but I wasn't going to carry that book around after I saw what Mrs. Nussbaum had written in it. So I tore out the title page and most of the chapter about the Ice Man, and then I buried Mrs. Nussbaum's book at the bottom of a garbage can filled with disgusting, half-eaten lunch leftovers.

After I abandoned the abridged version of *Male Extinction: The Case for an Exclusively Female Species*, I tucked my stolen pages beneath my garbage-bag rain slicker and into the waist of my swim trunks. Cobie Petersen leaned in and put his hand on Kyle Breckenridge's bare shoulder and told him, "Next time you feel like calling someone names, just remember this romantic walk in the rain you took with me, dude. And, dude. Really. You should shave."

Of course Kyle Breckenridge cried and screamed the entire time he was out there strapped down in his underwear and getting rained on, but nobody could hear him; or if they could, nobody wanted to come outside in all this foul weather.

Everyone thought it was such a great Camp Merrie-Seymour for Boys rainy-day prank!

THE CABOOSE OF NATURAL SELECTION

I have lived, and lived, and lived again.

I could not tell this to anyone, Max. I only hope it is not unfair of me to tell you.

I'm doing this now because you've asked me to. Other people have tried to get me to tell them about my first lives, but I have always kept the terrible stories locked inside my library. I realize we have become brothers in this, and I hope it doesn't weigh you down. I'm not trying to give you anything you'll have to carry around for the rest of your life, but that's what happens to us after all, isn't it? We carry story upon story upon story.

We carry our stories because we survive, and survival is ultimately the most selfish thing we do. It is the opposite of extinction, after all.

The small family with the wagon shared everything they had with me.

In the most immediate sense, what they shared was their

food and water. They gave me the clothes I changed into—the first real things I had to wear since the day I crawled inside that refrigerator. They also gave me the story of the boy whose name was Ocean. But what was lifesaving to me, I think, was Garen's and Emel's willingness to allow me to be with them in that difficult space between leaving everything behind and going toward something that was unknown to all of us. I don't know why they took me with them, or maybe I'm afraid to guess why—that they did this because I reminded them of a boy who'd been killed for cursing God.

Still, I don't know where I would have gone if they hadn't allowed me to walk with them.

I will tell you this: When we came over the final pass in the mountains and stood at the edge of the road we'd been following, I looked out across the endless plain of the flat valley below and what appeared there, clouded in the haze of salty dust, was bigger than any city I'd ever seen. I saw a settlement that had been built beside some orchards. It spanned outward in perpendicular arrow-straight rows of perfect soft boxes that, once we came down from the rise and were close enough to see, turned out to be tents—all of them stamped in blue letters: UNHCR.

I could also see how the city of tents had been enclosed within a ring of heavy chain-link fence. There was something about that fence—I think—that said *stay out*, from whatever side you looked at it. Stay out of here; stay out of there, like it was an island surrounded by ice.

I had been pulling the wagon down from the pass, but when we got closer to the entry gate to the city of tents, Garen took the handle from me and trudged forward.

"I want to know something." I said, "We agree that it is impossible to think about the future or God when someone is shooting at you, right? I wonder if you can think about the future now?"

Garen paused a moment and shook his head.

"No."

"Can you think about God?" I asked.

"No. What about you? Can you think about those things?"

"I've been trying to," I said. "Nothing comes to me, though. I think it's too hard to think of anything you haven't seen before."

"You could, but it's almost as though you would have to make up a new language to do something like that," Garen told me. "How could you make up words for things you've never seen?"

"Sometimes I think about that, too," I admitted.

We only carry old words.

The closer we got to the sprawling city of tents, the more the noise and clamor of the people inside it rose like smoke from a fire, or flies from a garbage heap. At the front gate stood a patrol of guards who wore uniforms I had never seen before, and spoke English with British accents.

I asked one of the guards what UNHCR stood for. His answer was, "Hey! You speak English really good!"

"It can't possibly stand for that," I said.

The guard smiled and told me this was the United Nations Refugee Agency.

I didn't really know what he meant by *refugee*. Were we looking for refuge; or were we running away from something, so we didn't care where we ended up, refuge or none? I had only run away once, from Thaddeus at the gate, and I was pretty sure Garen and Emel and their baby had only run away one time as well; and I think that they did it reluctantly. So who could say why, exactly, we had come here, and what hopeful refuge the place might offer?

We went into the city of tents. At that time I had no idea how long I would end up living there. How could anyone know that?

Garen and his family followed a few paces behind me with their wagon. We passed through a chute formed between two long tents that were built so they butted up to the chain-link fence at either side of the gate. At the end of this chute stood more guards carrying rifles.

The first guard asked how many of us there were in my family, and I told him that we were not a family. I saw a sign at the end of the chute with two opposing arrows on it, one labeled FAMILIES and the other ORPHANS AND INDIVIDUALS.

I pointed back at Garen and Emel and their baby with my thumb.

"They are a family," I said. "I only followed them here."

"Do you have a family?" the guard asked.

I shook my head.

"Okay, then. It will be okay, boy. What's your name?"

"Ariel."

"Okay, Ariel. Let's come with me."

The man took me away, to the tent on the right side of the chute. I looked back at Garen and Emel, who were talking to another guard. I waved to them as I went inside the long tent.

I never saw the little family with the wagon again after that moment.

I spent the next nine months in a tent filled with orphan boys, my next family. The oldest among us were sixteen or seventeen years old; the youngest ones were three. This arrangement—the hierarchy of an exclusively male society—put me in a very difficult spot of having to do whatever the older, bigger boys told me to do. This mostly included taking care of the babies—the smallest boys who could not do anything for themselves—or stealing from the other families living in the tent city, cleaning up after the older boys, and so on.

It was a painfully difficult nine months. The tent was pregnant with filth and unfairness.

I was born again when Major Knott took me away from that place.

- - -

Igor Zelinsky, Leonard Fountain, was a pus-oozing nuclear leper, emitting enough radiation that if you stuffed his clothes with popcorn kernels, you could open up a fucking movie house. At least, that's what Joseph Stalin told him.

Joseph Stalin was angry about all the time the melting man was wasting.

Mistakes are the locomotive engine of natural selection. Leonard Fountain was its caboose.

Up in the sky above the highway, a rectangular prism glinted in the sunlight as it hovered, watching Leonard Fountain, watching as he drove, accompanied and alone through the Kentucky woods.

And Crystal Lutz, playing the William Tell Overture on her accordion, rode along with the melting man.

SIM

MONDAY, MARCH 5, 1888—*NEW YORK*

We have settled into what we both hope are permanent accommodations in the Empire Hotel, a remarkable establishment owned by our benefactor and investor, Mr. Jonathan Seymour.

The icehouse below contains enough food provisions to last the entire establishment one full year—an untested claim that Mr. Seymour is proud to make—and remains at a constant temperature sufficient to preserve our friend, Mr. Katkov's beast.

Poor Katkov. And still, after these years, Warren and I continue to refer to the thing as *Katkov's Beast*.

Since Mr. Seymour brought us to New York,

we have placed the small man in permanent storage. Jonathan Seymour and I have engaged in partnership, the purpose of which is to fund scientific and medical research. And here we are again—research! The arrogant endeavor to control more and more of our shrinking world.

I have opened a small medical practice as well, and my dear Mr. Ripley Reed Warren has returned to his passion—he writes for the *New-York Times*.

We are very happy here; the city is magnificent.

I must admit that it took a good deal of persuasion—and no small amount of financial enticement—for Mr. Seymour to entice us to agree to a sea voyage to America, but when all had been said and done, Mr. Warren and I both arrived at the conclusion that shipping advancements have provided some remarkable improvements since our ordeal on the *Alex Crow*, some eight or so years ago.

We have come very far.

In settling into our new home together at Mr. Seymour's Empire Hotel, I have had more than several personal meetings with the man. He is quite odd, not to the point of being a danger, and I am entirely convinced it is the effect on his psychology of living in such opulence and comfort. In any event, it is Jonathan Seymour's peculiar conviction—as the deranged Mr. Murdoch had theorized when we first saw the beast on the Lena Delta—that our little ice man is some earthly incarnation of Satan himself.

What I believe to be the origin of Katkov's devil is of little consequence. Consider this: The thing did not exist at all in the eyes of the world until I rescued it from his icebound prison. In doing so, I feel endlessly confident the small man is destined to serve some greater, as yet undiscovered, purpose.

Satan or aberration of nature, let Seymour believe what he chooses—including the preposterous concept that the cells and the structures of Katkov's creature can somehow be, in his words, "reinvigorated."

Despite the gloomy weather that hovers over the city, there is a promise of spring in the air, and with it Mr. Warren and I share a hopeful optimism for our future here at the Empire.

R.R.W. and I walked together through the park and dined before bed.

Tuesday, March 13, 1888—*New York*

The terrifying irony of our situation has come full circle, hasn't it, my dear?

From ice, to ice, fooling ourselves as always.

I think I will die without you. This is hell.

This morning came the news that Mr. Warren had been found. We are trapped inside the Empire, whose lower floors are nearly buried in snow. The city is without heat and electricity, and travel is impossible due to the snowdrifts, some of which exceed twenty feet in depth.

Yesterday afternoon, my great friend Ripley Reed Warren left the Empire Hotel, determined to go to the offices of the *Times*, and he never came back to me. I was so consumed with worry, but had convinced myself Mr. Warren had taken shelter at his place of employment. The police came to notify us today that R.R.W. had been discovered buried in a bank of snow on Seventh Avenue. He must have stumbled in the tremendous winds and was swallowed by the relentless snowfall.

This is the most terrible thing that has ever happened to me.

What will I do now?

What will I do now?

- - -

From *Male Extinction*: *The Case for an Exclusively Female Species*:

In early 2002, Dr. Jacob Burgess, a senior research scientist employed by MSRG and working within the semiautonomous Alex Division's de-extinction laboratory, obtained approval from Chief Operating Officer Harrison Knott to investigate the viability of reversing the extinction of a hominid species that was discovered and preserved by Alexander Merrie during an Arctic expedition in 1881.

Burgess had successfully produced a variety of extinct annelid as well as one mammal, *Rattus macleari*, in earlier trials. Both of Burgess's initial attempts at de-extinction focused on the regeneration of males, since there were reasonable concerns expressed regarding the impact of reintroducing potential breeding populations. Later, these considerations were determined to be scientifically impractical as far as the progression of the program was concerned. Knott instructed Burgess and Alex Division to attempt reintroduction of both male and female specimens of the Polynesian crow, *Corvus polynesiensis*. The birds—called Alex crows—thrived within their captive environment at MSRG/Alex.

The hominid specimen—Merrie's so-called Siberian Ice Man (SIM)—was a unique individual of undetermined classification and origin. No similar specimens had ever been reported as having existed. Merrie's original drawings of the SIM animal detail proportional skeletal and muscular characteristics that suggest the primate, which stood erect at a height of 1.15 meters (45 inches), was entirely bipedal, and walked upright. Furthermore, the SIM organism preserved by Alexander Merrie was a fully formed adult male.

Although photographic and filmic verification of the creature exist, MSRG/Alex have not publicly released documentation to verify the presence of Merrie's original SIM specimen.

Archival searches of the *Illustrated London News* from 1881 provide one illustration of the specimen on display at an entertainment venue near Whitechapel. The striking feature of Merrie's Siberian Ice Man is that the creature appears to have short, thick horns growing from the animal's occipitofrontal skull.

Dr. Burgess himself cannot respond to inquiries regarding the SIM de-extinction attempt, citing contractual obligations to MSRG/Alex, although the records of other de-extinction programs are a matter of public record. Dr. Burgess, Harrison Knott, and Colton Petersen, legal counsel, subsequently testified to the joint congressional Committee on Environmental Anthropogenesis in 2008 as to the results of those well-publicized de-extinction trials. Former and current MSRG/Alex employees, however, verify that Burgess's experiment succeeded in producing a viable male SIM offspring—an exact living replica of Merrie's 1880 discovery.

The de-extinction process for vertebrates generally depended on the laboratory formation of a viable blastocyst developed in vitro, then monitored and sustained for a period of five to ten days.

The first SIM blastocysts, produced from active stem cells whose nuclei were redesigned with a fully diploidal set of SIM chromosomes, had been implanted in common chimpanzees, but the pregnancies never came to term. According to sources actively employed at MSRG/Alex in 2002, Burgess implanted a ten-day-old SIM blastocyst into his own wife, who was newly pregnant with Dr. Burgess's own child, a son, named Max.

THE BOOK OF MAX AND COBIE

"The book is worse than *chipped*. It's about *you*," I said.

"What do you mean, it's about me?" Max asked.

Cobie Petersen raised his hand and waited patiently for us to pay attention to him. "If it's about Max, is there stuff in it about him *dealing himself a hand of solitaire*?"

Sometimes talking to Cobie Petersen and Max was pointless, unless I wanted to talk about masturbation, which is something I truly never wanted to talk about.

"Hey," Max said. "Did you just make that one up yourself?"

Cobie Petersen nodded. "Yep."

"I like it. Solitaire. That's pretty damn good," Max said.

"Thanks. I tried, man. It's been fun."

"Got any more?"

"I wrote down a few more on Mrs. Nussbaum's index card."

"She's going to think all we ever do is *drop off our babies at the fire station*."

"Dude. That's totally gross," Cobie said.

Max laughed. He was stoned. Well, we all were, actually.

If there was anything at all redeeming or hopeful in our condemnation to the hell of Camp Merrie-Seymour for Boys, it was that I finally felt as though Max and I were brothers, and for the first time since coming to America, I believed I had made a friend in Cobie Petersen. On the other hand, I was completely sick of shared open toilets, beanie-weenie casserole, taking showers with other boys in a spider cave, and sleeping every night next to four other Jupiter kids and our snoring, inattentive counselor Larry.

It was past midnight, and the three of us had snuck away from Jupiter and hiked around to the opposite side of the canoe lake to smoke a joint. The heat and humidity were smothering, and bugs were everywhere, flying into our hair, pelting our skin, diving into the flashlight beam that shined on the pages I read.

We sat on the shore, shirtless, with our bare feet in the water.

I sighed and waved the pages I'd torn from Mrs. Nussbaum's book in front of Max's face. "I'm not kidding, Max. She even mentions your dad, too, Cobie. Look."

Since it was past midnight, it was technically the morning of the second day of our final week at Camp Merrie-Seymour for Boys. Our parents would be arriving on Saturday to take us home to beds that were not covered in plastic, and bathrooms with private showers and doors we could lock.

Still, if there was a light at the end of the tunnel, it wasn't shining bright enough for most of us to see.

The day after the thunderstorm hit during week four, the interplanetary games had resumed. As I suspected, Jupiter won the swim relays, but just barely. Robin Sexton would only paddle with one arm because he was afraid of getting lake water in his mouth. Cobie Petersen had told us he peed in the lake at least once or twice every day during swim practice, and Max couldn't resist adding that he could swim and also *conjure the microscopic spirits of millions of future Maxes* all at the same time. Max confidently told us there was so much of his sperm in the canoe lake that we'd all better keep an eye out for the *Pequod*. This was one of those things that neither Robin Sexton nor Trent Mendibles understood, since Max's reference to the *Pequod* didn't have anything to do with video games or online social networking platforms. But the comments about all the sperm and pee in the lake were among those things that Robin Sexton selectively chose to "hear." So Robin Sexton kept one hand firmly pressed over his mouth, which made him swim in circles somewhat, and slowed down Jupiter's relay team significantly.

And Trent Mendibles told Max, "You're such a freak. I hate you so much. I can't wait to get the hell away from you assholes."

I chose not to believe Max's claim about all the sperm he'd deposited in the canoe lake. Well, most of it. Who could ever tell with Max, though? But I was certain every boy at Camp Merrie-Seymour for Boys had peed in the canoe lake at least once. What could anyone do about it? It was camp, and camp was brutal.

I'd almost forgotten about the chapter I'd stuffed into the bottom of my duffel bag until I got down to the last of my clean laundry. In any event, reading it around Larry or the other boys would have caused trouble, so I decided to take it along with us when Cobie Petersen asked me and Max to sneak out of Jupiter with him one last time before the liberation of the campers.

"*Liberating the campers* sounds like slang for jerking off, too," Max had said.

Cobie Petersen took a big drag from the joint and passed it over to Max.

"I'm really going to miss you guys when they let us go home this week," Cobie said.

"Dude. Don't be dumb." Max told him, "We live three miles away. We can *walk* to your place. Let's hang out as soon as we get back."

"You should read this," I said.

"Dude. I'm too stoned to read," Cobie Petersen answered.

"I can never remember what I read when I'm high, even if I like it," Max said. He exhaled a big billowing cloud out over the water of the canoe lake. "You should just tell us about it."

So I tried my best, despite how stoned I was, to explain to Cobie Petersen and Max what I'd read in the chapter about the Siberian Ice Man from Mrs. Nussbaum's *Male Extinction: The Case for an Exclusively Female Species.*

Apparently, according to Mrs. Nussbaum, Natalie Burgess—my American mother—gave birth by Caesarean section to my brother Max and a de-extincted Arctic ape man on the same day in a medical lab at Merrie-Seymour Research Group/Alex Division. This happened to also be sixteen days before I was born on the other side of the world, in a place that was arguably less civilized than Sunday, West Virginia, or America, for that matter. We didn't have frozen ape men, snore walls, and de-extincted worms or crows where I lived in my first life.

But the Siberian Ice Man, who had been dead and extinct, had come back to the people of earth, thanks to my godlike American father and the equally godlike people at Alex Division.

I hadn't known Natalie Burgess very long, but who could *ever* get to know that woman, anyway? I can only imagine she thought that being a surrogate birth chamber to some other species of animal—Mrs. Nussbaum called him SIM—was "no big deal," or something people simply shouldn't make a fuss over.

She would be fine.

Natalie would always be fine, as long as nobody paid any attention to her.

The chapter called "The Strange Case of Dr. Alexander Merrie's Siberian Ice Man" claimed that both babies—Max and SIM—were healthy and thrived under the care of the Burgesses. Natalie even breastfed the de-extincted creature.

No big deal.

The SIM, however, matured more rapidly than his human womb-mate, Max, so that by the time both boys were approaching two years in age, the SIM was in the middle of puberty, sexually developed, and had sprouted horns. He was also completely unmanageable, frequently climbed on top of Natalie—and even Max—in almost constant attempts to have sex, and had caused significant destruction to the Burgesses' home. And again, I am certain Natalie would have thought it not too much bother at all.

The sources who provided information to Mrs. Nussbaum for her book also confirmed that the SIM disappeared around the time it would have turned two years old. Vanished. The general theory was that Jake Burgess, my American father, and Alex Division had decided to euthanize the troublesome animal, which was something Alex Division did to the majority of the output of the de-extinction programs.

Natalie Burgess probably didn't mind that so much, either.

"Awww . . . ," Max said, "I had a twin brother? And he was horny all the time, too. That must be where I get it from. That kind of gives me a boner."

Max grabbed his crotch and adjusted himself.

"Dude. You're high," Cobie Petersen told him. "It was a monkey."

"Or *something*," I said.

"Anyway, Mrs. Nussbaum's stupid," Max said. "Alex Division doesn't euthanize the majority of the Alex animals. They turn them into biodrones."

"Sounds like nobody at Alex Division knows what the other people there are doing," I said.

"Which is probably why they chipped one of us. Or all of us," Cobie Petersen added.

My stomach churned.

"Don't say that," I said.

Cobie Petersen stood up, wobbling just a bit. He said, "I'm going swimming."

"You'll get all your shit wet. Then you'll have to sleep in wet underwear," Max said.

"Not if I take them off first."

Max shook his head. "Skinny-dipping? That's pretty gay."

"Dude. They make us take showers together. Skinny-dipping in the lake after midnight is probably the least gay thing we've done all day at Camp Merrie-Seymour for Boys."

Cobie Petersen had a point.

So we all stripped off our clothes and jumped into the cool water, where I set adrift the pages I'd torn from Mrs. Nussbaum's book.

I'M STILL THE SAME OLD GUY
I'VE ALWAYS BEEN

"You are driving. You are driving, and you haven't slept in two days, Leonard," 3-60 said.

It was true. Ever since the melting man left the woods near Slemp, Kentucky, he'd been driving nonstop, and was now somewhere east of a place called Beckley, West Virginia. The lava, red-eared turtles, and kangaroos had gone away, but the hotel inside Leonard Fountain's head remained as full of noisy tenants as it had ever been.

Leonard Fountain wanted to pull over and sleep.

"Keep driving, you idiot!" Joseph Stalin said.

"Where are my timers? Where are my timers?" the melting man said.

"You left your timers in the back of the van, Leonard," 3-60 said.

"Keep driving! Enough of these distractions!" Joseph Stalin scolded.

"You are pulling over. You are pulling over," 3-60 narrated.

And Crystal Lutz began playing the Wedding March on her accordion.

"You are getting out of the car," 3-60 said.

"Van. It's a van," the melting man corrected.

"You are getting out of the van."

"Quick! Look up!" Joseph Stalin said.

The melting man did as he was told. He stood in the middle of the road, and when he looked up he saw the thing in the sky that had been following him. But this time, the rectangular metal object did not vanish, it hovered a while, making the faintest buzzing sound, as though to say to the melting man that it knew he could see it, and it wanted Leonard Fountain to know it was watching him, too.

Then it rotated and disappeared.

An old station wagon whizzed past in the opposing lane. It honked at Leonard Fountain.

"Don't forget you are standing in the middle of a road," 3-60 told him.

"I won't forget I'm standing in the middle of a road," Leonard Fountain said.

"And the speed limit here is sixty miles per hour," 3-60, who was always so pleasant and patient, reminded him.

Leonard Fountain unlatched the rear gate on his atomic U-Haul and climbed into the sweltering toxic steam of the cargo area to look for his timers, and maybe some of the used clothing he'd bought when he met Crystal Lutz in the thrift store.

He heard something.

"Your phone is ringing, Leonard," 3-60 told him.

"Huh?"

Nobody ever called the melting man.

"Don't answer it," Joseph Stalin said.

"I want to see who it is," Leonard Fountain protested.

It wasn't easy to find the phone, despite the ringing and ringing. The phone was buried beneath some of the filthy clothes the melting man had discarded up in Mom's Attic one time when he wasn't actually having sex with Crystal Lutz, but believed that he was.

"Huh . . . Hello?" the melting man said.

"Lenny? Is that you, Lenny? You've been calling this week. Sorry I missed your calls. I can't really carry a phone with me here at camp. The fuckhead kids I work with will steal it."

The melting man recognized the voice. It made him so happy to hear from his little brother.

"Larry? My gosh! Larry? How've you been?"

"Good, man. Good. Just dealing with a bunch of little shits here is all."

"Where are you?"

"Ah. I work at a summer camp for assholes. It's in the George Washington National Forest, right on the border of Virginia and West Virginia."

The melting man said, "Hey! I'm in West Virginia right now! I'd love to see you."

"No!" Joseph Stalin said.

"Really? That would be terrific, Lenny. It's been, what? Three years since I've seen you? I bet you've changed."

"Naw. I'm still the same old guy I've always been," the melting man, who had lost every hair on his body, and was covered with pus-oozing lesions, said. "I need to check the map. Where are you at, exactly?"

"The place is called Camp Merrie-Seymour for Boys. It's just a couple miles north of Lake Moomaw."

"Hang on. Let me write that down. Lake . . ."

"Beaver Dam," Joseph Stalin said.

"Moomaw," Larry said.

"You are writing. You are writing," 3-60 said.

"What's up, Lenny? Is something wrong?" Larry asked his brother.

"Oh. Uh. Nothing," the melting man said. "Look, give me a day or so, Larry. Is there anything I can bring you?"

Larry laughed. "Heh-heh. Yeah. A girl to screw. I'm so fucking horny here. This place smells like balls, and there's nothing but goddamned boys."

When Larry said *boys*, Leonard Fountain thought he said *beavers*.

Leonard Fountain wrote down *Camp Merrie-Seymour for Beavers, located a couple miles north of Lake Beaver Dam.*

Leonard Fountain was melting.

A LITTLE GAME OF STONES IN A GRID

A **seventeen-year-old** boy named Isaak ruled over the twelve other—thirteen, counting me—orphan boys who lived inside a drafty, leaking tent that became my home. This was my next family, Max, and it was not good. Isaak was a terrible, cruel, and demanding tyrant.

But what could I do?

This was the way things were now.

Let me tell you what it was like to live inside a tent full of orphans for those nine months. It was worse than being in a refrigerator. And it was as though every one of us were waiting to be born into a new life again.

Unlike the others who lived in the city of tents, the orphans came here without people or connections. We were the true refugees—waiting for the opportunity to run away again and again—and we had nothing to speak of, which is why Isaak and three of the other older boys—his sergeants—forced us to steal. It didn't matter what we stole, either; we only had to give things to the four boys who ran the tent just to keep them from beating us or taking what little we had—the clothes off our backs, our shoes. If they got mad enough, and a boy had already been stripped of his jacket and shoes, they would hover near at mealtimes so you would know not to touch your food or they would beat you at night.

They did worse things than that to some of us, too. And it all went unnoticed by the aid workers in the city, who were too busy to spend much more time than was necessary tending to us. There were more important things to take care of in the city of tents.

I will say that I had a sense of hope when I came there. Garen and Emel had given me new clothes to wear, the guards were nice and they spoke English to me, but when I entered the tent—the new boy among the thirteen others who lived there—I saw what this next life was going to be like.

The floor of the tent was covered with blue plastic tarps. I found out this was because so much water would seep in through the tent's seams during the winters when it rained and snowed. Against one wall was a stack of thin mats—the beds we'd sleep on, that had to be picked up every morning to save them from being trampled on and torn. There was a broom and several buckets—one for cleaning the floor (I found out all about this one), and two for carrying water in for the boys. The only other thing in the tent was an oil-burning heater that stood in the center of the floor.

There was nothing else inside, except for some of the boys who hadn't gone outside to play, to beg, or perhaps to steal things for Isaak and his friends. And as soon as I walked in, accompanied by a guard with a UNHCR patch on his uniform, all the collective eyes in the tent looked at me with suspicion and contempt. At least, it felt that way to me. How could I be certain? But I did learn from my American brother Max that no boy welcomes the addition of another boy with whom he might have to share his space—or anything else for that matter.

This was the new order of things.

The four older boys were sitting cross-legged on the floor. They were playing a little game where they tossed stones into a grid they had drawn on the tarp.

One of the orphan boys pointed at me and tossed a stone at my foot. "What's the dead boy's name?"

At first, I thought he might have recognized the clothes I was wearing and mistaken me for the boy named Ocean. I realized this was an absurd thought.

The guard, whose last name was McCauley, said, "Be kind, Isaak. The new boy's name is Ariel."

And that was my introduction to the king of the orphans and his sergeants.

Isaak stood up and looked at me. He was tall and his shoulders were square. The other boys got up, too.

Isaak put his hand on my arm. I knew right away it was not a friendly gesture. You know how you can just sense that kind of touch, like a live electric wire.

He looked at the others and said, "Come on, Ariel. We'll show you around. So you know what to do."

Of course I didn't want to go with them. What could I do?

Isaak walked on my left, so close our arms touched as he and the others who boxed me in like a captive led me through alleys formed between rows of tents, turning here and there, dodging people. I was instantly lost.

"Are you a good thief?" Isaak said.

"No."

"You are now," he told me. "Bring me something tonight, or you will pay."

"What am I supposed to bring you?"

"Surprise me. Make it nice."

"I don't think I can steal."

"Think again," one of the other boys said, and pushed me hard from behind.

Isaak stopped and pointed down another narrower alleyway. "Here we go. Let's take him this way."

We turned another corner and the boys ushered me inside a tent. It was mostly empty except for a heater and an electrical wire that connected to a small hot plate. The place smelled like food, tobacco, and sweat. This tent was smaller than the one the orphans lived in. I could tell it was home to one or two families by the rugs and clothing that were neatly laid out. At the back of the tent hung a carpet that served as a sort of flimsy room divider, which curtained off a smaller, darker place.

Isaak and the boys grabbed me tightly and pulled me toward the small room at the back of the tent. I resisted, tried to jerk away from them. When I turned my face back toward the doorway, one of the boys—his name was Abel—put his dirty hand over my mouth and nose, and shoved me forward.

"Shut up!" he told me.

I was so scared, Max. They pulled me behind the curtain and forced me down onto the floor while they punched my ribs and back. All the while Abel's filthy hand pressed into my face. Abel held me still by twisting his opposite hand into my hair. It hurt me, and I was terrified.

Instantly, I was sweating and crying.

"Don't make any noise," Isaak put his face right up to my ear and whispered.

The other boys pinned me flat on my belly. The thing I remember most was how bad they smelled, like piss and armpits. I was thinking that I wanted to ask them, *what are you doing? what are you doing?* But there was part of me that knew what the boys were going to do to me, even if I didn't want to believe it.

"Don't fight. Hold still or we'll hurt you more," Abel said.

Two of the boys pulled off my shoes and pants while Abel pressed my face into the floor, cursing me in a whisper and telling me over and over to shut up, to be quiet or they would beat me worse. Then the boys stripped off my sweater and undershirt, and Isaak climbed on top of me. Isaak braced his bare knees against my legs, straining to push himself up inside me. The other boys laughed and called me names.

It was sickening. I'm so sorry to be telling you this, but it's what happened to me that day.

I struggled and tried to move my body away from Isaak, but the boys holding me down were too strong for me. They kept telling me to shut up, and that it was going to be their turn next, so I better take it or it would only make things worse for me. Isaak grabbed my shoulders hard and forced himself all the way into me. I screamed, but Abel's hand sealed my mouth and nose, suffocating me, and Isaak pressed his chin against the side of my neck and slobbered on my face as he pushed and pushed and pushed.

Abel whispered, "You like it, don't you?" Then he jerked my head up and down, forcing me to nod, and laughed. "Well, I'm next after Isaak. You're going to like me even more."

Abel licked the side of my face. I shut my eyes and gagged down vomit.

"Shut up. Don't cry." Isaak's dripping mouth was right in my ear. "If you tell anyone, little chicken, we'll kill you."

"Hurry up," Abel told him. "Let me at him."

Isaak grunted and trembled.

Finally Isaak stopped. He put his teeth on my neck, panting and dripping his sweat on me.

I bit the filthy kid's hand, and he cursed and jerked it away from my face.

Then I screamed as loud as I could, over and over, cursing Isaak and telling him to get off me, to get off.

Someone came into the tent, shouting.

"Hey! What's going on here? What are you doing there? You again? Get out of here, you rats! I told you before! Get out!"

Isaak and the others ran past the curtain and the man who'd been shouting at them to get out of his home, leaving me lying there crying on the mats of what had been this man's bedroom.

The man yelled at me, "Get out, you little pig! Get out of here!"

Everything was a terrible blur.

I glanced at the man. He looked as though he wanted to hit me, but was afraid to touch me. It was the most terrible thing, Max. I tried to pull my pants on and fumbled at buckling the belt Garen had given me, but my hands didn't work and nothing went back into place. I remember that I was crying as I gathered up my shoes and the rest of my clothes in one hand, held my pants closed with the other, and ran outside into the daylight.

I'm sorry for giving this to you, Max.

Another of my lives ended that day.

After that, I hovered for so long between an old there—a refrigerator—and a distant somewhere else. Who knows where?

It was like that ridiculous gate we'd pulled the wagon through. We could have gone around it just as easily, but crossing through the thing—the actual gate—somehow gave a measure of significance to the passage that would not be diminished by doubt. The gate was certain, and we had gone through it, and that was that. And here I was now—lost, so lost.

I will tell you this, Max: I can't remember where I went after I came out of that tent. It was as though I moved through the city in a state of consciousness with neither identity nor language. Nothing made sense; no components could be categorized, defined, broken down. And at some point I found myself standing beside a spigot where a woman worked over a bucket, filling it up with water and wringing out a cloth to wipe the face of her child, and at that moment I knew who I was again, and remembered what happened to me and why I was standing there holding my pants up with one hand and my shoes and the rest of my clothes in the other while my belt dragged in the dirt behind me like a donkey's tail.

I managed to button my pants and thread the belt through the loops. Then I slipped my shoes back onto my feet and put on my pink undershirt and the dead boy's sweater. I don't know how long I stood there watching the woman and the bucket.

She held the cloth up to me and said, "Here, son. Do you want to wash your face?"

I must have looked terrible. I could feel the tightness of dirt where it had dried around my eyes after I'd stopped crying. But it was almost as though I couldn't understand what the woman was saying to me at all. I shook my head and turned around and walked away from her.

Of course I didn't know where I was going. How could I? The sky was fading to evening, and I was completely lost in that city of tents. But something occurred to me, Max, and it may strike you as the thinking of a crazy boy. I realized that I had to steal something for Isaak.

I'm sorry. It's irrational, I know. But I had to do it.

It was well past dark when I finally found my way back to the orphans' tent. The boys had already been fed, and most of them were lying on their mats on the floor, sleeping.

I'm not proud to admit any of this—or that I became a good thief. The things I'd stolen were hidden against my belly, tucked inside the sweater and pink undershirt Garen and Emel had given me.

Isaak and his sergeants sat nearest the heater, in the center of all the other boys. I hadn't realized how cold it was. I suppose I wasn't feeling very much at all. But the older boys instantly saw me when I stood inside the tent's doorway.

Isaak nudged Abel's shoulder with the back of his hand.

"Look, there. Our new friend has come back."

Everyone turned to look at me. I felt sick, like I would have thrown up if I had eaten anything at all that day. I looked down at the blue tarp floor and wondered how many times someone had vomited on it.

Isaak said, "Jovan, get Ariel a bed. He must be very tired."

And Jovan, one of the boys who'd held me down and stripped me that day, got up from his place near the heater and carried a mat to where I was standing.

Jovan said, "Did you bring something for Isaak?"

I nodded. I took my bed and placed it outside the group of orphan boys, who all made orbital rings that tightly packed them in a cluster around the heater. I put the mat against the edge of the floor so I could lie down facing all the others and keep my back against the tent's wall.

"You're going to be cold there," Abel said, and laughed.

Isaak laughed, too.

"Well, let's see what you got," Jovan told me.

Isaak kept his eyes directly on my face as I carefully stepped between the beds of the other boys. I would not look at him, but could feel his stare on me. I was sick and scared. Abel and Paul, the other boy who'd held me down for Isaak, scooted over slightly so I could stand in front of the bigger boy.

Abel nudged my foot with his. "Don't forget. It's my turn next."

I will tell you this, Max: I thought about fighting then and there. I knew they would kill me if I did.

Isaak said, "Did you bring me something, Ariel?"

I nodded.

I slipped my hand up inside my shirt and pulled out the thing I'd stolen for Isaak. It was a crucifix, made of wood, and as big as both of my hands together. On the crucifix was a painted plaster Jesus, small nails through both of his hands and feet. Plaster Jesus's head lolled onto his right shoulder, and his pale skin was streaked and smeared with rusty blood. To be honest, the blood looked real; I'd seen enough of it to know. And Plaster Jesus had an agonized and pitiful expression on his face, his eyes rolled upward as though confronting a tormentor with the question that didn't need to be answered: *What are you doing to me?* He wore a stained knot of rags slung around his hips that barely covered his groin.

Isaak turned the thing over and over in his hands. He nodded.

"This is nice. I can trade it for something good. Maybe some tobacco. Do you smoke, Ariel?"

Isaak kept staring at me, but I didn't say anything to him. I turned and went back to the place where I'd made my bed.

And Isaak called after me, "You're going to get cold there."

The older boys laughed. They knew what Isaak meant.

It hurt to lie down. I'd almost forgotten the beating I'd taken on top of the humiliation of everything else they had done to me. I put my arm across my eyes and tried to shut everything out. It was impossible.

This is how it was now, Max.

I will tell you this, Max: The Jesus was not the only thing I'd stolen that day. I also stole a short paring knife, which I wrapped in a rag and kept snugged away inside the waist of my pants. It was a strange and desperate thing for me to do, I think. Because I could never use a knife on anyone, not even if he was harming me. That's stupid, isn't it? Still, I hoped to believe that just having that knife would act as some charm of protection, a deliverance that would keep those boys from ever touching me again.

THE CAT AND THE MICE

"This is the most fucked-up, unfair competition I've ever seen," Max said.

"A bunch of bullshit," Cobie Petersen added.

We should have seen it coming.

Because Jupiter was so far in the lead of the interplanetary games, the counselors collectively decided to make the final competition worth so many points that any cabin who won the last event would be named overall camp winners. And there was a prize at stake, which was this: The boys of the winning planet—and their counselor—would get to take the Camp Merrie-Seymour for Boys van and spend the entire day Friday, which was our last full day trapped in our miserable planets, at the Little America Mall, where there was electricity and video games (which most of the boys of Camp Merrie-Seymour for Boys salivated over) and clean toilets and pretzel stands and teenage girls (which only a few of the boys of Camp Merrie-Seymour for Boys salivated over), and so on.

"We should have seen this coming," I said.

And Max said, "Yeah, but you never know."

On Wednesday morning during our sixth week at Camp Merrie-Seymour for Boys, the day before the contest was to take place, Larry gave us the disturbing news about the event before dispatching us to breakfast.

Max stirred his oatmeal sullenly. Cobie Petersen had a determined and focused expression on his face; he stared off into the woods, concentrating. Robin Sexton rocked back and forth slightly, dull eyed, plugs inserted, fingers twitching and stabbing at nothing, kite string dangling below his chin. And Trent Mendibles scratched his balls and tried not to listen to anything we were talking about.

The next day's event was going to be the longest and most challenging contest of the six-week session. And unfortunately, it was also quite possible that any planet would get lucky and win it. It was an orienteering challenge in the woods that sounded like the sort of event where Camp Merrie-Seymour for Boys might end up a few boys short when all was done.

Every cabin would be provided with a compass and a topographical map of the forestland around Camp Merrie-Seymour for Boys, along with written instructions detailing where the individual teams were supposed to go. Each planet had a personalized flag that had been hidden somewhere in the forest, all of them three miles away from Camp Merrie-Seymour for Boys. The instructions told us where to go to find our flags, which were hidden in different spots, so as to keep the planets from engaging in warfare or any other kinds of dirty tricks. So the game depended on the ability to judge distances on our own, use a compass to determine direction, and figure out what all the lines and patterns on a topographical map actually meant.

None of us had ever done anything like this before. But the planet finding their flag and returning it to camp first would win the competition—and the prize.

Six miles, considering the unlikely out-and-back shortest possible route, may just as well have been six hundred to some of the boys at Camp Merrie-Seymour for Boys.

I seriously doubted we'd be able to inspire Trent Mendibles or Robin Sexton to give it his best.

"We need to win tomorrow," Max said.

Cobie Petersen looked at Trent Mendibles and Robin Sexton, then shook his head. And he said, "I have a plan."

Of course Cobie Petersen had a plan. He always had a plan.

Cobie said, "Stay here. I'll be back in a few minutes."

And with that, Cobie Petersen stood up from the breakfast table and bolted off into the woods.

We didn't find out what Cobie Petersen's plan involved until the next day, after they sent the five boys of Jupiter out into the woods, alone with a compass, a map, and some impossible instructions to direct us to our flag.

We could all see—well, Max, Cobie, and I could—that Larry was stoned.

We had just gotten back to Jupiter from lunch, which Larry, as usual, did not attend with us.

Cobie Petersen raised his hand. "Having a good day, Larry?"

Larry fired a dirty look at Cobie.

"Why do you want to know?"

"I care about you, Larry," Cobie said. "I think I'll miss you in three days when we get to go home."

"So write me a letter, kid."

"You might be too busy with the fat boys."

"There's a fat-guy boss on level thirty-three of BQTNP that's like impossible to beat. It took me over a week," Trent Mendibles said.

"Really?" Max said, "That's fascinating, and also really sad all at the same time. And how do you propose helping us win the game tomorrow with all your awesome skills?"

"Fuck you, dude. I swear to God, before we go home you and me are going to go outside and have it out," Trent said.

"Have what out? Do you mean you want to go *upload some streaming data* with me? No thanks, I'm a solo artist."

"Dude, you're so fucking gross," Cobie Petersen said. "Anyway, I know exactly what these two dudes are going to do to help us win. I have a plan. They want to get out of here for one day just as much as we do, and so does Larry, I bet."

"I hate you all." Trent Mendibles plopped down on his cot—*crumple!*

Robin Sexton stared blankly at the ceiling and twitched.

And Larry said, "Sure, I'd like to go to the mall. But it's up to you fuckheads. Normally, the day before the last game is Carving Day, where we let the kids carve shit on the walls of the cabins. But after that Bucky fucker tried killing himself on day one, they told us no sharp shit allowed for the entire six weeks."

Cobie Petersen raised his hand. "Larry? I pledge allegiance to Jupiter, and to you, Larry. And I also pledge to not stab myself in the throat if you let us carve our names in the wall. Please? Are you guys willing to take the pledge of not stabbing ourselves with me?"

Our general, back in action.

Faced with three raised hands, because Trent Mendibles and Robin Sexton didn't care about anything, Larry sighed and sat up on his bed. And he probably would have given in to Cobie Peter-sen's Pledge of Non-Self-Injury, too, but at that exact moment we heard the jangling war cry of Mrs. Nussbaum trumpeting her arrival at Jupiter's door.

"Boys! Boys! Hello! It's me, Mrs. Nussbaum, coming to pay my *final visit!*"

I looked from Max, to Cobie, and back to Max again.

We were now, officially, all terrified of Mrs. Nussbaum. Af-ter all, there were more than enough reasons why: She seemed to know everything about us; she wanted to eradicate males—something we all happened to be—from the human species; and, most frighteningly, she knew that I'd read her book.

The screen door swung open.

"Are you all dressed?" she crooned.

The cat had landed on the planet of mice.

Here, kitty-kitty.

Cobie Petersen raised his hand. "Mrs. Nussbaum? It's a good thing you didn't come in five minutes later. Trent there was about to get into a fistfight with Max, and I just about had Larry talked into letting us carve our names in the walls."

"You mean *have it out* means he really wants to *fight* me?" Max said.

"Oh my!" Mrs. Nussbaum said, "Well, I think carving your names would be a lovely thing for you boys to do. But what's this about fighting? We can't have that! No fighting allowed! You boys are supposed to be friends!"

Trent Mendibles rolled over on his bed—*crumple!*—and faced the wall.

Mrs. Nussbaum looked at each of us, frowning slightly. Robin Sexton ignored it all. He just stared at the ceiling and mouthed inaudible lyrics.

Mrs. Nussbaum cleared her throat. "Larry, would you mind leaving me alone with our boys for a bit?"

"You can have 'em till Saturday, for all I care."

Larry stood up from his bed, a bit woozy and red eyed, and made his way out of Jupiter.

Mrs. Nussbaum sat down on the foot of Larry's bed, facing us.

"Sit down, boys! Let's chat, shall we? Max? Cobie? *Ahh*-riel?"

We sat on our beds.

Cobie Petersen raised his hand.

"Mrs. Nussbaum? What about those two?"

He pointed at the oblivious Robin Sexton and sulking Trent Mendibles.

"Yoo-hoo! Robin! Trent! Yoo-hoo!" Mrs. Nussbaum squealed.

"*Please make it stop*," Max whispered.

Trent Mendibles crumple-rolled over on his bed so he could see our therapist. Robin Sexton removed his toilet paper earplugs and sat up.

And Mrs. Nussbaum told them this: "You two boys can run along. Why don't you go outside and *play*? I would like to spend today's time concentrating on Cobie, Max, and *Ahh*-riel! I feel they need me more, at this point in their lives."

And when she said the word *lives*, I truly felt terrified.

"What are we supposed to play?" Trent Mendibles asked.

"Oh my! Why not just go outside and have a chat about *Battle Quest: Take No Prisoners*?" Mrs. Nussbaum said.

Trent and Robin looked at each other.

Trent Mendibles shrugged. "Sure. That sounds fun. Do you play, kid?"

Robin Sexton nodded.

And as they walked out, Trent Mendibles asked the twitching

kid from Hershey, Pennsylvania, "What's your user name? I'll look for you when we get home."

And that was that.

We were alone with Martha K. Nussbaum, MD, PhD.

"I wrote some more stuff on my index card, ma'am," Cobie Petersen, laying on his West Virginia–boy accent, said.

"I filled up a whole side of my second one," Max added.

I'd never revisited my choice about where I'd rather be than at Camp Merrie-Seymour for Boys since our first session with Mrs. Nussbaum.

"That's fine! That's fine! But, honestly, boys, I'd rather talk about something else today. Would that be all right with you?"

Mrs. Nussbaum smiled and made eye contact with each of us. I glanced away as soon as her eyes met mine.

"What would you like to talk about today, Mrs. Nussbaum, ma'am?" Cobie Petersen asked.

"Oh, Ariel! Is something bothering you? You seem nervous," Mrs. Nussbaum said.

I didn't answer her. I was too afraid. I shook my head.

Mrs. Nussbaum cleared her throat and smoothed her white doctor's skirt past her porcelain knees.

"Tell me—what did you think about my book, Ariel?"

I felt the blood drain from my head. I was suddenly so cold.

I didn't know what to do, so I just shook my head again and shrugged.

Mrs. Nussbaum was not pleased.

She said, "So it seems our Ariel has reverted back to his non-speaking behavior. That's a shame, poor boy. I'll bet you've plenty of stories to tell, don't you? About where you came from? Or perhaps the sad things that happened to you in the refugee camp, you know, before you met Major Knott?"

I felt dizzy. I also felt Cobie Petersen and Max looking at me, but I didn't raise my eyes from the floor. She was playing a game, and she was about to make me cry, too, and I suddenly hated her.

"Tell me," Mrs. Nussbaum said, "you boys don't truly belong here, do you?"

"I've been saying that for six weeks," Max said.

"And why do you suppose your parents sent you here, then?" Mrs. Nussbaum asked us.

Max said, "Because it's free."

Mrs. Nussbaum smiled and shook her head.

"No, no, no . . ."

Then Cobie Petersen raised his hand and said, "Ma'am? I think I know why, Mrs. Nussbaum, ma'am."

"Oh?" Mrs. Nussbaum's voice returned to her usual delighted squeal.

Cobie Petersen looked Mrs. Nussbaum directly in the eye and said, "Because I think at least one of us is chipped, and I reckon Alex Division is kind of scared of you, ma'am, if you'll excuse me for saying so."

Mrs. Nussbaum continued smiling, looking at each of us. She said, "Well! I suppose they'd never get away with something so predictable as sending me a six-toed cat! And you boys make such handsome biodrones."

Then Mrs. Nussbaum leaned forward and put her face directly in front of each of us, as though we were all living television cameras. She said, "Tell me—Jake, Colton? Would you really do that to your *own children*? Your very own sons? You would, wouldn't you?"

And that's when I threw up, all over my shoes and socks, and the dirty pine floor of Jupiter.

FOX IN THE SNOW

Alex, our pet crow, attempted suicide one time by trying to drink a bottle of our dad's gin.

He did not succeed. Alex the crow ended up knocking the bottle down from the bar rack, causing it to shatter and dump its contents all over our living room floor.

Natalie cleaned it up.

"Oh, Alex," Natalie said, as though the two words could adequately sum up all the emptiness inside her.

And from his perch in the corner, Alex said, "Leave me alone. I'm *working out a long division problem.*"

My brother Max was a powerful influence.

I don't know why anyone would want to keep a suicidal pet in the first place—where's the fun in it? You always have to be so careful around them. But so many of the creatures Jake Burgess brought home from his de-extinction lab were bent on offing themselves. I'm still not certain if that made no sense, or if it made perfect sense. When you're *extinct*, you're doing what you're *supposed* to do—a sort of biological imperative, a drive, like reproduction. When someone stops you from being extinct, I could easily understand why the drive to return to where you came from might be a strong motivator to self-destruction.

In carrying all these stories, I can't help but feel this powerful connection between them: the desire to *save* others; cruelty and choice; selfishness, control, and the loss of will.

Poor Alex. He's such a sad bird.

I hope you don't feel bad because I gave you my story about what happened to me in the city of tents, Max. There's nothing anyone can do about these things now. And you needn't feel guilty about hating me when I came here, either. There's only so much a person should be expected to put up with, and Jake and Natalie make you—us—put up with quite a lot, I think.

I learned to survive in the city of tents. I became something of a fox—a shadow that moved so quietly and could disappear so quickly. During the first two weeks I lived in the orphans' tent, I hardly slept at all. I was always terrified that Isaak, Abel, and those other boys would come back for me again, especially at night.

One morning, during my third week there, Isaak told me after the beds were stacked that I would have to get a bucket and wash the floor of the tent from one end to the other. I didn't mind working; they'd assigned me plenty of chores since my first days, and for the most part I never spoke to them or argued one time about the things they told me to do, whether it was sweeping up, washing some of the littlest boys' faces and hands, and even doing their laundry sometimes. But on the day I was told to wash the floor of the tent, it was very warm and all the boys had to go outside so I could do the work.

And when I was nearly finished, Isaak and the other three older boys came back for me. Isaak and Abel stood in one of the doorways to the tent; Paul and Jovan stood in the other. I pretended to ignore them, despite my being trapped.

Isaak said, "Ariel, it looks like you're almost finished here."

I kept my head down.

"Almost," I said.

"That's good enough. You can be finished now," Abel told me. He and Isaak stepped inside the tent. Then they shut the door flap and tied it closed behind them.

"We have something we want you to do. Remember, Ariel?" Abel said.

I felt sick.

And I knew I wasn't prepared to use my knife on one of the boys. I couldn't stand the thought of it. Paul and Jovan came inside and loosened the flap door so they could tie it shut.

I dropped my rag in the bucket and ran at the doorway as fast as I could.

This surprised Jovan and Paul. Maybe they were not used to the boys in our tent resisting them. Even I could calculate the odds well enough to know it was a stupid thing to attempt. I tried forcing my way between Jovan and Paul so I could get out through the open tent flap. I knocked Paul down, but Jovan clipped me in the lips with his elbow. I felt and tasted blood in my mouth, and then I fell against Jovan as he wrapped his arms around my chest.

I was not going to let them hold me down again. Before Abel and Isaak were halfway across the floor, I spun around and broke free of Jovan's grasp. I saw how I'd smeared some of my blood onto the boy's face and undershirt, and I was happy for it.

I tore through the flap doorway and ran.

They chased me for a while, but I did not look back, so who can say? It felt like they chased me. I was certain the older boys were there. And I knew that in the crowds and between the tents, my smaller size gave me the advantage. I had learned to find my way through the city of tents, and there was no way Isaak and the others would ever catch me again.

This is how it was in the city of tents. By staying careful, and always watching, I managed to stay out of the filthy hands of Isaak and his sergeants. And I kept to myself, not talking to the other orphans unless it couldn't be avoided. Because there was always the possibility of having to carry someone else's terrible story, of feeling compelled to save someone, and I didn't want to think about who among the other boys were targets for Isaak and Abel and their friends.

But I continued to steal for them. I had to, Max. It was a means by which we came to some difficult mutual accord. I would never trust them, though, and felt certain Isaak and his sergeants were merely waiting for an opportunity to do what they wanted to me again. So I learned how to make it so those opportunities never happened. Like I said, Max, I became a fox, a shadow.

I felt guilty about stealing things, but it had to be done. Eventually, I learned to make excuses for taking the most pointless items—a small bag of clothespins, a book about Greece, a colander. Sometimes Isaak would get angry and tell me he was going to make me pay, but he and the other older boys never did their dirty things in front of anyone else. I think they were too afraid the rest of us might realize we outnumbered them. They were a hunting pack, and their strategy was based on isolating individual prey out from the group.

I had them figured out.

At the end of my eighth month, the city of tents found itself in the grip of a terrible winter. But I was about to be born, Max.

Snow fell on us for three consecutive days. It was the bitterest cold I'd ever felt. Even with the heater running and our tent closed up, it was impossible to keep warm. The circle of beds on the floor of our tent constricted like a fist around our little heater.

Until that winter, I had only seen snow in photographs. So you can imagine how wonderful it was at first, and how terribly cruel it became very soon after that. Everything was frozen hard—the ground was crusted in white, and there was even ice at the edge of the floor along the wall inside the orphans' tent.

Some of the boys didn't have shoes. They suffered tremendously.

And there was never enough food to keep us satisfied, Max. The relief workers didn't like to come out in the cold, either. Who could blame them? So on the third day of the snowfall, our lunch had been served very late, which caused us all to question whether or not there would even be a dinner.

I sat on the floor, shoulder to shoulder among the other boys, hugging my knees to my chest with my feet and face pointed at the heater. I always sat away from Isaak and his boys, 180 degrees separating us, and I'd try to keep my face positioned so our heater would block Isaak from looking at me. I saw Jovan stand up. He walked to the rear wall and grabbed one of our water buckets. I could tell by the way Abel looked at him that they were planning something.

The water pipes had frozen the day before, so the only way for us to get drinking water was to fill our buckets with snow and bring it inside to melt by the heater. The deepest, cleanest snow was on a small hillside at the outer perimeter of the tent city, just inside the chain-link fence.

"Give it to him." Abel pointed to a new boy named Étan, who was sitting near me.

Étan wiped his nose on the back of his sleeve. He was small, maybe twelve years old, with dirty straw-colored hair and a coat that was too big for him.

"Come on," Jovan told the boy. "You need to learn how to bring the water."

I think everyone knew what was happening except for that new boy.

Jovan and the kid went out into the cold.

Maybe a minute passed, and then Isaak, Abel, and Paul got up from their post near the heater and followed Jovan and the new boy outside.

What could anyone do?

I looked around at the other boys sitting on their mats. There were nine of us left inside the tent, and I was the oldest. If that meant anything, I don't know what it was. It wasn't as though the others looked to me with the expectation I'd do anything to change the way things were. Like I told you, I never spoke to anyone in the orphans' tent, anyway. But I thought about my last birthday—the day I'd hidden inside a refrigerator. And my fifteenth birthday was coming up, too, Max, but it was impossible to think about the future, or God, or what warm air felt like pushed along by the winds of summer.

Nobody had the will to intervene.

I heard a boy whisper something to his friend, and the other only lowered his chin and shook his head.

Sick and afraid, without saying anything, I stood up and slipped out the flap door into the icy afternoon.

Nobody was outside in the cold. I could see Isaak and the others far down the row of tents, making their way to the hill by the fence. I cut across to a parallel row so I could catch up to them faster without being seen.

When I came to the end of the row, I turned along the fence and saw the boys out on the hill. They didn't notice me.

You know what I thought? It was funny how I knew I couldn't injure anyone to stop him from hurting me, but at the same time realized that I could not stay in the doubtful warmth of the orphans' tent and knowingly let Isaak and his boys harm someone else. This doesn't make me heroic, Max. Heroes make choices. I had no choice.

Étan's coat lay spread out on the snow. Abel was on his knees, choking the smaller boy and pinning him down on top of the coat, with Étan's shirt pulled up and twisted around the boy's struggling arms, while Jovan and Paul tugged at Étan's clothing. And Isaak stood at the boy's feet, unbuttoning his pants and laughing, telling Paul and Jovan to hold the kid's legs still.

Max, I held the knife I'd stolen on my first day. I'd wrapped the handle of it with the rag because I didn't want it to slip in my hand.

The boy was putting up a good fight. I thought he must have been braver than me.

Isaak was angry. Abel punched the smaller boy in the back of his head, and Paul and Jovan wrestled with Étan's kicking legs.

They were struggling so much they didn't see me as I walked right up to Isaak.

BOYS IN THE WOODS

Throwing up all over the place has a way of ending therapy sessions.

Larry was not pleased. He was sitting outside Jupiter when Max, Cobie, and I—covered from my knees down in vomit—came through the cabin's screen door and made our way across the grounds toward the spider cave. My feet sloshed in hot acid puke.

Mrs. Nussbaum, fanning the air in front of her nose, followed.

"What the hell?" Larry said.

Cobie Petersen shook his head grimly. "Puke. A bad one."

"Puke volcano," Max added.

Then, because I thought about puke volcanoes and smelled the hot stench vapors rising in the humid afternoon from my shoes and socks, I threw up again on the grass beside the dining pavilion.

And if I hadn't completely emptied myself out, I would have thrown up some more because I had to reach down and take off my sneakers and socks so I could toss them into the washing machine and get undressed without fouling my shorts and underwear with puke. It was a disaster.

"That was like a miracle or something," Cobie Petersen said.

"Perfect timing on the subject change, Ariel," Max agreed.

I showered, and Cobie Petersen and Max took the janitor's bucket and mop and went to work in Jupiter, which was a touching and very brave thing to do.

The day of the final Camp Merrie-Seymour for Boys competition came.

They sent us out after breakfast. Each team was given a nylon backpack with our map, directions, compass, and food. They gave us food because they anticipated most teams would be gone for at least six hours. Max and Cobie, who wore our team's pack, theorized that while we were gone the counselors would be getting wasted and drunk, and maybe even having an orgy or something with Horace's last condom.

The other planets had all scattered in their separate directions into the woods.

Cobie, who told us to not be in a hurry because rushing something like this magnifies the degree of error, spread our map out on the dirt while I read the first line of instructions to him.

"Fifteen hundred meters southeast from starting point to Sugar Creek ford point, marked with wooden sign and pink trail ribbon."

Cobie Petersen took our compass and laid it on the map beside the compass rose. Then he took a small pencil they'd put in our team's pack and drew new lines on the map.

Max asked, "Dude. Are you *trying* to get us lost?"

"Compasses are off about ten degrees from actual north here. It's called declination," Cobie explained.

"How do you know that?" Max asked.

"I just do, is all. I'd never make it home some nights if I didn't know shit like that."

"Someone's going to die for sure," Max said.

Robin Sexton rocked side to side, his eyes half closed, nodding his chin.

Trent Mendibles, uncooperative as usual, had his back to us, hands on hips while he stared silently at Jupiter. Larry sat on Jupiter's front steps, his arms folded across his chest.

Exasperated, Larry said, "Are you fuckheads going to get going, or what?"

Max whispered, "That guy's such a dick. I am so sick of Larry."

We folded up our map, and Cobie Petersen, our general, led us off into the woods of the George Washington National Forest. And although I trusted Cobie Petersen's leadership, I also knew we were not moving in the right direction.

I said, "I hope it's okay if I say this, but isn't southeast more *that way*?"

I pointed off toward our left.

"I know that," Cobie answered. "We're taking a little detour first."

This was Cobie Petersen's plan in action.

It didn't take much convincing at all to get Robin Sexton and Trent Mendibles to agree to wait in the woods near the well house while the three of us completed Jupiter's mission without them. Cobie Petersen made a reasonable point: Nobody ever specified in the rules that we all had to stay together.

All Jupiter needed to do was get our flag.

Cobie Petersen persuaded Robin Sexton and Trent Mendibles to hide in the woods by bribing them with the bottle of vodka we'd stolen from Larry. He instructed them: "You two can have as much fun as you want drinking and talking about online fantasy games while the rest of us go out in the copperhead- and bear-infested forest to win the prize for Jupiter. Only, you both better be here when we get back. And keep your clothes on after you start getting drunk."

Trent Mendibles snapped out of his constant agitation. He actually smiled at Cobie Petersen, and said, "Hey, thanks, Petersen. You're an okay dude."

Trent Mendibles lifted the bottle of vodka in front of his chest like it was some fantasy broadsword, magically charged for beheading ogres and stuff.

Cobie Petersen raised his hand and nodded at him. "Fellow Jupiterian and hairiest dude I know, I salute you. Just remember: Keep your pants on. That stuff will make you do crazy shit."

When we'd put enough southeasterly distance between our deadweight castaways and us, Max said, "Dude. Are you serious? They're going to die if they drink that much vodka. We'll get in so much fucking trouble."

Cobie Petersen laughed. "The bottle is ninety percent water. I dumped almost all the vodka out yesterday when we were at breakfast. Those idiots will sit there all day *pretending* to get wasted. And when we get back, I'll bet you anything at least one of 'em's going to be naked, too."

"Are there really copperheads out here?" I asked.

We found our first marker—the one tied near the bank of Sugar Creek—in less than twenty minutes, which was good time considering we had to make our way through hilly and thick woods. And although Cobie Petersen claimed to have no experience orienteering with a compass and topographical map, I couldn't imagine anyone being much more adept at it than he was.

The next instructions told us to follow the creek downstream for one kilometer. At that point, we had to cross Sugar Creek (we were smart enough to take off our shoes and socks before doing this) and look for a fallen jack pine, and use it as a bearing for the next leg of the trip, two kilometers south, which would take us across Route 600.

I read from the numbered sheet we'd been given. "It says: 'Be sure to look both ways before crossing the highway.'"

"Duh," Cobie Petersen said. "Two more kilometers should just about get us to the flag."

"Sounds like the flag's going to be on the other side of that road, because there's no other steps after that," Max pointed out.

"We've totally got this, dudes. There's no way anyone's going to beat us," Cobie said.

He was right, too. None of the other teams could possibly cover three miles as efficiently as we did. And although I was a little bit worried that even 90 percent–diluted vodka might get Trent Mendibles and Robin Sexton into some serious trouble, I also knew that leaving them behind was the best possible strategy if Jupiter was actually going to win this game.

In about one hour we had our flag. As Max had predicted, it was sticking up on the opposite side of Route 600.

The flag was about as tall as Cobie Petersen, hoisted on a white fiberglass pole, like you'd see on a golf course. And written across the triangular red flag, in thick black hand-printed marker, was JUPITER.

I pulled the flag stick out of the ground, and the three of us slapped high fives all around.

Then Cobie Petersen said, "Let's go pick up those two dudes, then get this thing in. We'll be sitting there *hours* before anyone else shows up."

"Wait," Max reminded us. He held out his arms to hold Cobie Petersen and me from walking forward. "Remember to look both ways."

Max was right. There was a car coming.

Well, it sounded like a car, but it was actually an old, beat-up U-Haul van that was rattling down Route 600 toward Cobie Petersen, Max, and me.

MAJOR KNOTT

Near the front gates of the city of tents stood two large administrative buildings. The buildings were more substantial than tents; they were permanent structures with actual doors and windows, wired with electricity, and comfortably heated.

The soldiers who came out to the hill that afternoon took those of us who could walk into one of those buildings. They separated us into different rooms: me, Paul, Jovan, and Étan.

Isaak and Abel were carried on stretchers to the camp's hospital.

I had stabbed them both in the legs—in their thighs to be exact, twice to Isaak, and three times to Abel, as deeply as I could jam that little knife into them. It was a mess. There was blood all over my hands and on the sleeves of my sweater, and the snow where it happened looked like candy.

I say *where it happened* as though I were a detached observer from the event, but I know this is not the case. I can still feel the thickness of the boys' muscles as the knife went in, how the handle turned slightly and wanted to slip from my grasp when they jerked away in horror and shock. It was all over in a matter of seconds, Max. The screaming was terrible. Everyone screamed, except for me: Isaak, Abel, Jovan, Paul, and Étan—barefoot and half naked, bleeding from his mouth and nose where Abel had been striking him.

And I was so mad when I did it, Max. It was as though my head and my heart were swarms of angry wasps. It was all I could do to stop myself from killing Isaak, and especially Abel. But I can't tell you either boy deserved it. Who am I to say who deserves anything in this life? I'm still confused by the whole thing—all those nine months I waited between lives in the tent of orphans.

So I sat in the room, alone, seated at an empty table for I don't know how long. I was shaking, but not from cold, because I remember how my hair stuck to the back of my neck with my sweat. I was also crying, with my head resting on my forearm, when the man came into the room and sat across the empty table from me. He put a bottle of drinking water down beside my hand.

This was the first time I met Harrison Knott.

"Are you thirsty?"

Major Knott was British. His voice sounded nice, you know the way English people sound, like they could never say or do anything mean at all.

I wanted the water, but my hands were shaking too badly, and they were still covered in Isaak's and Abel's blood.

"Here." Major Knott opened the water bottle for me and gave it to me. "We should get you washed up."

"How are they? Isaak and Abel?" I asked.

"That's an odd thing to ask," Major Knott said.

Major Knott placed his hands flat on the table. "Well, I'm certain they won't die. They won't be walking for a while, but they won't die, Ariel. Your name is Ariel, right?"

I nodded.

"Is the boy all right? Étan?"

"He'll be fine."

"The others—Paul and Jovan—you should never let them go back with the orphans."

"And why do you say that?"

I took a drink and looked at Major Knott.

"You know what they were trying to do to Étan. They were going to rape him, like they do to some of the rest of us."

"You?"

What could I say? He had to know what Isaak and the others had been doing all this time.

I nodded.

"Why didn't you tell anyone?" he asked.

I shook my head. "I don't know. I was new. Isaak—the boys beat me and held me down. It happened on the first day I came here. I didn't know what to do, so I waited. Somehow, I thought I would figure out what to do, but nothing came to me. I couldn't think about the future, you know? And then I tried to forget about it, probably the same as anyone else, if you ask the others."

"Would you like to see a doctor or something?"

"I'm not hurt."

"I meant someone to talk to. Maybe you should talk to somebody."

"I'm talking to you. I don't want to talk to anyone else. I'm tired of everybody. I'm sorry I ever came to this place. I should have died a dozen times by now."

Major Knott leaned back in his chair and sighed.

He said, "I apologize, Ariel. Come on, then, let's get you washed up."

Major Knott pushed away from the table and stood, obviously waiting for me to get up, too. And I thought, what was this man apologizing to me for? What could he have ever done—or not done—that would make anything different for me?

I was still shaking when I got to my feet. Major Knott patted my shoulder and said, "You'll be okay, son. Everything's going to be okay now."

Major Knott took me to a bathroom with tiled walls. It was so clean, it was like a hospital. He showed me how to run the shower, then left me there alone and told me he'd wait outside and that I could take as much time as I wanted to.

Let me tell you how pure it felt to stand under that hot water, Max. It was almost as though I were being born again. Do you know, this was the first time I'd bathed in hot water since my fourteenth birthday?

When I came out, Major Knott was waiting in the hall for me. I was wearing my pink undershirt; I'd left the sweater Garen had given me on the bathroom's floor. There was too much blood on it.

Major Knott understood what I'd done. He knew the orphans had nothing more than the clothes we wore. He said, "I'll see if we can get your sweater cleaned for you. But it looks as though we'll have to find you some new clothes, anyway. How would that be? You may have to dress like a soldier, though."

"I'd rather not dress like a soldier."

Major Knott looked at me and nodded. "Well, perhaps a doctor then. We'll find something else for you to wear, son."

———

I never went back to the orphans' tent after that day.

Also, I never asked what happened to Isaak and his friends. I only know that they did not go back to the orphans' tent, but Étan did. So maybe things were better for the boys there, at least for a while, until someone else like Isaak showed up. Because that's the way things usually work out if you wait long enough, isn't it?

For as long as I'd lived in the misery of the orphans' tent, and before that with Thaddeus and the soldiers and then the small family with the wagon, I'd forgotten what it felt like to be indoors, inside somewhere quiet and warm.

Major Knott's offices were like a palace to me.

We had dinner that night in a small kitchen for officers, and when I told Major Knott it was the best food I'd eaten in my entire life he laughed and said there was something terribly wrong with that. But it was the truth, and Major Knott's comment made me feel confused, and also afraid that he was going to kick me out and send me back to sleep on the frozen floor of the orphans' tent with the other boys.

I mean, why wouldn't he do that? It was where I belonged, after all. Major Knott knew the truth about what had happened that day on the hill—as well as what Isaak and his sergeants had been doing to some of us before then—so why wouldn't he send me back? Everything was fixed now; the way it was supposed to be. No more trouble.

Sometimes there is something endlessly selfish and cruel in saving others, Max.

Do you know what I thought about while we ate dinner? I thought about sitting in a chair at a table. I couldn't remember the last time I'd sat in a chair to eat. And I missed the feeling of that little knife I'd wrapped in a rag and kept tucked inside my belt for eight months, too. Sitting across from Major Knott, wearing my pink undershirt, I suddenly felt naked and embarrassed.

Major Knott asked, "How did you come to learn English so well?"

I shrugged. "In school. I also learned to speak French. I like languages."

"And you came here to the camp on your own? You don't have any family?"

I shook my head.

"I walked here with a man and his wife. They had a baby with them. That was more than eight months ago now. They gave me these clothes and let me walk with them."

"You've been managing well since coming here?" Major Knott asked.

I thought about that word—*managing*—and how ridiculous it was. I wondered if Major Knott actually thought I could have been the manager of the events of my past eight months. And there was something about the things the major said to me that made me feel guilty and afraid. Maybe it was just because I hadn't spoken to anyone since coming here, so now, faced with this assault of words and sentences, I found myself seeing again the events of my first day in the orphans' tent, and I could smell those dirty boys and taste Abel's hand over my mouth.

"It's the worst place I've ever been," I told him, "I wish I could go home."

After dinner, a soldier brought a set of powder-blue hospital scrubs and some new socks for me to sleep in. Major Knott waited for me to change, and then gave all my dirty clothes and even my shoes to the soldier, along with instructions to do the best he could with them.

I didn't realize how filthy my things were until I'd changed into the sterile hospital uniform. It felt soft and loose—like the Pierrot costume I'd worn for so long—and the socks were so warm on my feet. Major Knott let me sleep on a couch in what he called a "break room." There was a refrigerator, stove, coffeepot, and even a television in it. He told me I could stay there until he figured out the best thing to do with me, and he promised to find somewhere better so I wouldn't have to go back with the orphans. I'd just have to be patient and trust him, he said, and wait for things to work out.

As far as I was concerned, the couch in the break room was the nicest place I had ever been in my life.

THE BEST THING TO DO WITH ARIEL

I came to feel much better about things, Max, but what did I know?

You know what I realized the first day I spent in Major Knott's office, Max? That up until the very day of my fourteenth birthday, I never once considered an alternative to this life. And since that afternoon in the schoolhouse, it seems I can hardly think of anything else. I should have peed in the refrigerator. I could still be there if I did.

My new life began on a couch in Major Knott's break room, where I could watch television in English, and sleep with real dreams. Real dreams, Max—imagine that! In the orphans' tent, I never actually slept; I hovered just below the surface of frightened awareness, always ready to run off, to vanish. But here, for the first time since before I'd hidden inside that refrigerator, I dreamed about things I had no words for and had never seen. And it made me feel so good.

The clothes I'd taken off were cleaned and returned to me, and Major Knott also gave me socks and new underwear, which I had to get used to, but he let me keep the hospital scrubs so I had something to sleep in. And every morning, I brewed American coffee for Major Knott and the other people who worked in the administrative office.

I couldn't help but think about the boy named Ocean, whose clothes I wore and who also at one time made coffee for people in a different life and a different world.

Every evening before he'd leave me alone to watch television until it put me to sleep, Major Knott and I played chess. I beat him only one time, and he complimented me, even though I can't be certain if he was just playing weak to let me win. We talked about science, the world, and about the company Major Knott managed in America, called Merrie-Seymour Research Group, in particular, a part of its labs called Alex Division.

"Do you ever wonder how much of a footprint we leave, Ariel?" Major Knott asked me one time while we played chess.

I looked down at the floor. I thought maybe someone had carried in mud.

"What do you mean?" I said.

"There's not a single thing on this planet—not an organism, a sea, a river or lake, and even the weather that surrounds us, that hasn't been changed by human beings. For good or bad, we're in charge of the rate at which everything changes now. Every living thing, and the majority of nonliving systems, too," Major Knott explained.

"We've become our own God, I suppose."

Major Knott said, "In some ways. But in other ways, we've trapped ourselves, and if we're not careful, the whole thing could fall apart."

"What happens if we *are* careful?" I asked.

"If we're careful—and smart—we can control everything to our benefit. We decide on weather patterns, forestation versus desert-ification, we can shape evolution, decide on extinction, make the world exactly the way we want it to be. All for the best, of course. That's part of what we do at Alex Division," Major Knott said.

"Sounds like an important job."

"Even more than you might imagine, I would guess," he told me.

"I can't imagine anything that I haven't got the words for," I said, "but I do like science."

"And languages, too," Major Knott added.

I smiled and nodded.

Max, I never wanted to leave the building. In fact, I had not gone outside for nearly a week. I was too afraid of being stranded out there, of having to go back to the orphans' tent. When I did finally go outside into the city of tents, it was with Major Knott. He took me to the hospital to be examined by a doctor.

It was very uncomfortable for me. The doctor looked at and touched every part of my body, and took X-rays, too. Then Major Knott walked with me to where the soldiers got haircuts. The barber cut off nearly all my hair and he shaved the light fuzz off my face with a straight razor. Of course, that was completely unnecessary, but the barber and Major Knott had a laugh over my getting a shave, and told me that all boys always remember the first time they shave.

Major Knott said this was the first step for me on my journey to a new family and a new home.

My next life.

Major Knott kept telling me to be patient, that he'd found the best thing to do with me. Still, I desperately wanted to know what he thought was *the best thing to do with Ariel*. But I trusted him completely. Why wouldn't I? Major Knott had given me more than anyone ever had in my entire life.

The snow had melted, and the alleyways through the city of tents were transformed into swampy canals of mud. As we walked from the barber's, I felt like a new person—a different one. I could smell the menthol of the shaving cream on my face, and I daydreamed that Major Knott would take me to live with his family.

"Are you married?" I asked him.

"Yes," Major Knott said. "My wife is American. We have a home in West Virginia. Do you know where that is?"

I nodded. "In the eastern United States, between Virginia and Ohio. Do you have any children?"

Major Knott chuckled. "No. No children, Ariel. Why?"

"Oh. I was just wondering," I said.

The following day Major Knott took me to see a dentist named Dr. Mather. He spoke with an American accent. I had never been to a dentist in my life. It frightened me when Dr. Mather put his hands and metal instruments in my mouth. He could tell I was very nervous; I was shaking.

I will tell you, Max—I almost started to cry. I couldn't see the point in putting things inside my mouth.

Dr. Mather said, "I'm going to have to extract a couple of your teeth, Ariel."

I started to get up from the chair, not because I was going to run, but because I felt like I was going to vomit.

Dr. Mather put his hand on my chest and said, "It's okay. You won't feel it at all. I'm going to give you a shot. Really, it's nothing."

The dentist called Major Knott into the examination room and both men looked at X-ray images of the inside of my mouth, while

Dr. Mather pointed from image to image with a surgical-gloved hand.

Dr. Mather spoke to Major Knott as though he were my father, which I suppose Major Knott had become after the day on the hill.

He said, "The boy is afraid. Do you want to stay in here? Maybe say something to him?"

So Major Knott stood beside the armrest of my chair. He put his hand on mine and I instantly felt better, safe.

Major Knott said, "It's not a terrible thing, Ariel. I'll stay right here the whole time. Would that be all right? Or if you feel very troubled, we can go home and come back some other time. What do you think?"

When Major Knott offered me the opportunity of ending this, and when he talked about going *home*, which was my little room with the television and coffeemaker, everything seemed to get vastly better.

"I'm sorry," I said. "What will it be like to have some of my teeth taken out?"

Major Knott smiled. "There's nothing to it. I'll be here the whole time."

"Okay, then. Thank you."

To be honest, I don't even remember anything at all after Dr. Mather put the gas mask over my mouth and nose. The next thing I knew, I was lying on my couch-bed in my scrubs, covered in blankets while the television played a science-fiction program from England. And there was cotton gauze that tasted like medicine in my mouth.

HAPPY BIRTHDAY TO ME

My fifteenth birthday came four days after our visit to the dentist. I didn't say anything to Major Knott about it, so he must have found out from the information that was written down during my physical.

To tell you the truth, I tried not to think about it at all. A birthday has a way of making you condense everything that's happened in a previous year into something like a small pill, and then it forces you to swallow it. It had been one year since I playacted the part of Pierrot for my classmates and later hid inside a refrigerator after the slaughter at the schoolhouse.

On my fourteenth birthday, exactly one year earlier, I believed it was a miracle that I was alive.

On my fifteenth, I wasn't so sure that it was anything other than an accident, Max.

But on that morning Major Knott and the entire staff of the UN administrative building came into the break room while I was sleeping. Major Knott carried a cake with fifteen candles on it, and everyone sang to me.

I had never seen a cake like that, Max. Also, the singing terrified me. Think of what it was like for me—I was asleep, wrapped in heavy blankets, and then suddenly I was assaulted by all these noisy grown-ups carrying something that was in flames.

It took me a while to figure out that what was happening wasn't a nightmare. And when I did, I felt so sad for all the things I had left behind in my first lives. That's a funny thing to admit to, isn't it? But you can't expect to be pulled from one life and emerge into another and carry along anything with you besides all those stories that never go away.

Major Knott could tell I was overwhelmed. After they finished singing to me, he put the cake down on the table where we played chess every night.

Major Knott rubbed his hand in my hair and said, "Happy birthday, Ariel."

I looked at him, then at the fiery cake.

"Thank you."

"You're supposed to blow out the candles and make a wish," Major Knott said.

It was very confusing, Max. And I couldn't think of anything to wish for, either. What else could I possibly want?

There was so much to think about, and yet everything I considered was something I did not want. It would only make me feel worse to contrive a wish that could never come true—to go back home, to make things revert back to the way they used to be, to never have come to the city of tents in the first place. But I got up from my couch-bed, stood over the burning cake, and blew the life out of all those little candles. Then people clapped, and we all had cake and coffee for breakfast.

It was nice.

And after everyone left and we were alone, Major Knott told me he was going to take me to America to live with a new family, they were going to adopt me, and that I would have a brother who was my age. Well, sixteen days older, but you already know that.

Happy birthday to me, right?

Major Knott seemed surprised that I didn't look happy. He asked me, "What do you think about this, Ariel?"

I didn't know what I was supposed to think about this. There was an awful lot for me to think about. I didn't want to leave. I know at the time it was a foolish sentiment, but I wanted to stay there and live in that small break room forever, until it was safe to come out—just like the refrigerator. But I had an overriding sense that it would really never be safe to come out, right? And I didn't want to go away from Major Knott, either. I was so tired of being saved and saved again and again. Couldn't I just stay in one place—frozen there forever?

It felt like the wind had been knocked out of me.

I sat down on the couch and looked across at the remains of the cake.

"Is something wrong, Ariel?"

I shook my head. It was all I could do, but the effort fell far short of convincing Major Knott that things were perfectly fine.

I didn't want to answer him because I felt so sad about everything. I thought about all the terrible stories I'd been carrying with me, and it was suddenly too much. I didn't believe I could carry anything else with me—at least, I did not want to try. I knew I would start crying if I said anything, and that would be unfair to Major Knott. He had done so much for me. He was too nice and didn't deserve my making him feel bad. But who am I to say what people do or do not deserve?

I shook my head again and looked down at my feet, the gray socks they'd given me, sliding this way and that way on the cool slick floor of the break room.

Major Knott pulled a chair around from the table and sat down right in front of me.

"I understand this is going to be a drastic change in your life, Ariel, but you just don't see how fantastic everything is going to be for you from now on."

There's a word for you: *fantastic*.

Think about what it really means: unreal, imagined. Why would anyone think *fantastic* was a good omen of my future?

I realized I was pouting. My chin was down and I wouldn't look Major Knott in the eye.

He put his hand on my knee and said, "You'll like the Burgesses. Jake Burgess works with me, in West Virginia. I'll take you to his house and you'll see. His wife is named Natalie, and their son—your new brother—is named Max. He's a funny kid, Ariel. You'll have a good life there. It's a beautiful place, and I live quite close to them—your new family."

"You do?"

Major Knott nodded and smiled.

"We'll see each other often. I promise, Ariel. And the Burgesses have a very clever pet—a crow, named Alex."

So what do you think, Max? Maybe they should have changed my name to Alex, too—all things considered.

SOMETHING MORE LIKE FONDUE

The same year that Jake Burgess was perfecting the genetic diversity and de-extinction of Polynesian crows, while his wife was pregnant with Max and a hominid monster discovered in a block of Siberian ice in 1880, a woman I never got to meet was pregnant with me on the opposite, less civilized, side of the world.

Most things, including the Siberian Ice Man, aren't ever really *discovered*; we just were never looking at them in the first place. But, like the Siberian Ice Man who developed alongside my brother Max inside Natalie Burgess's womb, these things we humans credit ourselves with *discovering* were actually always in plain sight to begin with, it's just nobody ever took the time to look at them.

And that same year when Max and I were born, my American father, Jake Burgess, also stumbled upon a process for manufacturing a new variety of carbon-polymer composite whose molecules were arranged in such a way that when it was shaped in precisely determined dimensions, the material could absorb all visible light. It could become, at certain angles, absolutely invisible to the human eye.

The Merrie-Seymour Research Group and Alex Division used the carbon-polymer composite to construct small mechanical drones.

Their drones were everywhere, watching and listening.

One of the drones had been following a man named Leonard Fountain, who had been one of Alex Division's first—and highly flawed—human biodrones, for a very long time.

\- - -

"Why are three polar bears with a Soviet flag hitchhiking on the side of a road in Virginia?" the melting man said.

"Probably climate change," Crystal Lutz offered.

"Do something right for once in your life. Shoot them. Shoot all three of them!" Joseph Stalin told him.

"You're slowing down. You're slowing down," 3-60 said.

"I am slowing down," Leonard Fountain agreed, "and it *is* hot, too. Maybe Crystal has something."

The melting man shifted in his seat. He felt the gun in his back pocket. He wanted to do something right for once in his life.

"Pull over and shoot them!" Joseph Stalin ordered.

The melting man eased the gun from his pocket.

The three polar bears carrying the Soviet flag stood beside the road and watched as Leonard Fountain's U-Haul van slowed to a stop in front of them.

"Do polar bears speak English?" Leonard Fountain wondered aloud.

"You are waving to the polar bears. You are rolling down your window and gesturing for the three polar bears to come to you," 3-60 said.

Actually, the three polar bears were not polar bears, but boys from Camp Merrie-Seymour for Boys. And their flag was not a Soviet flag, but a triangular red vinyl pennant with the word JUPITER written on it.

In the melting man's hand was a small chrome-plated .380 semiautomatic. And inside the melting man's head was a brain that had become something less of a brain and something more like fondue.

OUT FOR A WALK WHILE
OUR PORRIDGE COOLS

The U-Haul van slowed to a stop in the middle of Route 600, directly in front of where we stood.

"Do you think he'd be willing to give us a ride back to camp?" Cobie Petersen asked.

"There's nothing in the rules that says we can't hitch a ride," Max said.

"I thought in America, people always tell kids to never get in cars with strangers," I said.

"Loosen up, Ariel," Max argued, "besides, it's a moving van, not a car. Nothing bad ever happens to kids in moving vans."

When the van stopped, the shadowy figure behind the wheel rolled down the driver side window and stuck his arm out, waving for us to come around to him.

I carried our flag. Cobie Petersen and Max followed me out into the road and we walked around the front of the moving van so we could see what the driver wanted.

I think the three of us simultaneously recoiled as though we'd all been slapped when we got a clear view of the man behind the steering wheel. And the truck itself gave off the hot smell of rotting meat and maggots.

"Holy Jesus," Max whispered.

"Something's wrong with that guy," I said.

I have seen some things more repulsive than the man at the wheel of the van, but they were all either nonhuman or dead. The melting man was outside of both of those group classifications. He wore a plaid hat with a narrow brim that turned down in the front, and his head was bandaged around with stained medical tape that attached small plastic windup timers to his ears. The lack of eyebrows and eyelashes made him look almost fishlike, and his skin burbled with oozing pink blisters. A small worm-trail of blood slithered a sluggish path from his right nostril toward his upper lip.

Cobie Petersen, mouth slightly open, looked at Max, then me, then he spit down onto the asphalt between his feet and grimaced.

"Hello, friendly bears!" The melting man said, "Do you need a lift? Where are you heading?"

"Shoot them, Leonard! Do something right!"

"Oh. Uh. No thanks, but thanks anyway," the tall bear said, backing away slightly. "We're just out for a walk while our porridge cools."

"Dude, I'll play three bears with you, as long as I'm not the mom," the small bear—the one without the flag—said.

If the melting man had eyebrows, they would have gotten closer together. He had a sudden thought. He pointed at flag-bear's chest. The melting man happened to be missing the fingernail on his pointer.

"You are pointing at the bear. You are pointing at the bear with the green camp T-shirt on."

"Hey!" The melting man said, "That's exactly where I'm heading!"

Each of the bears was wearing a Camp Merrie-Seymour for Boys log-fonted T-shirt, with adhesive Jupiter name tags.

"Jupiter?" the tall bear said.

"Unclick the safety, Leonard."

"You are unclicking the safety. You are—oh, Lenny, you are going to shoot the bears."

"Ha-ha! No! Camp Merrie-Seymour for Beavers!" The melting man bounced up and down in his seat. This was all like a scene from a hallucinogenic dream.

"Um. Stranger danger, guys," small bear with no flag whispered. "Looks like the dude's *freeing some kittens in the disco* there."

"Do it, Leonard. Shoot them. Now."

Tall bear said, "Yeah. Okay, well, bye now."

As the three bears backed away from the melting man's truck, he waved again. "Wait! No! I'll give you a ride to Camp Merrie-Seymour! Don't be scared, little bears!"

"It's okay. Really," tall bear told him.

"My brother's there. He works at Camp Merrie-Seymour for Beavers. He invited me to visit. Maybe you know him?" the melting man asked.

"I doubt it," small bear with no flag said.

"You have unclicked the safety. Your finger is on the trigger. You are holding the gun."

"His name is . . . Uh . . ."

The melting man couldn't seem to remember. He rubbed his forehead with two fingers and popped some blisters, which made pus run down the bridge of his nose.

"Dude. Really. You should probably towel down or something," the tall bear said.

"Larry! His name's Larry!" The melting man looked overjoyed. Well, he looked like a hairless, infected, overjoyed fish with a bloody nose.

"Larry? Our Larry?" the small bear without a flag said.

"Yes! Do you know him?" the melting man asked.

The bears looked at one another.

"Small world," tall bear said.

"Your finger is on the trigger."

"Make them get into the van with you, then take them out into the woods and shoot them, Leonard."

"And what about the Beaver King? Do you bears know if the Beaver King is there with Larry, too?" the melting man asked.

The tall, friendly polar bear scratched his head and spit on the roadway. "I think Momma Bear and Baby Bear and I need to be getting back to Jupiter."

"No! Wait!"

"You are raising the gun. You are raising the gun."

Suddenly, the melting man jerked his head, the way someone would if he was being screamed at. He said, "Bears, this is Crystal Lutz, my girlfriend. She's really good at the accordion. Crystal, meet the talking polar bears. Um? What did you say your names were?"

The tall bear raised his hand and said, "Poppa Bear, ma'am."

There was nobody else in the van with the melting man.

Small bear with the flag whispered, *"We really need to go."*

"Now, Leonard! Now! Do something right!"

The melting man behind the wheel moved his right arm again, and when he raised his hand up to the window, he pointed a pistol.

"You are shooting. You are shooting."

Welcome to America.

UP IN THE WOODS A WAY UP THERE!

"Those were the nicest talking polar bears I've ever shot," Leonard Fountain said.

"You should have forced them to come with you, and shot them somewhere else!" Joseph Stalin, as always, was angry at the melting man's incompetence.

"Oh!" The melting man's feelings were hurt. He was nearing the breaking point with Joseph Stalin. He pounded the timers into the sides of his head. Naturally, this hurt very much, and caused him to bleed from his ears, too.

"You are winding the timers. You are winding the timers. You are driving. Keep your eyes on the road, Lenny!" 3-60 said.

"How could I force three polar bears to come with me? There's only enough room in the cab for me and Crystal," Leonard Fountain whined.

"Idiot!" Joseph Stalin said.

"You are crying. Oh. Poor Leonard, you're crying," 3-60 said.

"I'll play something happy for you, Igor!" Crystal Lutz said.

Crystal Lutz played something on her accordion that did make the melting man happy. It was an old Boy Scouts campfire song he remembered from when he was a boy. The song was called "I Met a Bear (The Bear Song)."

And Leonard Fountain, the melting man, Igor Zelinsky, wept and smiled and sang and bled from his nose and ears and got an erection as he drove down Route 600 toward Camp Merrie-Seymour for Bears and Beavers, and the timers ticked and ticked and ticked.

The other day I met a bear,
Up in the woods a way up there!

AMERICAN AIRSPACE

Three days after I put the fire out on the cake Major Knott brought me while I was asleep, we rode in a troop transport vehicle that took us on a rocky road west out of the valley of the city of tents to a military airfield where we boarded an enormous plane filled with American soldiers who were all so happy to be going home.

I was numb and in shock. I had nothing but the clothes on my back, a small plastic sack containing my pajama scrubs and two pairs of socks and underwear, and a brand-new American passport that identified me as Ariel Jude Burgess. I didn't wonder about how things like new identities and passports could happen so fast. Major Knott could make anything happen, I was convinced.

To be honest, I didn't want to go to America, Max. This is an appalling thing to say, but in many ways I felt as helpless and as swept along by the tide as I did on that first day in the orphans' tent, when Isaak and Abel and those other two boys took me with them.

"I have never been on an airplane before," I admitted to Major Knott.

I sat by the window. He told me all boys like to sit by the window on airplanes. I desperately did not want to throw up on Major Knott. And the plane was so noisy. Behind us, a group of soldiers began singing a song about a prostitute named Ruby.

They were drunk.

"Are you excited?" Major Knott asked.

"I'm really very scared," I said.

"There's nothing to be frightened of, Ariel. You'll see. You're going to love it."

I knew I was definitely not going to love it.

And when the plane took off, and I looked out the window at the world slanting this way and that below me, at the great silver wing rising up and then pointing terrifyingly down at the smaller and smaller gray-and-brown grids of towns and cities below us, I could feel myself being torn away from something I would never be able to return to.

What could I do?

I closed my eyes and wished for sleep, but everything was noisy and the plane shuddered and dipped and all I could think about was how scared I was. And Major Knott, who knew everything about what was happening to me, put his hand on mine and told me everything was okay, and that he would always be here whenever I needed him.

Nothing is true though, is it, Max? Because everything is really something different than we think it is.

I was every bit the same as that crow, forced to come back, to be saved again and again and again.

I was flying, and I never wanted to fly again. I never wanted to talk again. Does that make sense to you now? I'm sorry. I'm sorry for these terrible stories. There's nothing you or anyone else can do about them now.

The library has been built, right?

The shelves are full.

And as the plane began to descend, my head felt as though it were splitting apart. I didn't sleep at all for the entire way. When I needed to pee so bad I couldn't stand it, I climbed over Major Knott's gawky knees and he didn't stir at all. And making my way to the toilet, a soldier stopped me and he told me how lucky I was. He said, "Welcome to the United States of Fucking America, kid. Do you know how lucky you are?"

And I said I didn't really know how lucky I was, so I asked him if he knew how lucky I was, because I'd really like to know.

And he said, "That's a good one, kid! I don't know, either!"

You never know, right, Max?

So I asked him if he'd let go of my sleeve, because I was about to pee in my pants, and they were the only pants I owned.

Then the soldier got angry and he said, "You don't have to be a dick about it. It's not my fault your country is fucked up. Do you want my pants or something? Here. Take everything we own."

The soldier shifted in his seat as though he were going to take his clothes off.

I told him no, I actually just wanted to pee.

I think it was the fact that I was actually holding my dick that he let go of me. Otherwise, I could tell he wanted to continue having a discussion about how fucked up my country was compared to his, and how I was going to take everything I could get my hands on once I came to America.

Welcome to American airspace, kid.

But as we came down, lower and lower, I was certain something was wrong with me. I had felt pain before, but nothing like this. I was convinced I was dying. I shook Major Knott awake and told him what was happening to me.

"It's okay, Ariel. Let me take a look," Major Knott said.

Then he took a small instrument out and looked into my eye. He had something in his hand that was about the size of the remote control for the television in the break room in the city of tents. He pushed some buttons. Major Knott told me to close my eyes, and he pressed his thumb on my temple and made small circles in my hair. I felt a buzzing, a slight tickle, and Major Knott put the little device on the side of my jaw. Then he slipped the thing back into his jacket pocket.

"Is that better?" Major Knott asked.

I don't know what he did, but whatever it was worked.

I took a deep breath.

"Yes," I said, "I'm feeling better now."

Behind us, the soldiers sang and sang.

BRINGING YOUR FLAG BACK HOME

When someone is shooting at you, it's impossible to think about the future or God, and you don't really care about bringing your flag back home, either.

The man shot six times. I counted them all: one, two, three.

Four.

Fivesix.

Max's frequent obsession with escape routes may have sunk in. When the man raised his pistol and aimed at us, Max, Cobie, and I scattered and ran in separate directions.

I dropped Jupiter's flag in the middle of Route 600.

I think I only made it thirty or so feet into the woods on the other side of the road. Everything seemed to slow down tremendously. My legs weighed tons, and I couldn't seem to move. It was all so much like the afternoon I'd hidden in a muddy irrigation ditch with Thaddeus.

And I lost one of my shoes in the brush. Four steps later, my foot got twisted up in some weeds and I tripped. I lay there against the ground, panting, unable to suck in enough oxygen, listening, listening. My gasps were so loud I couldn't hear anything else, so I held my breath until it felt like my lungs would implode. Everything was so quiet. The shooting had stopped, and if Max and Cobie were anywhere near me, they weren't making a sound.

I took a breath, held it in.

As I lay there, I tried to think about directions: where I had come from, and where I was going, where was the man in the truck, where might Cobie Petersen and my brother be? I found myself wishing I could tell them about some of the stories I knew, that this is what happens when somebody shoots—how you have no choice, really, because when you're alive you only know how to do one thing. When you're not alive, I suppose you only know how to do one thing, too.

Then, off through the trees I heard singing.

The other day I met a bear,
Up in the woods a way up there!

Then the motor on the old moving van started up, and I waited and listened as the sound of the truck receded down the road.

It seemed as though several minutes passed. It may have only been seconds. Who could tell? I rolled over onto my back and stared up through the treetops.

Something glinted in the sky just above the trees, hovering directly over me. It looked like a small silver box that gyrated and then vanished into the blue.

"Max?"

I sat up.

"Max? Cobie?"

Something moved in the trees behind me.

"I'm over here," Max said.

"Are you okay?"

"Yeah. Are you?"

"I lost my shoe. Do you know where Cobie is?"

And from farther off in the woods came Cobie Petersen's voice: "That fucker shot me, guys."

"Well, at least your left hand seems to be okay," Max said. "Thank God for that."

"Yeah. It's a miracle," Cobie Petersen said.

Of the six bullets fired at us, only one of them had found a mark. It went directly through the center of Cobie Petersen's right hand. I felt terrible for him; the thing looked awfully painful. Cobie held his bloody hand palm up, with the fingers half curled in paralysis. The flesh around the wound was drained, and his wrist was swollen straight down from the thumb joint.

Max sacrificed his shirt and tore strips from it, which I used to wrap Cobie's hand as tightly as I could. I had done this sort of thing before, after all. But I would not go back to look for my lost shoe. Although none of us said it, we were all afraid the crazy man with the gun was coming back for us.

So between my missing one shoe and Cobie Petersen's wounded hand, the trip back to Jupiter through the woods proved difficult and slow.

"What are you boys doing here, and why do you only have one shoe?"

"Huh?"

"I said—why do you only have one shoe?"

The man who'd been watching the three of us wade through

Sugar Creek seemed angry over the fact that I was carrying only one shoe. My other had been abandoned somewhere behind us near Route 600.

Of course we didn't see him standing there until he spoke, we were all so intent on watching our footing on the slick algae-covered rocks on the creek's bottom. And when we did see him, there was little we could do. You can't just take off running like crazy when you're balancing, knee-deep in the middle of a stream.

For all any of us knew, we could have just walked directly into the man with the gun again. We froze there, shocked speechless in midstream.

"You there—are you hurt or something?" the man pointed a stick-finger at Cobie.

Cobie Petersen just said, "Huh?"

"What is *wrong* with you kids?"

What was wrong with us was that we'd narrowly escaped with our lives after being shot at by a melting man inside a U-Haul van, and now we'd come face-to-face with one of the strangest human beings I'd ever seen.

"Is that the Dumpling Man?" Max asked.

Cobie Petersen shook his head and whispered, "No. No horns. I don't know what he is, though."

The man was skeleton thin and stood at least six and a half feet tall, wearing bib overalls, barefoot, and shirtless. His skin glowed in the dapples of sunlight like fresh snow—the whitest man I had ever seen—and his straight and lifeless shoulder-length hair was absolutely colorless.

"Are you all dumb? I asked if you was hurt," the white man said.

"Some crazy dude shot at us back there by the road," Max said.

We still hadn't moved from our spot in the middle of Sugar Creek.

"Is it bad?"

"I don't think so," Cobie answered.

"Well, come here. Let me see if I can help some."

Marshmallow Jeff did not turn out to be the child-killing monster that Larry had described on the night we sat by the fire and told scary stories. In fact, he was probably one of the kindest human beings I'd encountered since coming to America. He even carried Cobie Petersen on his back all the way to the edge of Camp Merrie-Seymour for Boys, and I got to wear Cobie's shoes, as opposed to stumbling around and hurting myself.

"Do you really carry marshmallows around everywhere?" Max asked him.

"Naw. That's dumb. I don't even like marshmallows," Marshmallow Jeff said. "The name comes from this."

He stuck out his paper-white arm and turned it over in front of us.

"They still making up stories about me to scare you kids?"

"I called horseshit on the story as soon as he said it," Cobie said.

Marshmallow Jeff, who'd never owned a pair of shoes in his life, told us the counselors at Camp Merrie-Seymour for Boys made up stories about the man living in the woods, just to keep the boys in camp from wandering too far from their home planets, and that he'd never worked at the camp, and didn't know the first thing about the nonsense that took place there.

"It's like a prison camp for insane teenagers," Max said.

"Well. What's wrong with you three, then?" Marshmallow Jeff asked.

We walked for several moments, each of us trying to come up with some kind of answer for that, and finally Cobie Petersen offered: "One of us got shot through the hand, one of us doesn't talk, and one of us is obsessed with practicing his five-digit multiplication tables. Other than that, we don't belong at Camp Merrie-Seymour for Boys."

Max nodded. "Practicing my five-digit multiplication tables. I like that."

We got back to the cinder-block well house after dark, flagless, and in last place. And Marshmallow Jeff said good-bye to us there, explaining he was as afraid of the boys at Camp Merrie-Seymour for Boys as they were of him, present company excluded.

Every other planet had beaten us back to Camp Merrie-Seymour for Boys; and Trent Mendibles and Robin Sexton had given up waiting for us, convinced that we had only intended to ditch them in the woods with a bottle of piss-tasting water, just so we could laugh at them.

THE MELTING MAN AND THE BEAVER KING

Everything Joseph Stalin told the melting man was coming true, right before Leonard Fountain's eyes.

The Beaver King really *was* hiding out in a place near the Little America Mall, which Leonard Fountain had driven past on his way to Lake Moomaw—Lake Beaver Dam. And Poppa Bear himself affirmed to the melting man that the three bears also used to live where his younger brother Larry worked, Camp Merrie-Seymour for Beavers.

It was all working out, and the melting man's masterpiece would finally be put to good use.

"You are driving. You are driving," 3-60 said.

And Crystal Lutz played her accordion and sang along with Igor Zelinsky:

> *He said to me, "Why don't you run?*
> *I see you don't have any gun."*

Whereas the melting man had been weeping earlier, now he was very happy.

Joseph Stalin was happy, too.

He said, "You are finally going to amount to something, Leonard!"

"You sound like my father," the melting man said. "I hate my father."

"You are driving. You are driving. Oh, Lenny, you've lost another tooth!" 3-60 said.

It was true. One of the melting man's large molars had dislodged from the mushlike putty of Leonard Fountain's infected gums. The melting man nearly choked on it, and when he spit it out onto the dashboard, it left a black gooey smear of pus and blood.

Leonard Fountain—Igor Zelinsky—was exhausted.

Actually, Leonard Fountain wasn't merely exhausted, he was nearly dead. He only had one more thing he needed to do, then everybody would finally be satisfied with Leonard Fountain.

"You see the posts of the camp up ahead on the left," 3-60 said. "It is getting closer. It is getting closer."

The melting man's atomic U-Haul had finally arrived.

"You are parking on the side of the road," 3-60 narrated.

And Leonard Fountain looked across the street at the electric metal gates that were swinging open—almost as though to invite him in—between the hewn log posts and the sign that read:

Camp Merrie-Seymour for Beavers
Where the Beaver King Has Been Hiding from You!

So this was it, Leonard Fountain thought.

This had to be it.

And as the gates to Camp Merrie-Seymour for Beavers swung open, a black Town Car pulled out and then paused before turning down Route 600.

Leonard Fountain noticed the license plate on the car as it rolled through the gate. It was a personalized plate that said NUS BOMB. But Leonard Fountain was too far gone to actually read the plate. He didn't need to, because the only thing he could see was BVR KING.

"That's him!" The melting man was so excited, he urinated bloody piss all over himself.

Martha Nussbaum was leaving Camp Merrie-Seymour for Boys for the weekend before the fat kids came. In fact, Martha K. Nussbaum, MD, PhD, was leaving Camp Merrie-Seymour for Boys and Alex Division of Merrie-Seymour Research Group for good. Her bags were packed, and she had a one-way, first-class ticket on Lufthansa.

"The Beaver King!" Joseph Stalin said.

The melting man spun the U-Haul van back out onto the highway and followed the Beaver King.

"Don't fuck this up!" Joseph Stalin said.

Leonard Fountain began to cry again. "I promise not to fuck this up, Dad."

"You are crying. You are crying," 3-60 said.

And Crystal Lutz played a song called "Warm Leatherette" on her accordion. She sang to Igor Zelinsky as he pursued the black Town Car down the road:

Quick—Let's make love. Before you die.

And in the air above the melting man's poisonous vehicle a small metal object hovered along, watching, watching.

Somewhere not terribly far away, sitting in separate offices at Merrie-Seymour Research Group's Alex Division facility, Colton Benjamin Petersen Sr., Jacob Burgess, and Harrison Knott were watching it all unfold; had been watching even as a lunatic from a botched droning experiment fired a pistol at their own sons.

"Pull the plug?" Colton Petersen asked.

"I think he's past the point," Major Knott answered.

"You are melting. You are melting," 3-60 said.

Leonard Fountain was liquefying behind the wheel of his festering U-Haul van.

"Activate the switch, Leonard! It is time!" Joseph Stalin commanded.

The timers ticked and ticked and ticked, and Crystal Lutz played wildly. The melting man forced the van up closer and closer to the tail of the black Town Car ahead of him.

"Oh, Lenny! Your phone is ringing again!" 3-60 said.

"Huh?"

It was all so much, inside and outside the melting man's head, all at once.

Leonard Fountain looked at his phone. His little brother was calling. He'd forgotten about visiting his little brother, like he said he was going to. There were more important things to do now.

"Don't answer the phone!" Joseph Stalin told him. "Activate the switch! It's time, Leonard! It's time!"

"You are driving. You are driving. You are answering the phone," 3-60 narrated.

"Huh . . . Hello? Larry?" the melting man said.

"Hey, Lenny. You nearby? I thought you'd be here by now."

"Something came up."

"Get off the phone!" Joseph Stalin shouted.

The melting man steered with his knee and pressed the timers into his head.

Crystal Lutz played and sang.

Flying fish leapt up from the asphalt sea of Route 600. They flitted along beside Leonard Fountain's van. They smiled at him, and several splattered—*thunk! thunk! thunk!*—into the windshield.

The melting man was melting.

"Sorry, Larry. I gotta go."

And it was on the John Lederer Bridge that the melting man lost sight of the Town Car, which was speeding on its way to Dulles Airport.

Here we see the melting man, a flawed biodrone from Merrie-Seymour Research Group, being decommissioned by remote control.

Here, kitty-kitty.

So much for the John Lederer Bridge.

So much for the melting man.

One step closer to male extinction.

Mrs. Nussbaum noticed a bright flare in her rearview mirror; it was like one of those annoying traffic-signal cameras firing machine-gun flashbulbs at an inattentive line-crosser.

One day, humanity won't need such devices, she thought.

OUR LAST DAY IN JUPITER

On the way back to Camp Merrie-Seymour for Boys with Marsh-mallow Jeff, it was Max who concluded that we had come full circle: that the six weeks of hell here began with a kid getting shot through the foot and would most definitely come to an abrupt end with another being shot through the hand.

And Max said, "Camp Merrie-Seymour for Boys, Where Boys Rediscover the Fun of Being Shooting Victims!"

So our six-week captivity at Camp Merrie-Seymour for Boys ended pretty much the way it began, with Larry being mad at us and calling us all a bunch of fuckheads.

The thing that made him especially angry, besides Cobie Petersen actually being shot, was that Mars won the final challenge.

Nobody liked the Martians.

To be honest, none of the planets in the Camp Merrie-Seymour for Boys solar system liked one another at all.

And nobody got to spend the entire day Friday enjoying the freedom and consumerism of the Little America Mall due to the mysterious vaporization of the John Lederer Bridge, which was pretty much the only way to get from Camp Merrie-Seymour for Boys to the Little America Mall and all its pretzel stands and sensory stimulation and so on.

And when the three of us did come back to Jupiter after dark, Trent Mendibles sprang up from his crumpling bed, fists balled, and ready to throw punches at Cobie, which he probably would have done if Cobie wasn't all covered in blood and pale.

"What in the name of fuck happened to you?" Larry demanded.

Cobie Petersen raised his hand.

"Got shot by an asshole in a U-Haul," he said. "Do you have a brother, Larry? Because when we were out there, the fucker who shot at us said you were his brother."

"Lenny?" Larry said, "You saw my brother Lenny?"

"Well, he didn't say his name, but he did look like you, except for all the sores and stuff on his face," Cobie Petersen said. "And then he shot me."

"And he was bat-fucking-shit crazy," Max added.

Cobie Petersen stretched out on his bed. Larry, deflated, sat with his face in his hands, mumbling something about quitting this shithole job.

"Larry?" Cobie Petersen said, "Will you just promise to never call anyone else Teacher's Pet? It will always be special to me."

"Or fuckhead, too," Max added.

"Fuck you, guys," Larry said. "Lenny had a head injury when he was a kid."

My brother Max nodded knowingly. "Head injuries can answer a lot of questions that genetics are just too afraid to ask."

After they loaded Cobie Petersen into the same ambulance that had transported the camp's first martyr, Bucky Littlejohn, carloads of alerted parents began showing up like funeral motorcades to take their supposedly reformed sons back home to safer realities that could be paused and rebooted.

Colton Benjamin Petersen Sr. and Jake and Natalie Burgess arrived at Camp Merrie-Seymour for Boys early Saturday morning. They rode up from Sunday in a carpool van that belonged to Alex Division.

They had obviously stopped at the hospital Cobie was taken to, because Cobie waved a white-gauze-wrapped hand at us from the third-row seat.

Colton Petersen stuck his hand out to us. "Ariel and Max! Very nice to meet you boys! You're quite a team! Quite a team!" Cobie's father said. At the time, I didn't think much of it. Max and I talked about it the next day, though—how strange it was that Mr. Petersen knew exactly who we were, and that we had been such a good team at the games, because we had never met any of the Petersens before Max and I came to Camp Merrie-Seymour for Boys.

And then I saw Major Knott standing beside the driver's door on the van, alone in the gravel parking area.

Even though he'd promised we would see each other often, this was the first time I'd seen Major Knott since arriving in Sunday. It was understandable. I told myself that he must have wanted me to adjust to my new family, and he was so busy, after all.

Still, just seeing him made me feel wonderfully happy—as though I'd been reunited with my real father after such a long time. I couldn't help myself; I ran over to him and hugged him. Then I felt bad because I hadn't so much as said hello to Mom and Dad before running off.

"Ariel! Look at you! You look splendid!" Major Knott said.

I felt my eyes getting a little wet, but I willed myself not to cry.

"How have you been?" I said.

"Well, I've missed playing chess with you," Major Knott said.

"Me, too."

"We'll have to set up a game, then. What do you say?"

"That would be good."

We walked across the grass toward my parents. Natalie was limping. I found out later she'd been hit by a car crossing the street in Sunday, but she said it was nothing to worry about and that she'd be fine.

On the drive back to Sunday, I sat between Cobie Petersen and Max in the third row of the van.

"We smell really bad," Max said.

Cobie Petersen agreed. "I noticed that."

I nodded, too. These are things that happen to boys at camp.

I pointed at Cobie's bandaged hand.

"Is that going to be okay?" I asked.

He nodded. "I still have lefty to solve my math problems."

Cobie reached over and put his arm around me and patted Max. He said, "I'm glad I met you gents. Made it all worth it."

Then Max put his arm across my shoulders and hugged me and said, "It really wasn't so bad. It would have been worse if you weren't there."

So I put my arms around Max and Cobie, but I didn't say anything.

And we did smell really bad.

Max asked me, "And when we get back, will you tell me all the stuff that happened to you before you came here?"

"You don't want to know that, Max."

"Sure I do. If we're going to be brothers, then you should tell me. Only wait till after I take a shower. I want to put on some clean clothes that don't have my name written in them, and, dude, I really, really need to *propagate some of my lucky bamboo.*"

I laughed and shook my head. "You are so gross, Max."

SUNDAY IN SUNDAY

Here are all the stories I shelved in your library.

I never thought you'd want to hear these things, Max.

And here's what I found out: The terrible stories are the same as the extinct beings that Dad brings back to life—each one pulls from the original, which never loses weight in the replication. So they all remain equal in substance for us to carry around—the boy in the clown suit, the men in the schoolroom, a refrigerator, the little dog, a coffee server named Ocean, the boys in the city of tents—populating and overpopulating, filling all the libraries inside every one of us.

The night we came home from Camp Merrie-Seymour for Boys, I told Max my entire story, which began on my fourteenth birthday in a field where my friends and I—we were such children then—found the skull of Mr. Barbar's ram.

Max and I sat alone in my room in the dark.

The stories went through the night, past midnight. Sometimes Max would ask a question—about what it was like traveling with the soldiers in wartime, if I was ever afraid, things like that—but he listened, even though at times the things I said made him uncomfortable.

When I finished, we sat in the dark not saying anything for I don't know how long. Then Max, his voice a little shaky, said, "I'm really sorry I was such a dick to you, Ariel."

What could I say?

"It's okay, Max."

"Do you want me to sleep in here? I mean, I'll sleep on the floor if you're afraid or anything."

"It's okay. Really. You don't need to do that, and I'm not afraid. But thank you, Max."

"Are you sure?"

"Yes."

I wanted to make it okay for Max, but I wasn't sure if there was anything I could do. These things happen.

On Sunday morning, while for the first time in six weeks I was asleep in a regular, non-plastic bed, Max came in and threw himself across my feet. He woke me up, took one of my pillows to prop up his head, and complained about how six weeks of getting up at dawn had ruined him for life, and did it do the same thing to me?

I told him I wasn't sure, and that he should come back later and ask me after I woke up.

But he stayed there, lying across my bed, and we talked about things. It was a morning like I had never had in all my previous lives, and it was very nice.

Max had left the door open, and Alex, our dead-and-alive pet crow, flapped his way in and landed on my windowsill. The bird pecked on the glass twice, then turned a beady eye at me and Max and said, "Kill me now. God! I really need to ditch some squids."

"Do you teach him all that?" I asked.

"Not the suicidal stuff," Max said. "I don't know where he gets *that* from."

"The other, though."

"Yeah. Pretty awesome, huh?"

"It's something. That's for sure," I said. "*Ditch some squids?*"

"Kind of poetic, isn't it?" Max said.

"Ditch some squids," Alex, our crow, echoed.

I really did not want to be talking to Max about this so early in the morning. Not ever, actually.

"And, anyway, don't tell me *you're* not totally relieved to finally be back home. Don't lie, Ariel. But I realized last night in the shower I was kind of out of practice after six weeks."

"Really. You don't need to tell me what you do in the shower, Max."

"Maybe everyone knows, anyway. Maybe it's like Cobie said— and we're all chipped, and we're just putting on one hell of a show for everyone at Alex."

"I wish you wouldn't say things like that, either," I said.

And Alex, our crow, hearing his name, bobbed his sad little head up and down and said, "Round up the buffaloes! Round up the buffaloes!"

I put my arm over my eyes and sighed.

"This house is insane," I said.

"You love it, though," Max said. "But I have been thinking about what Cobie said. And Mrs. Nussbaum, too. Because what if they actually *did* do it to one of us? Or all of us? They would do it, don't you think? They're just crazy enough, between Mrs. Nussbaum wanting to oversee the extinction of all males, and

Dad wanting to oversee the resurrection of anything he can save. And who even knows about what kinds of things Cobie's dad or Major Knott are after?"

I didn't say anything. I wished I was still asleep. But Max turned onto his side and grabbed one of my feet and continued, "Don't you think it was weird how Mr. Petersen knew exactly who we were? And that we were *such a good team*?"

"Of course he'd know who we are, Max. Maybe Dad showed him pictures."

"Of you? There aren't any."

"Well, you. You plus one equals I have to be Ariel, right? The team thing was just a coincidence," I said. "Anyone would have said that."

"Anyone? Okay. But Mr. Petersen did ask Dad one thing about you. When you were over by the van hugging Major Knott."

I felt myself reddening, thinking about how everyone had been watching me and Major Knott.

"He asked Dad if you ever had another episode after the one on the airplane." Max shook my foot again and said, "What's an *episode*?"

The niceness of the morning, of being there in my own bedroom and talking to my brother, suddenly turned to ice.

Of course I knew what it all meant, even if I didn't say anything to Max about it. They had been using me; I was another surveillance drone, maybe something worse, not quite a person, I suppose; not quite a crow.

I took Max's bicycle and rode over to Major Knott's house that morning before Jake and Natalie got out of bed. Or maybe they weren't even home; who could say?

Max wanted to come with me, but I talked him out of it because there was only one bicycle, and I told him I needed to talk to Major Knott alone. I didn't know how to get to Major Knott's house, though, so Max had to give me directions, which I wrote in black pen on the back of my left hand.

Also, I wasn't very good at riding Max's bike. I crashed turning the corner on Stoney Creek Road, which was the street Major Knott's house was on. I scraped my elbow pretty bad on the pavement and dripped a little trail of blood droplets up the road.

Max told me Major Knott's house was the second or third house on the right. He didn't know the house number, but he told me it was a one-story brick house with a white door, which pretty much described every house I saw on Stoney Creek Road.

Naturally, the first door I knocked on was not connected to Major Knott's house.

The woman who answered the door was a dark-skinned Asian lady, who was about four inches shorter than me. She was wearing a lacy pink nightgown that was nearly transparent and reached the tops of her feet. Her hair was rolled up in curlers of all different sizes and colors, and she had a lit cigarette hanging from the corner of her mouth.

I was afraid of her. I knew right away I must have guessed the wrong house, and thought she would be mad at me, so I just stood there with my mouth open, dumbly staring at the lady.

"What happened to you?" she asked.

"Huh?"

"You're bleeding. What happened?"

"Oh. Uh. I crashed on my bike. Well, my brother's bike."

The woman sucked on her cigarette and turned her chin so she wouldn't exhale the smoke on me. She blew it out her nose inside her house.

"Come in. I have something you can put on it."

She swung the door wide.

"Oh. No, I wasn't looking for help. I was looking for a friend of mine. He lives on this street somewhere. His name is Harrison Knott."

"The English guy?"

"Yes."

"He's a friend of yours?"

"Yes."

"Well, come in. I still have something you can put on your arm. Unless you want to bleed on his porch, too."

I looked down and noticed the little splotches of blood I'd deposited beside my foot on the painted concrete porch.

"I'm sorry." I could feel myself turning red.

The woman sucked on the cigarette again.

"Don't be."

The smoking woman took me into her kitchen, where she ran warm water over the scrapes on my arm. She washed off my wounds with her bare hands, all the while sucking on her cigarette and carefully blowing the smoke away from me. She turned the water off and said, "Stay there."

What could I do?

I stayed there with my arm in her sink.

She grabbed a clean dish towel from a drawer and then patted my arm dry.

"Does that hurt?"

"No. Well, yes. A little."

Then she wrapped the towel around my arm and led me over to her small dining room table.

"Sit down," she said.

I sat down.

She disappeared into a hallway behind me. It was all so strange. I couldn't understand why the woman would so matter-of-factly take a kid into her house—a bleeding kid—and then try to help him without even hesitating or thinking about it.

When she came back, she had some antiseptic spray and two flesh-colored bandages, about the size of index cards. I thought about writing *Inside a refrigerator* on one of them before she stuck it on my arm.

"You're not from here, are you?" she said.

"From *here*?"

"Yeah. Here. West Virginia. America."

"Oh. How can you tell?"

She exhaled smoke. "You have an accent. It's cute."

"You're not from here, either," I guessed.

"How can you tell?"

"The hair curlers?" I asked.

The woman laughed and smoothed the bandages over my scrapes.

"You shouldn't leave these on, but you don't want to bleed on the English guy's house. Take them off today so you can get air on that road rash."

"Is that what it's called?"

"That's what kids here call it," she said. "What do kids call it where you come from?"

"An accident."

She took the cigarette out of her mouth and dropped it in an ashtray that looked like an orange abalone shell.

"The English guy lives in the next house that way."

She pointed at her kitchen wall. There was a painting of two dolls hanging on it.

"Thank you," I said.

"If he's your friend, how come you don't know where he lives?"

I showed her the writing on the back of my left hand.

"It's my brother's fault." I said, "He gave me bad directions."

Major Knott was having coffee on his porch and reading the Sunday newspaper when I rode up Stoney Creek Road and deposited Max's bicycle on the corner of his front lawn near the driveway.

If he was surprised to see me, he didn't show it. And if I was happy to see him—which I wasn't—it didn't show, either.

"Ariel! Good morning!"

I stood in the grass at the bottom of the steps leading up to the porch, not really sure of where to begin.

So I said, "What did you do to me?"

Major Knott's smile dissolved. He folded the newspaper and placed it on the table.

"Do you want to sit down?"

He pushed a chair out from the side of his small table.

I looked over my shoulder to where Max's bike lay in the yard. Major Knott's wife was in the garden, bent over a row of tomato bushes. She was young and pretty, just like I'd pictured the type of woman who'd be attracted to Major Knott. I almost had the feeling someone was watching us.

Someone was always watching us, I suppose.

I climbed the steps and sat down beside Major Knott, and said it again: "What did you do to me?"

Major Knott's tone was unapologetic. He turned his hands up and said, "I brought you to America."

Inside his office, Major Knott said this to me: "Suppose you were flying in an airplane. Just you, the pilot, and someone you love, someone you care about very much. Do you have someone like that, Ariel?"

I thought about Max, but I didn't want to say anything to Major Knott about people I cared for. It was all a trick, an accident of my survival, anyway.

He continued: "And suddenly the pilot jumps out of the plane, so the two of you are left up there, alone in a plane with no pilot. What are you going to do? Crash, or learn to fly?"

I didn't answer him. Why should I? Did he think I was stupid, even after I'd figured out what he'd done to me?

"Someone has to fly the plane, Ariel. Someone has to keep us from crashing, because it's certainly going to happen if we don't. That's why we—your father and I, and the rest of us—do what we do. We have to figure out the controls."

So that was it: controls. Extinction, de-extinction, drones and biodrones, a chipped boy rescued from a tent full of orphans, even *girl sperm*.

And he actually thought this was flying the plane.

I said, "Show me how it works. You know, what you did to me, the thing you put in my head when you took me to the dentist."

"Sit down here."

Major Knott wheeled his desk chair out for me, and I sat facing a computer monitor. He took out the little controller he'd used on the plane to make my headache stop and handed the device to me. When I looked at it closely, I saw my name—ARIEL JUDE BURGESS—printed along one side.

The thing actually looked like a touch-screen cell phone. He told me to press the home button and the panel lit up with an array of colored and numbered buttons.

"Touch that green one and watch the monitor," he said.

What I saw looked like I was standing in a hall of mirrors: the computer screen inside a computer screen, inside another and another, infinitely. I was looking out my own eyes at an image of looking out my own eyes. Forever.

"The home button turns it off," he said.

I turned *Ariel Jude Burgess* off.

I sat there for a moment, just thinking about all the things I wanted to say, and not knowing where to begin. I was shaking; I felt myself starting to cry.

"How could you do something like that to me?"

I honestly didn't think he would answer me.

Then Major Knott said, "I'm sorry, Ariel. But I took you out of that place, too."

"You fucking destroyed me, is what you did. You can't just use people like that."

And then I thought, what a stupid thing to say. Apparently Major Knott, my father, the Merrie-Seymour Research Group could use people—or birds, cats, frozen devil-monkeys, and flying invisible boxes—any number of ways they wanted to.

Major Knott looked hurt. He put his hand on my shoulder but I pushed him away.

"Look, Ariel—"

"No. You look. What am I to you? A cat? A crow? Some fucking experiment so you can take the controls? I'm a human being. You can't just—How could you do this to people?"

A tear dripped from my chin.

Major Knott lowered his voice. "I'm sorry. I do care about you, Ariel. I do. You have to know that."

What could anyone ever know?

"Did you do it to Max? To Cobie Petersen?"

Major Knott swallowed and shook his head. "No. You were the first person for Alex Division. Well, the first one in ten years. I promise. I'm very sorry, Ariel. We weren't going to use you anymore. I promise. What can I say? I'm so sorry. You weren't supposed to know. Nobody should have known."

MAX AND HIS BROTHER

I hadn't seen Major Knott since the Sunday morning when I rode Max's bicycle over to Stoney Creek Road. I went back there one time to bring some flowers to Mrs. Le, the cigarette-smoking woman who'd bandaged my arm after I crashed. I suppose I still couldn't figure out why some people will go out of their way to help a complete stranger and, on the other hand, why others will treat someone they care about as though they're disposable objects.

And I know Major Knott cared about me, which made the whole thing even more puzzling.

Before I left his house that day, Major Knott gave me the little controller that turned *Ariel Jude Burgess* on and off. He promised—for whatever that was worth—that there was no other way for Alex Division to use me, to look through my eyes and hear what I was hearing, and he told me I could do what I wanted to with the device. When I rode away, I almost felt as though Major Knott expected me to go steal something and bring it back for him, as Isaak did, even if it was something completely worthless, like a bag of clothespins, just to affirm Major Knott was at the controls and the plane was flying just fine.

I kept Major Knott's device for a few days, and then I threw it into Dumpling Run without telling anyone my last, little, terrible story. Why should I give something like that to Cobie Petersen or Max? There was no way to fully trust or believe Major Knott, anyway, and like Cobie said, maybe all three of us really had been chipped.

Who would ever know?

After coming home from Camp Merrie-Seymour for Boys, Max and I spent most of our free time over at Cobie Petersen's house. And whereas Major Knott had given me credit for figuring out how I'd been used by Alex Division to keep an eye on my own father and also to watch what Mrs. Nussbaum, who mysteriously vanished that summer, was doing with the boys at Camp Merrie-Seymour for Boys, I figured something else out, too—and it was something nobody at Alex Division had caught on to.

It was this: Cobie Petersen's two younger sisters, Kelly and Erica, were the girls Mrs. Nussbaum referred to in her book about male extinction—the ones who'd been created with *girl sperm*. That was another story that would never leave Ariel's library.

Erica, who was almost fifteen, liked me very much—I could tell. And I liked her, too, which gave Max sufficient reasons to tease us both incessantly.

In September, before the fall session of our tenth-grade year started at William E. Shuck High School, Cobie Petersen took me and my American brother Max out coon hunting with him and his dog, Ezra.

I don't think Max or I wanted to actually see Cobie Petersen kill a raccoon; we just liked spending time with him.

Cobie was the only one in our hunting party who carried a rifle. Shortly after midnight, as we trudged through the dense woods along the bank of upper Dumpling Run, Cobie Petersen stopped us by raising his hand and saying, "Gents, I do believe coon hunting's a bust tonight."

"The three bears are going to go home empty-handed," Max said.

"It's a great night to be a coon," I said.

"And a sad night to be a talking bear," Cobie added.

And as though to punctuate our misjudgment with an exclamation point, Ezra immediately started howling and barking, running wildly through the brush after what sounded like a monstrous raccoon.

"Oh, shit," Cobie said. "Let's get this one."

And the three bears took off in the direction of Ezra's baying.

Here is the Dumpling Man, who in another life was called Katkov's Devil, the Siberian Ice Man, another immigrant in Sunday, another one of the things Jake Burgess and Alex Division brought back from the dead—like me.

The pale thing with horns and hands sat hunched down on a branch six feet over our heads in the West Virginia woods.

Cobie Petersen aimed his rifle at the snorting creature as Max shined a blinding flashlight beam at the thing in the tree.

"*See? I told you he's real,*" Cobie whispered.

Ezra barked and barked.

The thing looked exactly as I pictured it from Mrs. Nussbaum's book and from Cobie Petersen's scary story. But after hearing all the legendary rumors about the Dumpling Man, I never would have imagined him to be less than four feet tall, which is a rather generous estimation of the little horned man's height.

Still, he was kind of scary looking. I suppose if I had been more infused with biblical images, I may have thought, as others had, that here was the devil himself, but I found myself feeling sorry for the small, naked, and sparsely white-haired creature.

Who could say how long he'd been trapped in ice, only to end up here in Sunday without any say in the matter at all?

"*Don't shoot him*," I whispered.

"I'm not going to shoot him," Cobie Petersen told me. "If I was going to shoot him, he'd already be dead."

Then Cobie snapped his fingers at Ezra, who instantly stopped barking and sat down.

"Then what are we going to do with him?" Max said.

The Dumpling Man cocked his head at the sound of Max's voice, then he leaned forward from his perch, straining with his big amber eyes to see us three boys below him.

"Nothing," Cobie said. "Leave him alone."

"*It would be cool if people could see him*," Max whispered.

"Why?" I asked.

Max shrugged. "Yeah. Probably not."

Then the Dumpling Man said, "I don't just let *anyone* find me, you know?"

And my brother Max raised his hand above his head, straining to lift himself as high as his tiptoes could get him, and held his fingers out just below the little man.

The Dumpling Man smiled a toothy grin that seemed to split his head in two. He reached down and touched Max's hand.

And Max turned off the flashlight that had been shining on Katkov's beast, and said, "Let's just leave him alone."

So much for extinction.

epilogue:
MASON-DIXON-BRAND SAUERKRAUT

Here is a fishing lure, wedged between two flattened rocks at a depth of three feet in a slow bend of a creek called Dumpling Run.

The lure is what boys here call a plug, carved from basswood with an inset glass-bead eye, painted red at the diagonal slash of the mouth with hexagonal dots of yellow to mimic the scales on a minnow trailing back along its tapered length.

A double hook dangles from the front, a triple from the tail.

When the three boys uncover it, they are hunting crayfish for bait. The epoxied wooden lure has been wedged between those unmoving flat rocks in Dumpling Run for more than half a century.

- - -

Here is Natalie Burgess, standing alone in aisle seven of the Sunday Walk-In Grocery Store. The sauerkraut she prefers, Mason-Dixon brand, has been moved to a lower shelf.

Outside the market, cars speed by along South Fork Route. Natalie's Volvo is parked across the street.

- - -

Here is a handful of dirt—just dirt from a field where I played with my friends on my fourteenth birthday. And here, too, are all the things in the terrible stories we pile and pile in our library that is always at capacity, and also is never full—ice, dogs, cats, coffee, clowns, and crows.

- - -

Here in the frozen room beneath the Empire Hotel, among vast stores of food provisions is a doctor named Alexander Merrie. He smokes a pipe as he sits hunched over his journal and writes an entry to a man who will never read it.

Thursday, July 30, 1903—*New York*

I had to look back in my journals I'd kept during the *Alex Crow* expedition to be certain just how many years it has been since Mr. Warren and I brought Katkov's beast out from the ice. How would I have ever guessed where I would be today?

There are times—many of them in my life—when it has been impossible to think about the future.

Lately I find myself wondering more and more about the stories that have been frozen—for how many years before Mr. Warren, Murdoch, and I first caught a glimpse of you?—in the timelessness of your captivity. And it was purely out of the need to allow the one thing that was a certainty be known—that you existed at all, man, devil, or beast—which drove us to bring you back as evidence of our reason, and our stewardship of this world. And so I've come more often to sit here among Mr. Seymour's impossible stock of food, and look at you while I write. It brings me back, in my mind, to that spring on the Lena River Delta when I myself crawled from the ice.

Twenty-three years today! And sadly, fifteen of those years have passed since Mr. Warren was lost to us.

It's a sort of a birthday, I should say—a birth from the ice, into ice, and now, only to wait to be born once again. And when that happens, what stories we all will have to tell!

- - -

Here is our pet, a crow named Alex, who should not be alive, taunting a neighbor's cat through an obviously opened window.

- - -

Here is an immigrant kid, a second son named Ariel, who has lived, and lived, and lives again, in a place called Sunday.

ACKNOWLEDGMENTS

Someone once said this to me: "*Careful Is My Middle Name* will NOT be the title of your memoir, Andrew."

That someone is actually Julie Strauss-Gabel, the editor and publisher of *The Alex Crow*. I must thank Julie for an uncountable assortment of things—among them, for her intelligence, dedication to producing the best books possible, for being patient with me, for asking the best questions, for making me be a better writer, and for pulling me in when I became a little less than careful. Also, for giving me the title for the memoir I will one day write: *Careful Is My Middle Name Is Not the Title of This Memoir.*

If I did write a memoir, I'm pretty sure—given its title—it would not be very boring, but I would feel obligated to name names, which would not be very careful of me. And if my life were a movie, I would cast it as follows:

- The no-bullshit golf partner—played by Amy Sarig King.
- The reliable, understanding, and calm therapist—played by Michael Bourret.

- The conspiratorial drinking buddy—played by Michael Grant.
- The other boy in Christa Desir's and Carrie Mesrobian's "Boy Cabal"—played by Ted Goeglein.
- The incredible survivors who introduced me to Ariel Burgess—played by my English-language learner students.
- The people I love most in this world—played by Jocelyn, Chiara, and Trevin Smith.

You all give me so much, and I am incalculably thankful.

Oh . . . and the crow is played by Oprah, our hen, who just sits there and stares.

There's something a little off with that bird.

THIS IS THE TRUTH. THIS IS HISTORY.
IT'S THE END OF THE WORLD.
AND NOBODY KNOWS ANYTHING ABOUT IT.
YOU KNOW WHAT I MEAN.

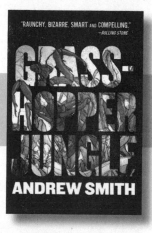

Boston Globe-Horn Book winner

"Raunchy, bizarre, smart and compelling"
—*Rolling Stone*

"A literary joy to behold . . . reminds me of Kurt Vonnegut's
Slaughterhouse Five, in the best sense."
—*The New York Times Book Review*

"An absurdist *Middlesex* . . . and is all the better for it. A-"
—*Entertainment Weekly*

"Nuanced, gross, funny and poignant, it's wildly original."
— *The San Francisco Chronicle*

"Once you get lost in *Grasshopper Jungle* you won't want to be found."
—*Geekdad.com*

★ "Filled with gonzo black humor."
—*Publishers Weekly*, starred review